Ghost of the
Murder Mamas

Ghost of the Murder Mamas

Dream Collins

www.urbanbooks.net

Urban Books, LLC
300 Farmingdale Road, N.Y.-Route 109
Farmingdale, NY 11735

Ghost of the Murder Mamas

ISBN 13: 978-1-64556-139-2
ISBN 10: 1-64556-139-9

First Trade Paperback Printing December 2020
Printed in the United States of America

10 9 8 7 6 5 4 3 2 1

Distributed by Kensington Publishing Corp.
Submit Orders to:
Customer Service
400 Hahn Road
Westminster, MD 21157-4627
Phone: 1-800-733-3000
Fax: 1-800-659-2436

Ghost of the Murder Mamas

Dream Collins

Prologue

Do you know what pain is? Most people swear they do, and if asked, they can rattle off tons of examples of what they think it is. The word *pain* is defined as "physical suffering or discomfort caused by illness or injury." At least that's how the dictionary describes it, but that isn't entirely true. Life has taught me a different meaning of the word. Pain is an unpleasant experience that motivates you to do something; usually it's to protect parts of you that are damaged. And we're all damaged creatures, right? Some of us just more than others. But pain is a survival mechanism of fundamental importance: it plays a crucial role in our lives and eventually molds us into whoever it is that we become.

At least for me it did. See, outsmarting niggas has always come easy to me. Some would say it's my gift, one of the things I do better than any bitch I know. I was born to get in a nigga's head. Shit, why else would God bless me with this gorgeous face of mine, a banging body, and a pussy niggas have killed to claim? I'm not being conceited. Shit, these are facts. If anything, I'm the exact opposite. I recognized there are plenty bad bitches in this world—I have a beautiful collection of them myself—and I've made it my business to make sure that they get everything they want and deserve. The thing that separates me from most is the things I want and deserve extend much further than a trip here or there, a new designer bag or pair of designer shoes. Most females fall for those empty promises these niggas out here tossing around and get left with nothing but a wet pussy and an empty designer bag void of cash.

Shit, not me. A nigga can't sell me a bridge. I buy lakes. I can purchase my own bags, and I damn sure ain't hurting for no shoes. You should see my closet. It's every girl's dream. But there is always a price to pay in order to live in luxury. Most go the square route and spend nearly half a decade of their young adult life piling up debt, studying at a university. Just to receive a piece of paper that tells the world they're worthy of sitting at some boardroom table. But if you're like me, you hustle your way up to the top. When I say hustle, I mean no holds barred, by any means necessary. See, when people think hustler, they instantly think of a man. Some hungry, young thoroughbred standing over a stove, working his wrist counterclockwise, hoping those couple of ounces of coke lock and birth an empire. But what people fail to realize is that the greatest hustler ever created was a woman.

Ever since Eve in the garden, a woman's ability to persuade with just her words has changed mankind. She can gain everything and destroy a multitude. We're not even talking about the power of the pussy, which has been known to start a war or two. See, women rule the world, at least I do mine, but Lord knows I've been through hell and back. So every day I toast to this life, but bottles of Henri Jayer Richebourg aren't cheap, and neither is my time nor the breathtaking view of the Atlantic Ocean from my penthouse. And I intend to remain right here, because I abide by the rules. Rule number one, never put your heart over your hustle, and rule number two, never break rule number one.

That's the key to my success, and I've passed these jewels on to the young ladies in my circle. I don't lie to them, and I won't to you. I once fell victim to the deceit of my heart, and it almost cost me everything, but luckily, I was able to regain control. No longer do the ghosts of my past haunt me. Now it's just a cautionary tale I share with the ladies that join my exclusive sorority. . . .

Chapter 1

April 2008 . . .

"Under my umbrella, ella, ella, eh!"

Nubia sang in unison with her younger sister, Zuri, as they coasted through the city, bobbing their heads. The sun had finally decided to show its face, and the streets were filled with people out savoring the first day of beautiful weather in the city. The candy apple–red BMW 325i stood out as it danced through traffic. The new toy was almost as gorgeous as its driver, Nubia, who sat behind the wheel, enjoying the slight breeze blowing through her signature blond weave.

With her light skin sprinkled with freckles, her green eyes, which she hid behind a pair of designer shades, and the pink lipstick that matched her nails, Nubia was captivating. In fact, nothing and no one equaled her beauty. Not even Zuri, who was a few years younger than her sister. Zuri had darker skin and wore her hair in four big cornrows that she braided into two, so that she had one to hang over each shoulder. Her body had just begun to bloom, and her sense of style wasn't on her sister's level quite yet. But every street nigga who had struck out with Nubia was waiting on deck for Zuri.

Nubia was having none of it, though. Like a mother hen, she was overprotective when it came to Zuri. She had been taking care of both of them since she was sixteen and Zuri was just twelve. That was when their father had started serving life in a federal prison for kidnapping and murdering a neighborhood drug dealer, and their alcoholic mother had abandoned them. They hadn't laid eyes on either of their parents in two forevers. After their father's arrest, they had been sent to live with their father's mother in the Gowanus Houses in Brooklyn, but she hadn't made much of an attempt to raise or supervise either of them. Eventually, Nubia had assumed the responsibility no one seemed to want, and she'd done whatever she had to do to make sure they were good. She had moved herself and Zuri out of the Gowanus Houses and had set up what could be seen only as a comfortable life. Nubia had fought tooth and nail for it.

Nubia had a natural hustle about herself and was a quick study, so anything she didn't know, she learned fast, like how to turn coke into crack. Something she had discovered most young hustlers around her way didn't know how to do. Most resorted to buying "hard," or "cook up," as it was called on the streets. Seeing a business opportunity, Nubia had taken full advantage, and before long she'd started pulling in a couple hundred dollars a week off her culinary skills alone. She was fearless, street smart, and she taught Zuri how to be independent, to take care of herself, and survive in the world. She put her younger sister up on all the game guys in the streets would come at her with. She never sugarcoated anything and knew Zuri would have to learn on her own, but she didn't hold her tongue about hustlers she deemed off limits.

Nubia pressed the volume button, lowering the music inside the car, then looked over at her sister. "What's up wit you and that dusty li'l nigga Trav? Why he always all up in ya face and shit?"

Caught off guard by the line of questioning, Zuri pretended she hadn't heard Nubia clearly. "Huh?"

"If you 'huh,' you can hear."

"I don't know. He just does. He cool, though," Zuri answered.

But in Nubia's eyes, he was anything but cool. Trav was a young wannabe and was never going to be from their old block. He hung around all the hustlers, thinking it made him real. But it didn't. He didn't hustle, bust his gun, or nothing. He was just there to be a gofer for the niggas on the block who were getting money. They would send him to the store when they were hungry, and they'd send him for weed when they wanted to smoke.

"He follows you around like a little puppy. I know you ain't give him no pussy," Nubia said, pushing her point. There were a lot of things she wanted to teach Zuri, and not giving it up to a man that couldn't provide and had no cred was one of them.

"Hell no. You trippin'," Zuri said. She shifted in the seat of the BMW and adjusted her clothes. She was wearing shorts, and between the heat of the sun and Nubia's questions working her nerves, she was all sweaty and her thighs were sticking to the leather seat. Zuri didn't know what was worse, her sister thinking she let Trav hit or Trav following her around, even thinking he had a chance.

Nubia cut her eyes at her sister, indicating she didn't believe a word Zuri was saying. Truthfully, she did, and she was just having fun at her little sister's expense. But she still wanted to drive her point home that Trav was a no go.

That only made Zuri deny it harder. "For real, NuNu. I'm dead serious. That nigga couldn't even get a whiff of this." She didn't hide the fact that she wasn't a virgin from her sister, but Trav was definitely not getting in her panties.

"Oh, okay, 'cause I was about to say . . . ," Nubia began, her face serious, then trailed off.

"Say what?" Zuri turned in her seat to face her sister, unsticking her thighs so quickly, it hurt. She winced, both at the pain from the seat and the accusation.

"That I know I taught you better than that," Nubia said with a smile across her face. She had schooled Zuri plenty of times on the dos and don'ts of the streets and the who's who and who's not. Nubia had faithfully preached that if you fucked with a bum nigga, it made you a bum bitch. She was never going out like that, and she wouldn't let Zuri, either. They were boss bitches, and that was all a real nigga wanted on his team.

Zuri rolled her eyes now. Nubia loved being right, and Zuri couldn't hold it against her, because she was. "I thought we was going shopping. What we doing over here?" Zuri said, noticing that they had turned onto their old block.

They had made it to Hoyt Street. Zuri had been so caught up in defending her honor, she hadn't noticed where Nubia was going. Ever since they had moved away, even though it wasn't far, Zuri and Nubia had tried to avoid the old block. In their minds, there was no point in reliving bad memories or holding on to bad ties. In the new life they had, Nubia was about her business, and Zuri was learning to get like her.

"We are. I just gotta go see Brown for a second," Nubia said, adjusting her glasses in the rearview mirror. She fumbled in the cup holder for her lip gloss and reapplied it, keeping one hand on the wheel and using the other to make sure her full lips caught the light of the sun.

Zuri rolled her eyes.

They pulled up in front of the corner store at Hoyt and Baltic and immediately spotted Brown exiting the store, with a menacing look on his face. He was talking on his cell phone while a brown-skinned, bowlegged female dressed in a pair of tight jeans and pumps trailed closely behind him. By his facial expression, Nubia could tell he wasn't happy about what he was being told over the phone. Upon spotting Nubia's car, the female turned away from Brown, lowered her head, and looked the other way. Nubia got out of the car, and Zuri sank in her seat. She could already tell where this was going.

Brown was a fly young hustler with a slim but muscular frame, and despite his young age, he had gained respect in the streets. He was seen as a nigga on the come-up, one who was following in the steps of his father before him. Brown's father, Roman, had once owned the streets of Brooklyn. The eighties were his time. At the height of the chaos that had ruled the city, Roman had reigned supreme, running drugs in and out of Brooklyn, having the gangs do his dirty work, keeping his hands clean and the cops at bay. The whole borough had been his. But when the feds had come in and cracked down, he'd had nowhere left to hide. He died in a shoot-out with the FBI, cementing his status as royalty. He left Brown behind to inherit his kingdom, and even though he was young, Brown was already living up to the family reputation.

Like his father, Brown had smooth dark skin, chinky brown eyes, and a bright white smile. He wore his hair cut low, with more waves than the Pacific on a windy day. Brown stayed fresh, dressed in a red T-shirt that fit him perfectly, jeans, and sneakers to match. He wore gold Cuban links around his neck and carried himself like a boss, something that was very appealing and sexy and had earned him the nickname Pretty Brown from all the females in the neighborhood. He kept Nubia looking good as well: she was always draped in the newest designer clothes, shoes, and handbags. This was something other females had taken notice of, and they were constantly trying to knock her out of her spot, but that was never going to happen. Nubia knew females loved his G'd-up attitude, and she did too, but he was her gorgeous gunner, and she didn't appreciate the females being a little too friendly with her man.

Brown cracked a slight smile, showing off the gold bottom teeth he was rocking today, as Nubia exited the car and stalked toward him. He ended his phone conversation while stepping away, putting distance between himself and the female in his face, to meet Nubia halfway. He knew her like the back of his hand and could see she wasn't happy. Nubia was normally on chill, but she always wore her emotions on her face when it came to him, good or bad.

"Who's that bitch, Brown, and why she think you a dentist?" Nubia asked as soon as she got close to him, making sure she said it loud enough that the female would hear.

Brown chuckled as a sheepish grin adorned his face. "Dentist? What you talking 'bout, Ma?"

"She must be, cuz she all in ya face, showing all her teeth, smiling and shit," Nubia said, cocking her head to the side to let Brown know that she wasn't stupid.

"What up, NuNu? Where Zuri at?" a voice shouted, breaking the tension.

Zuri groaned. She had been avoiding interrupting the showdown between Brown and Nubia, but she looked up in disappointment to see Trav leaning against the broken pay phone in front of the store. He spotted Zuri and waved like a little kid who had found his or her parents in the crowd at a school play. He was so embarrassing. She went back on her phone.

Nubia didn't respond or acknowledge the fact that Trav had interrupted her conversation. She went on grilling Brown, head cocked, waiting for an answer. Brown chuckled again and pulled her reluctant body in for a hug, and Nubia relaxed. She was still mad, though.

"That shit ain't about nothing, Ma. I ain't out here chasing no chicks. I'm out here chasing a check. She probably out here looking for a new baby father," he said, peeking back over his shoulder at the female, who was now talking to the group of young corner boys dressed in different shades of red who were hanging around the store.

Nubia pulled away. "Yeah, well, don't get fucked up, you hear me, Brown?" she warned. "What you doing out here on the block, anyway? Ain't that what you got them niggas for?" she questioned, looking over toward the group of teenagers posted on the block.

"Fuck that. Niggas ran up in my spot last night, took work, money, all that shit. So I'm out here getting all this money, letting niggas know ain't shit sweet. I'ma run down on the first muthafucka I even think had something to do with it."

Nubia's mouth fell open from shock when she heard that news. "What?" There was no way that anybody in Brooklyn would have the audacity to run up on Brown, a true street legacy.

"Yeah, it's a dirty game, Ma, but I can play foul too," he said, flaring his nose in anger.

Nubia knew Brown wouldn't hesitate when it came to gunplay, and so did everyone else in the streets. She knew he wouldn't rest until he found the person who was responsible for the robbery. "Just be careful out here. I don't want nothing to happen to you," she said, voicing her concern, and placed a hand on his shoulder.

He grabbed her around the waist, then pulled her to him again. This time Nubia noticed the bulletproof vest under his shirt and the gun in his waistband as she pressed up against him.

"Whatever, blondie. You know I'm good out here," he told her.

Brown always loved that hair color on her, and he loved to see her act like that over him. It showed how much she really cared. Plus, it reminded him of her softer side, which was rarely on display. Nubia had to be tough in her line of work. Hustlers would see her pretty face and assume she was a pushover. But she refused to be gamed out of her bread when cooking up product. She was as serious about her money as they were about theirs, and those who didn't know quickly found out. Nubia wasn't afraid to put some money in the streets to send a message that she wasn't to be played with. Brown loved the fact that she had her own hustle and didn't just rely on him. That only made him do that much more for her.

"What's up, though? Whatchu need?" he asked.

Nubia pulled back from his embrace and shot him a dirty look. "Don't talk to me like I'm one of your customers. And what makes you think I need something?"

Brown tossed his head back and laughed at her smart remarks. "Cuz you don't even be over here like dat, so I know you up to something. Just go easy on a nigga's pockets."

Nubia was so attracted to his gangster charm, not to mention that she loved how he was smelling as good as he looked. "I just need a li'l cash. I promised Zuri I would take her shopping, but that was before I knew about what had happened to you. I'm good. Never mind."

Brown put his arm around her shoulders and walked her back over to her car. "So you came to rob me too?" he joked before reaching into his pocket and pulling out a roll of cash. He counted off fifteen hundred dollars and handed a thousand of it to Nubia, then walked over to the passenger-side window. "What up, ugly?" he shouted, banging on the car door.

A startled Zuri looked up from her phone and smiled. Just like all the rest of the females in the streets, she had easily fallen under Brown's spell. His charismatic ways and looks were unlike those of any boy her age. Although he was only a few years older than her, his maturity made the gap in age seem much bigger to her. He always showed her love and looked out for her, not just because of Nubia but just because.

"Hey, Brown," she called as she rolled down the window.

"Trav over there," he teased.

"So?" she answered, showing her disinterest.

Brown reached into the car and dropped five hundred dollars in her lap. "Here."

"What's this for?" Zuri asked, surprised by the pile of tens and twenties in her lap.

"Your sister said y'all going shopping. I know how she get in them stores. She be wildin'. You gonna need that to keep up," he said with a nod and a smile, then turned back toward Nubia. "I'ma come by the crib later. I need you to do something for me."

"For you or to you?" Nubia said seductively, flirting with him and trying to cheer him up some.

"You crazy," he said, cracking a brief smile. "For real, though," he explained. "The shit I got stashed at your house, I need you to bag that up and make a couple of drops for me. You still be carrying that thing I gave you for when you make ya runs, right?"

"Of course," Nubia answered.

"Good. I wouldn't know what to do if something happened to you, Ma." The sincerity in his voice made her body tremble as she stepped into his embrace and he palmed her butt.

"I know," she said. "I got you, baby. I love you."

Brown kissed her lips softly. "I already know. Now get ya pretty ass outta here before I have to kill one of these li'l niggas for staring too hard," he joked, looking back at the group in front of the store.

Nubia gave him one more kiss, then walked around the car, swaying her ass harder than usual, knowing he was watching. She hopped in her car and pulled off the block.

Nubia and Zuri laughed and joked as they entered the lobby of their apartment building, fresh from their shopping spree, with bags in hand. Their small two-bedroom apartment sat above a beauty-supply store in the middle of the block. The two of them had been staying there for a few months now. Brown had helped Nubia find a new place after she decided her old apartment was starting to draw too much attention from all the traffic running in and out. Since moving, she had switched up her routine some. The slight change had made her feel better and had slowed down the revolving door of traffic.

Although Brown didn't live there, he spent a lot of nights there, but he didn't serve anyone out of the new apartment or have anyone meet him there. Nubia didn't, either. She couldn't chance the police raiding her apartment and sending her to jail. That would leave Zuri all alone in the world. Just the thought of this broke Nubia's heart into fragments.

The two sisters were as close as two people could be. Their love was unconditional, and their bond was unbreakable. Zuri looked up to Nubia like any young sister would, but their connection was deeper than the norm because of the motherly role Nubia played in her life. And for her part, Nubia adored her baby sister. She saw in Zuri all the things she wished for herself, and she was determined to make a better life for them, but especially for Zuri. There was nothing they wouldn't do for each other.

"I gotta pee," Nubia cried out as she raced up the steps to the second floor, causing Zuri to laugh.

"You was killing those grape sodas in the mall," Zuri called after her.

"Shut up and open the door for me," Nubia insisted as she danced in place in front of the door to their apartment, trying not to pee on herself.

Zuri's hands were full of bags as she reached in her handbag. She fumbled the keys, and they fell on the hallway floor. As she bent down to pick them up, she heard a muffled scream and looked up to see a solidly built man wearing a black hood and ski mask with his hand over Nubia's mouth and a gun pressed to her head.

"Open the door right now, or I'ma kill this bitch!" he barked out.

Zuri could see the fear in her sister's eyes as tears began to form in her own. Her heart was raging in her chest, and she froze with fear.

"Don't play with me, li'l bitch. Open the door!" the man's voice roared through the hallway as he turned the gun on her.

Zuri's hands trembled from nervousness, with the gun mere inches from her face. She had never been in anything like this before. Tears flowed freely down her face, and she felt a sinking feeling in her stomach at the sudden chill of a gun being pressed against the back of her neck. Out of the corner of her eye, she saw another masked gunman standing behind her, silent. His silence made her blood run cold from terror. She tried to calm herself down and follow the stocky gunman's instructions but couldn't stop her hands from shaking.

"Take the keys from her," the stocky gunman ordered.

The quiet gunman snatched the keys from her, opened the door, and shoved her into the house forcefully. The man holding Nubia followed close behind, still aiming his gun at her head. Once inside the apartment, he tossed her onto the floor of the living room.

"Where the money and the bricks?" he shouted, waving his gun back and forth at the two sisters.

"I don't know what you talking about," Nubia cried out, black tears smeared on her face as her mascara ran.

"I look stupid to you? You think we here by accident? Bitch, I know who you is. Don't play dumb with me. Now, where it's at?"

Nubia shook her head. "I swear I don't—"

"NuNu!" Zuri screamed in horror as she watched the stocky gunman strike her sister in the face with the gun before she could finish her sentence.

The pain was like nothing Nubia had felt before. Blood instantly filled her mouth, and she could feel that her front teeth had cracked. She spit the tooth chips and the blood on the carpet as she moaned in agony.

"Now, I ain't gonna ask you again," he said in a menacing tone. "Matter of fact, I'll find it. If either one of them move, kill dem bitches," he stated coldly to the silent gunman. Then he began searching the apartment for the stash.

"NuNu, are you okay?" Zuri cried out, seeing all the blood leaking from her sister's mouth.

Nubia nodded her head but didn't attempt to speak as she continued to spit up blood.

The silent gunman showed no sign of any emotion; his body language remained stoic, and to Zuri, his eyes were piercing and filled with evil intentions. His quiet demeanor was frightening as he aimed his gun at them. He held it tight, and his trigger finger seemed to twitch with anticipation. He scared her more than the gunman who had been barking out orders.

Finally, the stocky gunman returned to the living room from the back of the apartment. He held a small duffel bag in his hand. "I knew these bitches were lying," he said, looking over at the other gunman and handing him the bag. "Money and bricks."

The quiet gunman looked in the bag, then nodded in approval. He slowly walked over to a bloody and battered Nubia and tossed the duffel bag at her feet. She looked down at it, then up at him through the tears in her eyes.

Boom!

Nubia's body went numb as she watched her little sister's body fall limp to the floor, seemingly in slow motion. Her soul felt like it left her body. She could feel herself screaming but couldn't hear the noise coming from her mouth. There was a deafening silence in the room, a pause in time. It was like she had died from the same bullet that he had put in Zuri's head.

"Fuck you and that nigga . . . ," she heard the stocky gunman say, knowing her murder was a message for Brown. The two shots to her head that followed were only a formality.

The loud ringing inside her head was persistent and seemed to intensify by the second. It felt like someone was striking her brain like a gong. The noise was dwarfed only by the excruciating pain that accompanied it. The intensity of that pain caused Zuri to jolt from her unconscious state and let out an agonizing screech that echoed through the apartment as she opened her eyes. The room was still. Not only was the eerie quiet frightening, but it also amplified the ringing in her ears. Zuri placed her hand on her head and could feel the warm blood leaking from the side of her head. She pulled back her hand to see it covered in crimson.

The origin of her injury was lost in a fog of confusion and splintered memories. As things slowly came back to her, she could recall the sounds of giggling and laughter as she tried on clothes in a dressing room with Nubia and the taste of the Cold Stone Creamery ice cream she had. The last thing she remembered seeing before the world went black was a fiery red flash. Then it all came back at once, and her chest felt like a hundred-pound weight had fallen on it as a wave of emotions washed over her. She had been shot by a pair of intruders who had been waiting for her and Nubia when they returned home. Fear instantly set in. The absence of sounds in the apartment really unnerved her now. There were no moans, no muffled whimpers or cries for help, nothing but dead silence. Zuri looked to her right and saw Nubia's lifeless body lying next to her.

"Nooo!" she screamed, using her blood-soaked hand to cover her mouth.

The shock of seeing the person she loved the most in the whole world with her brains painted all over the carpet was too much for Zuri to bear. She immediately began to gag, then emptied the contents of her stomach onto the floor as she cried from deep in her soul. A flood of tears ran from her eyes as the levee holding her together snapped. The room began to spin as she crawled over to her sister.

"NuNu!" she tearfully shouted as she shook her sister in a futile attempt to revive her. It was too late; Nubia was long gone. But this realization didn't stop Zuri from trying to wake Nubia. "NuNu, open your eyes, please," she begged, continuing to shake her. "You can't leave. Please don't go. Please don't leave me. Oh my God!"

Zuri refused to accept her sister's death, believing there was something she could do to save her. She mustered up enough energy to struggle to her feet. As she stood up, the room began to spin out of control, and she became lightheaded, then blacked out. When she collapsed to the floor, she landed in a pool of Nubia's blood.

The hard rain crashing violently against the window, along with the beeping of the machine in the quiet room, interrupted Zuri's peaceful sleep, causing her to crack open her eyes and awaken from the best rest she had had in a long time. Her eyelids felt heavier than normal, and it took a few minutes for the rest of her body to realize she had awoken. She felt slightly off balance, and it took a little longer for her eyes to adjust to the darkness of the room. She fought through the stiffness in her neck as she lifted her head and swiveled it back and forth, surveying the room. She noticed a shadowy figure seated in the corner, and she strained her eyes as she peered into the gloom.

"Who's there?" she called out in a raspy tone, her voice a whisper. Her throat burned and her mouth was dry, making it hard to speak. The shadowy figure rose from the chair and walked toward her bed. Zuri gripped her bedsheets as she instantly grew nervous. She sat up in the bed, her heart pounding in her chest.

"Be easy," the voice said before clicking on the small lamp above her bed. "It's me, Brown."

Zuri let out a sigh of relief. She thought it was one of the robbers, coming back to finish the job. Her relief quickly turned to anger. After all, Brown was the one the two masked gunmen had been looking for when they murdered her sister and left her for dead. "What are you . . . ?"

"Shhh," Brown said, stopping her in mid-sentence. "You shouldn't try to talk so much, Ma. You had a tube down your throat until yesterday."

"My sister," she whispered, ignoring his suggestion. She started to struggle in the bed, but there were so many wires attached to her body, she couldn't move much. Brown put his hands on her shoulders, holding her together.

"I know," he said, lowering his head in sadness and placing his hand on hers.

"No, you don't understand. I have to get outta here. I have to let my mother know. We have to plan her funeral," she said, tearing up at the thought. Even though her mother hadn't done much for her, she still felt the need to inform her about Nubia.

Brown shook his head and looked away, unable to find the words to say. How was he supposed to deliver the news that would crush her young life even more than it had been already? He was clearly grief stricken, and it hurt him even more to have to be the bearer of bad news. He felt a lump form in his throat. "I'm sorry, Zuri," he said from his heart, in a somber tone. "Nubia's funeral was two weeks ago."

"Huh? What? How?" she asked, confused by his statement.

"You been in a coma for about a month," he informed her. "I been coming up here every few nights to check on you."

Zuri felt like she had just gotten hit in the chest with a sledgehammer, as every bit of air had been knocked out of her lungs. Large teardrops began to fall from the corners of her eyes, like the beginning of a rainstorm, as she looked away from him.

Brown rubbed her hand, trying his best to console her. He had lost his girlfriend, but she had lost not only a big sister but also the only person in the world she had who cared about her. Seeing her cry made Brown's eyes tear up as well. The handsome hustler's presence usually filled up a room. He moved with a swag and an edge that could be felt as soon as he entered. But that was gone; the charm and the bright smile that normally greeted Zuri had been replaced by tears and sorrow.

"I just want to be left alone, Brown," Zuri said, pulling her hand away, still holding on to a bit of resentment toward him for bringing those men to her front door. He may not have pulled the trigger, but Zuri couldn't help thinking it was his fault.

"Zuri—" Brown began, only to be interrupted.

"Just leave," she stated coldly, refusing to look at him.

"I'm sorry, Zuri. I understand what you are going through. Just know you're not alone out here. I swear to you, I'm gonna find whoever did this and I'm gonna kill them. I'm gonna kill them for you, for NuNu. I promise," he said, knowing her attitude was a part of her grieving.

Hearing Brown's promise did absolutely nothing for Zuri. Killing whoever was responsible wouldn't bring her sister back, and at that moment that was all she wanted. Her world had just come crashing down, and nobody could fix it. Not even Brown, with all his gangster bravado.

Brown wiped the tears from his eyes. "I gotta go. I got my niggas downstairs, waiting on me. But I promise you, I'ma make this right. You ain't never gotta worry about shit from here on out. I gotchu. Believe dat."

None of what Brown was saying seemed to make a difference in the moment, and Zuri refused to look at him. She felt so many feelings running through her mind, she didn't know which one to give in to. She just knew that they all hurt more than anything ever had.

Brown stood frozen in the doorway for a moment, not knowing what else to say or do. He stared at a devastated Zuri and took a mental note of her pain, like he was using it to fuel his retaliation. "I'll be back to check on you in a couple of days. I'll let the nurse know you woke up," he said. Then he slowly closed the door, leaving her alone in the hospital room.

Zuri stared at the ceiling and let out a scream as tears raced down her face. Then she banged her balled-up fist on the hospital bed in a fit of rage and frustration. The streets had taken every person close to her in one way or another. She had experienced a lifetime's worth of heartache and tragedy in her short time on Earth and felt broken and defeated.

Maybe death would be easier than living, she thought to herself, contemplating ending it all. *Maybe Nubia was dealt the better hand. Why am I left here to deal with it all alone?* It was a question only God could answer, but at that moment, she didn't have much faith in Him, either.

Chapter 2

Five years later . . .

"Hatin'-ass bum bitch," Zuri mumbled under her breath as she positioned herself behind the curtain to the left of the stage. The screw face she sported was reserved for the petite redbone currently occupying the main stage at Daydreams, a hole-in-the-wall strip club located in South Philly.

Despite its sordid conditions and grimy reputation, a decent amount of money flowed through the doors of the sleazy club from time to time. It was the spot where all the local corner boys came to blow through their daily bread. Although her job wasn't like being in one of the hottest spots in the city, where the athletes, rappers, and all the real money played, it paid her bills, even if only barely. Zuri was one of the club's main attractions, Twenty-one years young, the beauty had an angelic face and a body ripped from the pages of the magazine *Black Men*. She was every dope boy's dream and received most of the attention from the customers who entered Daydreams.

That reality didn't sit well with some of the other dancers. In the cutthroat business of stripping, the women were fiercely competitive, and every dollar counted. Zuri knew this all too well. The petite redbone working the pole onstage right now had been trying to cut into her paper. This slim, tattoo-covered stripper had gone to great lengths to destroy Zuri's reputation by getting in the ears of some of the regulars and hustlers that frequented Daydreams, spreading lies about Zuri, trying to claim her loyal customers as her own. Word had quickly gotten back to Zuri, and she was waiting for a chance to check her about it.

"Give it up one more time for Diamond Eyes," the DJ announced as he lowered the music's volume slightly. The half-hearted cheers and whistles of the light crowd could just be heard above the speakers.

Zuri watched and waited as Diamond pranced around the stage, collecting the small number of bills scattered on the stage. When she noticed Diamond making her way backstage, she slipped back behind the curtain, out of sight, and waited for her to appear. Zuri didn't give the petite stripper a chance to make it all the way to the back of the stage before she had her pressed against the wall, with her hand in her face.

"Bitch, I thought I told you to keep my name out ya dick-sucking mouth?" Zuri barked. Zuri knew that maybe the club wasn't the place to be handling this aspect of the business, but in the years that had passed since Nubia died, she had grown into her own protector. Even though she was quiet, she was still able to handle her own, and her demeanor always gave her the advantage of surprise. No one ever saw her coming.

"Whatchu talkin' 'bout?" a startled Diamond asked, dropping the items she clutched in her hands.

"You know exactly what I'm talkin' 'bout. You out here running ya mouth to these niggas in the club, thinking it won't get back to me," Zuri stormed. She pushed Diamond's face together with one hand, her acrylics digging into Diamond's fleshy cheeks.

"I don't know what you talkin' 'bout," Diamond said, lying through her teeth but doing her best to sound convincing and unafraid. She tried to jerk her head out of Zuri's hands, but Zuri's grip was too strong.

The confrontation caught the attention of some of the other dancers backstage, and a bouncer rushed over and attempted to intervene. Their presence gave Diamond a little more courage, as she knew no one would let the two of them fight.

She puffed her chest up now, filled with heart. "You coming at me over some shit some random niggas in the club told you? Really, bitch?" Diamond yelled as she struggled even harder, knowing Zuri would have to let her go.

"Yeah, really, bitch! And this the last time I'm gonna tell you about my name in ya mouth. Next time I gonna fuck you up," Zuri snarled, digging her nails into Diamond's cheeks one last time to punctuate that this wasn't a threat anymore, but a promise. She let Diamond go.

"Whatever," Diamond snapped as she bent over to pick up the money she'd dropped, shaking out her hair and running a hand over each cheek. She sucked her teeth and rolled her eyes before walking away. Zuri didn't like making enemies in the place where she worked. It was messy, and it could fuck with her paper. But if other bitches were causing the mess and getting in the way of her money, what else was Zuri supposed to do?

The DJ's voice over the speakers caught Zuri's attention. "Now, brace yourself, fellas. The next dancer coming to the stage is none other than the lovely and sexy Heaven," he announced as the intro to Jagged Edge's "Walked Outta Heaven" began to play over the club's sound system.

Hearing her theme song, Zuri instantly pushed the altercation with Diamond out of her mind and shifted her thoughts back to her money. Just like Clark Kent emerged from a phone booth as Superman, once she broke through the curtain, Zuri disappeared and Heaven, the stage name she used, appeared. Strutting provocatively on to the stage like a sex kitten, she was full of confidence and ready to fulfill every man's visual fantasy.

Her two sides couldn't be more different. Zuri was reserved and unassuming, a bashful around-the-way girl in her day-to-day life. Heaven was a character she had created in order to thrive and survive in the seedy world of stripping. But she was quickly learning that it was impossible to keep the two separate. Men lusted over Heaven, and once they recognized her outside the club, that was all they saw her as. Zuri was slowly disappearing, no matter how tightly she tried to hold on to herself. With every month that passed, she was being swallowed whole by her alter ego. She wanted nothing more than to leave Philly in her rearview mirror, but she was barely making it as it was, and she feared the uncertainty that awaited her outside the City of Brotherly Love. After all, she didn't have much to fall back on when it came to work experience or education. After her sister's death, she had fled New York to stay with her mother, hoping the change of scenery would help. But she had quickly realized not much had changed with her mother's addictive ways, and just like before, she'd been forced to fend for herself, but now without Nubia there to guide her.

After an erotic performance that lasted a few songs, Zuri retrieved the bills that had been tossed her way in appreciation and headed off the stage the same way she had glided onto it, gracefully and seductively. Her naked body glistened as the club lights caught the specks in the body shimmer she wore. She swayed her wide hips as the DJ played the next record and announced the next group of dancers to hit the stage. Her feet were on fire, but she showed no pain as she clutched her money and strutted through the club, toward the locker room. The club was dead, which meant the dancers were aggravated and the men were being cheaper than usual. Zuri looked down at the cash in her hand with disappointment.

Scraps, she thought to herself. "And these bitches in here working my nerves," she said aloud, cutting her eyes at Diamond, who was back on the main floor, giving a dude seated directly in front of the stage a lap dance.

Zuri didn't want to be working tonight as it was. This night, more than any, was hard, and the nights would only get harder, as the anniversary of Nubia's death loomed on the horizon. She felt a sickening feeling in the pit of her stomach upon realizing she was going to have to work twice as hard to make half as much. That usually was how it went on dead nights like tonight. She purposely passed right by Diamond and grabbed the eyes of the guy she was entertaining. She wanted to beat her ass right there, but she never blew her cool in front of money, no matter how little there was to be made in the club tonight.

A light-skinned dude by the bar, dressed in a dark tee and jeans, reached out and grabbed Zuri's hand before she could pass him. "Damn, Ma. Can I get a dance?"

Everything in her wanted to decline, since he was a regular in the spot but never tipped. He always ordered the two-drink minimum and watched for free all night, while others spent money. Tonight he was stunting in a half-empty club with a small stack of singles, trying to get noticed and lucky. Zuri had peeped his game from the jump, but the thin wad of bills in her hand made her willing to entertaining his bullshit tonight. Just by looking at his clothes and shoes, she knew he wasn't about major paper. Not to mention the two broke niggas he was with, who looked more excited to see the show than he was. Neither of them had a single dollar in their hands, and they looked like they had been babysitting the same bottles of beer all night.

God, I hate wasting my time with these lame niggas. Fuck it, though. I'm 'bout to get this nigga's li'l bit of cash. I need it, Zuri thought to herself as she caressed his hand. "I got you baby. Just let me go freshen up some," she said flirtatiously, tracing her finger down the front of his shirt and flashing her pretty smile.

Zuri's beauty easily captivated men, casting a spell over them. Her light caramel skin was smooth and blemish free. Her doe-shaped eyes didn't need fake lashes to enhance them; they curled perfectly without any mascara being applied. Zuri's full, pouty lips drew men in, but her perfect set of pearly whites and her beautiful smile melted hearts. Her young body was fierce. Though she didn't have the biggest set of breasts, they blended well with her tiny waist and her curvaceous hips and ass. Most women paid for the sculpted body that she had got through genetics and the good Lord Himself. Hence the stage name Heaven.

"You know you too pretty to be working in here, right, Ma?" he said, holding on to her hand. "You need to come fuck with a real nigga and let me take you up out of here," he added, shooting his best shot.

Zuri was used to it; she had heard this same speech over a hundred times just this month alone. She always entertained it, anything to keep the money flowing.

"What makes you think I need to be rescued from here?" she asked as the song switched. She tried to tug her hand out of his, but he held on tight.

"You don't belong in this place, Ma. You should be somebody's wifey. Spend your days shopping and traveling. I can make that happen," he proclaimed boldly.

"Just let me go freshen up and I'll be back, I promise," she said, seeing his unwillingness to let go of her hand. She tugged a little bit more.

"Okay. I'll be right here waiting for you to get back, Ma," he said, trying to sound smooth, finally releasing his grip. Zuri snatched her hand back.

"Okay. Daddy," she said, then turned her back to him and rolled her eyes before walking into the locker room.

When Zuri came back from freshening up, the light-skinned man who had grabbed her hand and had insisted she dance for him and his friends was still in the same spot, with the same beer. She sighed. Truth be told, she hadn't done much in the dressing room. Zuri hated to admit it, but sometimes the job she had got to be too much. She loved being able to provide for herself and take care of her own, but when it came to the men, she wished there was a different way of dealing with them. Especially now. The thought of what Nubia would say about Zuri putting it down on a man with no money and no power for a few singles was enough to make Zuri nauseated. But a job was a job, so she walked over.

"Hey, baby. I'm back," Zuri said, placing her hand on the shoulder of the light-skinned dude. He was in conversation, and she needed to get his attention if she was going to dance. He turned to her.

"Sorry, Ma. You're going to have to give me a second. The men are talking," he told her, then went back to laughing with his friends.

Men, Zuri thought, trying her hardest not to roll her eyes. This was the lamest bunch of men she had ever seen in her life. But she needed the tips, and so while the so-called men talked, she swayed and gyrated her hips to the music.

"Yeah, it's crazy, fam," said one of the men leaning against the bar. "I can't believe they're letting him out.

With all that fucked shit he did, he must've given 'em something good to be let out that easy."

"Fuck you mean?" said the light-skinned dude. "He was in that bitch for a minute. That man got a whole RICO charge. Redd used to run these streets. No way he talked."

Zuri kept dancing, but she was intrigued. Growing up in Brooklyn, but specifically growing up around Brown and his family legacy of crime, she knew what it meant to have charges that heavy. Even though she had been in Philly for five years and there were always hustlers in and out of the club, she still felt left out of the loop. She started dancing a little closer to the group, and then she draped her hands on either side of the light-skinned man's neck.

"What's your name, Daddy?" asked Zuri. "You have me all worked up, and I don't even know your name." Zuri dipped back and forth in front of him and cracked an innocent smile. He laughed as she swayed her hips.

"I'm sorry, Ma. It's Ty," he said. "But you can keep calling me Daddy." He slapped her ass, and Zuri forced a smile to keep herself from grimacing. There was something about a man placing his unwanted hand on her body that made her furious. But she always put her paper before her feelings, so now she only moved closer to Ty.

"All I'm saying is the streets in Philly might start to heat up," Ty's friend said after taking another tiny sip from his beer. There was no way it wasn't lukewarm by now, and Zuri could almost taste the bitterness in her mouth. She wanted to throw up.

"What you mean?" asked Ty. He had started to disengage from the conversation his friends were trying to have with him. Zuri's breasts were too close to his face for him to focus completely on something else, and as he trailed his hands down her chest and around her waist to her ass, he was barely thinking about anything else. But Zuri was still totally tuned in.

"All I'm saying is that if a player like Greg Redd makes his way back on to the scene, shit is gonna shift, ya feel me? Ain't no way they're letting him out for no reason. I say he cut a deal," said Ty's friend with the lukewarm beer.

"Man, shut the fuck up," Ty said, his attention still mostly on Zuri.

She turned away from the conversation and back to him. It was strange. In that moment she thought only of Brooklyn and the fact that even though she had left it behind, she still knew more about those streets and those people than she knew about Philly and the men in front of her. Who was Greg Redd?

She sat on Ty and could feel him hard against her before she even started the lap dance. She chuckled to herself. Men were so easy. Zuri sat with her thoughts as she ground on him. She wondered what Nubia would say about her now. She was totally out of that life. The life that NuNu had tried to build for them was one of power and freedom. But to have those things, you needed to be in the know. Here was this conversation about some big drug boss, and Zuri didn't even know who or what they were talking about. Nubia would be disappointed. How was Zuri supposed to be in the game if she didn't know the players? She could feel herself grow hot, and she reminded herself that even though that lifestyle was what she had been groomed for, it was the same lifestyle that had killed Nubia.

"How about we take this somewhere . . . more personal, Ma?" said Ty, gripping Zuri's ass in his hands.

She tried not to roll her eyes. Thinking about Nubia had made her forget where she was and what she was doing. She stopped dancing and removed Ty's hands from her behind. "Actually, that's about it for you, baby, unless you have a couple more bills stacked somewhere I can't see," Zuri teased, knowing he didn't.

Ty's face twisted, and he reached up and grabbed Zuri by the back of the neck. She was stunned. Men in the club weren't allowed to treat the dancers like that. There were rules. Between the flashing lights, the loud music, and her hair covering Ty's grip, no one could see or hear what was going on, and no one was coming to save her. He yanked Zuri's face down to his level. "You better watch it with me, bitch," he spit in her ear before letting her back up.

Zuri was shaken. She hated thinking that men thought they could treat her any which way and get away with it. As she backed away from him, she could feel the rage building up in her. A million thoughts ran through her head in one second. What if she slapped him? What if she cracked one of those babysat bottles of beer over his head? He smirked at her, and her anger broke.

"Fuck you," Zuri said, and she yanked the money Ty still had in his hand.

"Take it, bitch," Ty said as he got up to leave. Then he just laughed. At the end of the day, Zuri had no way of winning this fight. He had the money, and she had a job, and even if he was fucked for grabbing her that way, she couldn't do anything about it, and he knew it.

His boys laughed with him, thinking shit was funny. They all walked away from Zuri, and even though she had the money, she felt like she had lost.

Zuri entered the busy locker room and let out a deep sigh as she sat down on an empty seat in front of a mirror that covered the entire wall. Naked women zoomed in and out of the locker room. While there, they scrambled here and there, making outfit changes and small talk at the same time. The muffled bass of the music made the room vibrate slightly as Zuri took a long look at herself in the mirror. Her natural beauty was hidden behind the makeup she wore. She was mentally drained. The club had become a place she dreaded going. At first, the money had been good, but it had slowed down so much lately that she had fallen behind on her bills. The club owner was a sleazy ex-hustler who didn't do much to attract new customers but continued taking a big cut of all the dancers' money. His way of doing business was getting old, but she didn't have much of a choice at this point. Most strip club owners were the same. But that meant that men like Ty, men who thought they could handle women however they wanted, kept coming in and fucking with Zuri's mental.

Zuri loosened the straps on her thigh-high lace-up boots with the eight-inch heels, thankful not to have them on any longer. She was done dancing for the night. As she started counting her small earnings, she noticed Scarlett approaching through the mirror. Scarlett was a thick Puerto Rican with a fiery personality and red hair to match her attitude and her name. She was one of the few dancers in the club that Zuri rocked with. Scarlett smiled as the two made eye contact through the mirror.

"Hey, boo. You calling it a night?" she asked, seeing Zuri in a relaxed state, with her shoes off, and not scrambling around like everyone else in the locker room.

Zuri sighed while counting the little bit of money in her hand from the unfortunate lap dance she had just given. She then added it to a small stack she had on the table in front of her. "Yeah. Girl, ain't no money in here tonight. I don't even know why I brought my ass up here." Zuri leaned back in her chair, and Scarlett playfully turned her around so they were face-to-face.

"I didn't expect to see you in here tonight. Bitches' faces hit the floor when you walked in. Shit, it already wasn't no money in here, but they knew whatever was in here, you was gonna clean up," Scarlett joked, causing the two of them to laugh.

"Clean up. Pss! I wish. This ain't cutting it no more, girl. Once I cash out, it really will be a waste of time," she said, counting the money for a second time and dreading having to give a cut to the owner. "Shit, I could have kept my gig at the mall for this. It don't work your nerves?" Zuri was exasperated.

"Yeah, it do, but you know me. A bitch keep a side hustle," Scarlett declared proudly.

"I need to get me one," Zuri confessed, shaking her head. "You always up to something."

"You should fuck with us. If you need some extra paper, I could definitely put you on," she offered. She smiled in a way that made Zuri think she must be up to something.

"On to what? And *us* who?" Zuri asked skeptically. "You know I don't fuck with everybody." She thought about the rest of the girls in the club; they were all so lame to her. For Zuri, the strip club was a means to an end, a stepping-stone to something bigger and better. She just didn't know what it was yet. But even though she didn't know what her finish line was, she knew it was better than whatever these bitches were doing. Scarlett, however, was different.

"Me and Jazz," Scarlett said. "We be hustlin' out in Atlantic City. It's a lot of money out there," she explained, bouncing her neck as she spoke, seeming to light up. Jazz was okay with Zuri too, but a hustle wasn't for her.

"Oh, hell nah. I don't know nothing about selling no drugs. I'll pass," said Zuri, shaking her head. She started to collect her things to get ready to go.

Scarlett laughed. "Girl, not that type of hustlin'. My cousin work at the front desk of the hotel at one of the casinos. He put me on. It's plenty of high rollers in dem casinos looking to have beautiful women on their arm for the night, and they pay like they weigh. Especially if they winning." Scarlett winked at her. Zuri couldn't believe it.

"Y'all selling pussy?" Zuri blurted out, giving her the side-eye.

Scarlett's mouth dropped open. They were all strippers, sure, but selling it was a whole different story. She pinched Zuri, not wanting that floating around the locker room. Zuri winced and smacked her hand away, but Scarlett smiled at her still.

"Damn, you tryin'a blow a bitch's spot," Scarlett said, looking over her shoulder, making sure nobody had heard. Then she corrected her. "It's escorting."

"Whatever you call it, I'll pass, Scar. I ain't knocking your hustle. Do your thing," Zuri said. She meant it. She liked Scarlett, and even though she wasn't going to sell pussy, she respected the ambition.

"Okay, but if you ever change your mind, just let me know," Scarlett said, hugging her. As she headed back out into the club, she spun around at the door to the dressing room and blew Zuri a kiss.

Zuri couldn't explain it, but Scarlett reminded her of Nubia. Definitely not because of her side hustle. It had more to do with her personality. Scarlett was bubbly and positive, something Zuri had never been able to develop as part of her attitude. She was just quiet, but she could stand up for herself when she needed to, and maybe that was enough. The dressing room was still crowded and bustling, but Zuri moved slowly as she finished packing her bag. Between the way Scarlett had framed things as an opportunity and the fact that the anniversary of Nubia's death was coming up, Zuri couldn't stop thinking. The déjà vu from the way Scarlett moved sat with her and took her back to that last day she and Nubia had spent together.

"Hey, Z," Nubia said.

Zuri was trying on clothes in the dressing room of the Gucci store.

"*Look at this,*" *Nubia continued before she touched the tip of her tongue to the tip of her nose and licked off a drop of ice cream that had somehow found its way from the spoon and to Nubia's bright face.*

Zuri cackled. "Girl, we can't take you nowhere, huh?" she joked. She pulled up a skirt that was definitely too tight on her full and curvy thighs. "Man, how does this fit on anyone?" Zuri pouted, exasperated. Nubia put down her ice cream on one of the padded suede benches in the dressing room and walked over to Zuri. If there was one thing about luxury shopping, it was that there was always going to be a place to sit, and Nubia loved that. And Zuri loved days like these. Just her and NuNu, strutting through the mall, with more money than they could spend in one place. But having her big sister there to help her adjust the pieces she was trying on and give her advice was her favorite part of the experience.

"*It's not you, boo,*" *Nubia advised her. "These white bitches just don't have ass." She went behind Zuri and tried to pull the zipper up over her little sister's growing hips. She got only halfway. With a move so quick it could have been a reflex, she managed to pull Zuri's stomach in and the zipper up all the way.*

"*Damn!*" *Zuri exclaimed, gasping, "How am I supposed to breathe?"*

Nubia rolled her eyes in the mirror when Zuri lifted her head and could see her. "Stop being dramatic. You're going to have to learn to deal with this shit. Being a bad bitch don't come easy," she explained, flipping her long blond hair over her shoulder with a comical flourish. She then put her head on Zuri's shoulder and leaned into the crook of her little sister's neck. "You look good," she said, squeezing Zuri's shoulders. "Let's get it."

"This is going to make those other bitches sick," Zuri said and giggled.

She loved that she and her sister were able to wear designer and were able to pay for everything with hard cash. Zuri kept the skirt on as she pulled the money Brown had given her from her purse. From behind her, she could hear Nubia kiss her teeth. Zuri turned around, confused. The expression on Nubia's face was one Zuri had never seen before. She looked tired.

"Save it, Z," Nubia said.

Zuri was still confused. "I thought we was gonna get it. I have the money right here," she said, counting the bills again to make sure there was enough.

"I know, boo. We gon' get it. But save your money. I got it," Nubia said, pulling out a stack of bills way bigger than what Brown had given her earlier. Zuri didn't even know how all that money fit in her purse.

"Shit, NuNu. Where did you get that?" she asked. Suddenly, what she was holding didn't feel like nothing. Just from looking at it, she guessed there had to be at least five stacks in Nubia's manicured hands.

"Don't worry about it, Z. Point is we got it, and now we can get whatever we want. You want the skirt, you get the skirt," Nubia said. She smiled at Zuri, but something in her eyes was dark. Zuri couldn't keep her emotions hidden for too long, and concern turned the corners of her mouth down. Nubia started laughing.

"What?" Zuri said, slightly annoyed to think that Nubia might be messing with her.

"Girl, I told you not to worry," Nubia reassured her younger sister. She started counting out bills and placed a small stack in Zuri's hands. "Listen, where I got it, how I got it, that don't matter. Point is we got it," Nubia said sincerely. "However you choose to make your paper, make it, Z, but never leave yourself open to getting violated. Watch your front and your back."

"Why I got to watch my back if that's what I got you for?" Zuri *joked, sticking her tongue out.*

Nubia laughed and got back to her ice cream. "Listen, I'm just saying, if I'm ever not there, you got to be ready. First step, let's see if you can't get out that skirt by yourself," she said, winking.

Zuri laughed, not knowing how ready she would have to be.

Zuri had zoned out. She looked around her now. The dressing room at the club had grown quiet. There was only a couple of dancers left now, and the energy was low. Zuri finished packing her bag, thinking about what her sister had said. She wished she could talk to Nubia, to get guidance. There was no way to know what Nubia would have thought about how Zuri lived her life now, because those men had taken that away from her all those years ago.

Chapter 3

Zuri walked out the front door of the club, wheeling her small roller bag behind her. She was dressed in a fitted T-shirt, a black pair of leggings, and a pair of Nike Air Max, and her face was free of makeup, but her natural beauty still caught the eye of every man she passed. After speaking to the bouncers posted out front, she headed straight for the parking lot where only the dancers were allowed to park. It was brightly lit and guarded by club security to make sure all the girls remained safe. Philly was a gutter city, where there wasn't much brotherly love being spread around. Anybody could be a victim. The robbers didn't discriminate, and strippers carried large amounts of cash on them when they left the club, making them prime targets.

After opening her car door, Zuri placed the bag inside, then slid into the driver's seat, happy to finally be heading home. She put the key in the ignition and attempted to crank up her car, but nothing happened.

"Come on! Not now," she shouted, then pleaded with the vehicle before attempting to start it up again. The same result, nothing. She banged on the steering wheel in a fit of frustration. "This is just not my night."

She pulled out her phone and began scrolling through her contacts, trying to see whom she could call to come pick her up. She knew calling anyone at this time of night would look like she was trying to creep, so she needed to choose wisely. She wasn't about to give up no pussy for a ride home, and she didn't feel like getting into it with a nigga after making him get out of bed this late. That made the choice easy: her best friend, Geisha. Zuri knew Geisha had to work in the morning and hated to wake her up, but it was an emergency. She dialed the number, but the operator picked up instead. Zuri's heart sank in her chest. Geisha's phone was off, and she would need to call someone else. She took a deep breath and scrolled down a few more times before settling on the number of a person she knew would come for sure.

Standing beside her car, with her arms folded, Zuri heard the loud music coming up the block before she saw the headlights turn into the parking lot. She let out a big sigh, partly out of relief but mostly from trying to prepare herself mentally for the ride home.

"What's up, Zuri?" said the guy with a caramel complexion and a neatly lined and groomed beard as he pulled up alongside of her. His hair was cut so low, he almost looked bald, but his line looked fresh.

"Hey, Waheed," she replied in a snobbish tone, then walked around to the passenger side of his car.

He just shook his head, but he was still happy that she had called. They hadn't officially been a couple in a year, but there wasn't much he wouldn't do for her, including getting out his bed at three thirty in the morning to drive across town to pick her up. Waheed was a sucker when it came to her. They had been dealing with each other off and on since she arrived in Philly. He was six years her senior, and at first, he had thought he could mold the pretty girl's young mind into what he wanted her to be, figuring his age and experience gave him the upper hand. But despite having a little weed hustle, Waheed wasn't a thorough enough street nigga, and he wasn't built to groom anyone. Once Zuri had got a taste of what other street niggas had to offer, she had quickly turned the tables on their relationship, and before Waheed knew it, he had been molded into her do boy.

"Damn. You would think I was the one that called you and woke you up out ya sleep," Waheed said, referring to the cold greeting he had received.

"I'm sorry. It's been a long night. Now this," she said, pouting and gesturing to her car. She knew just how to play him. A smile grew across his face. He loved it when he got to baby her.

"I understand, Ma. I thought I told you to get rid of that piece-of-shit car, but you never listen," he said.

He and Zuri both knew what their relationship had become, and as much as it pained her to listen to his annoying "I told you so," she knew it was the way that things were going to have to go down if she was going to get what she wanted from him.

"I know, Wah," she whined. "I wish I would have now."

Waheed readjusted himself in the seat next to her. She was stroking his ego, and even though he knew she wasn't being totally sincere, he loved hearing it, anyway. "It's all good. My manz is a mechanic. I'll have it towed to his spot first thing in the morning. You know I gotchu," he stated confidently.

Zuri knew he loved to feel like the hero, so she sat back and let him. She knew Wah like the back of her hand, and she'd known it wouldn't take long for him to offer to have her car fixed. Not only was he so predictable, but he also thought he could buy her heart, and both things were major turnoffs.

"So, you coming back to the crib with me?" he asked, rubbing her hand as he drove. She watched his fingers run across hers and cringed inwardly. As long as he kept his hand off her thighs and neck, she would let him play affectionate.

"Not tonight. I am way too tired. I just want to go home, take a shower, and go to sleep," Zuri replied, even yawning a bit to sell it.

"You can do all that at my crib," he continued, determined to get her to say yes. Wah hadn't had a sample of her goodies in a while, and after receiving her call, he knew tonight would be the night.

"Maybe next time, Wah," she said in a soft voice, giving him a false sense of hope. "All this shit with my car got me stressed out. I hated to even call you for my bullshit, but I knew if anybody would come through for me, it would be you. I always said you were too good. I hope ya new bitch appreciates you." Zuri was making a guess, but she was probably right. Wah kept a strong rotation of bitches, and once upon a time, he had dropped them all for her. She was sure he would do it again if she asked, but she definitely wasn't asking.

Wah ate up her words, using them to feed his ego. He loved Zuri, but the feeling wasn't mutual. She was honest about her feelings, but still he pursued her, ignoring everything she said.

"I'ma have to take a cab everywhere now. This shit is ridiculous." Zuri remained angry about her car situation. She had enough problems, and her car not working was the last thing she needed at the moment. It just felt like everything was piling up.

"You not gonna get your joint fixed?" he inquired.

Zuri looked back at the hand he kept on top of hers. She didn't want him to fix her car, but at the same time she didn't know what to do. "Yeah, but it's gonna take a minute," she whined again. "I got other bills I need to take care of."

Wah sighed deeply. He pulled his hand away from hers and placed both hands tensely on the steering wheel as he drove. "You always playing broke, Zuri," he muttered.

"That's cuz I ain't playing," she said seriously.

They grew quiet, and Zuri could make out the low buzz of the commercials playing on the late-night radio. They were at a red light, and the inside of the car glowed red from the fluorescence. She leaned her head back against the seat. They always ended up here, every fucking time. Waheed breathed in, preparing to speak, and Zuri mouthed the words with him, knowing exactly what he was going to say.

"Then whatchu up at the club shaking ya ass for if you ain't making no money? That don't make no sense," Wah said.

It was the same shit every time. Zuri knew the way men moved. When it was that first moment seeing her on the pole, they all wanted her, wanted to wife her up. But the minute they were given an inch, they would try to take a mile, and Wah was the same way.

"Don't worry about what I'm doing. If I knew I had to get a lecture, I would've called a cab," she barked, full of attitude, folding her arms across her chest. She would never let a man tell her how to make her money, but they all tried, anyway.

"I was just—" Wah started, his hands moving in front of him as he gestured to the air.

"How 'bout you leave me alone and just drive?" she said, cutting him off mid-sentence. This conversation was why she had been reluctant to call him in the first place. He could never just let her be.

The car grew silent once again as the two of them drove through the streets of Philly on the way to her apartment. Zuri tapped her foot and bounced her leg the entire time, something she did when she was stressed and upset. Wah recognized it, even though he didn't say a word. Eventually, he turned onto her block, pulled to the curb, and parked.

"Thanks for the ride," Zuri uttered as she reached in the back for her bag, trying to exit his car as fast as possible. Her duffel got caught in between the two front seats, and he had to help her get it through. She hated being in this position; there was nothing worse to her than this awkward shit. The bag was finally in her lap, and she opened the door and swung both legs out in one move.

"Hold up," Wah said, stopping her from getting out of the car by grabbing her by the wrist more roughly than he had intended to. "How about this? I'll pay for your car to get fixed, and you pay me back whenever you can," he offered, moving his hand from her wrist and interlocking his fingers in hers. "Just promise me you'll call more."

Zuri yanked her hand out of his, her wrist tender from where he had grabbed her. "No, thank you," she said quickly, refusing his offer. Then she stepped out of the car and slammed the door in his face.

Waheed opened his door and sprung out to meet her on the other side of the car before she could make her way inside. "Why not? What's the issue?" he asked, standing in between her and her front door.

"For one, I don't want you to, and for two, I don't know when I'd be able to pay you back. So, no thanks," she said, rolling her eyes and trying to push past him. They did this little dance so often, she was able to fake him out and moved past him. He spun around, grabbed the strap of her bag, and pulled her back. He did it rougher than he had meant to.

"I'm sorry, but hold up please. Why you in such a rush?" he said, still holding on to the strap of her bag. "Like I said, whenever you can . . . but if you can't, that's cool too. I just want to see you more," he said. "I know things between us didn't go how I had hoped, and I just want us to be a *we* again."

Zuri looked at him in the low light from the streetlamp above him. The light moved across his strong brow as he cocked his head. There was nothing more she hated than this weak and fake desire, but she couldn't deny that he was fine. Wah was the first man she had ever really loved. Well, maybe *love* wasn't the word. But they had spent so much time together, and they had so many memories and inside jokes. And even though there were things about her he didn't know, she knew him better than anybody else. It was moments like this when the sadness of the situation moved her. He was never going to understand that what they had was done. His words rang in her head. *I just want us to be a we again.* She pretended to give it some thought, already knowing she would accept his offer to help but not to be together. She needed it but didn't want to come across as desperate.

"How ya li'l girlfriend gonna feel about you helping me out, Wah?" she teased. Bringing up his new bitch was her favorite way to kill the tension. He couldn't spend time thinking about the past when Zuri threw his present in his face. He raised an eyebrow at her.

"I never figured you for a snitch," he responded, pulling her closer to him. Zuri knew he was all talk now, so she let him.

"But you figured me for a side chick," she retorted, sassing him about his obvious attempts to get her to spend the night with him. His face came close to hers, and she let him get just close enough before she turned her body away from him. She started laughing.

"Now see? There you go. Just let me get the car fixed," he demanded, letting her go and throwing up his hands in the dramatic way he always seemed to do things.

"Okay, okay, I accept," she said, finally getting him to smile.

"Cool. I'll take care of it first thing in the morning."
He stepped closer to her. "C'mon," he instructed as he
attempted to grab the duffel bag from off her shoulder.

"Where you think you going?" she questioned him,
rolling her neck back and grabbing his arm to stop him.

"I'ma walk you to your door. It's late," he replied. His
face was all innocent, but there was a hint of mischief in
his eyes.

Zuri chuckled, knowing what was up. Even when she
thought the coast was clear, he would still always be after
her. "I'll be okay. Ain't nobody gonna bother me over
here," she assured him. "You think you slick," she added,
causing him to smirk.

When they were halfway to her door, she glanced at
him and said, "Give me some weed. I know you got some
on you. I can smell it."

Waheed reached in his pocket, then removed a small
food-saver bag filled with loud that had a knot tied in it.
"Here," he said, gladly handing the bag over. His fingers
grazed her palm as he gave it to her, and he let them
linger there for a little too long.

Zuri stood in front of the door to her apartment, holding her keys in her hand, just staring at the bright yellow
paper on her door. She had seen it enough times while
she was growing up that she didn't need to read it to
know what it was or what it said. "Fuck," she sighed while
snatching the eviction notice off the door. She inserted
the door key in the lock, turned it, and entered her apartment. She was two months behind on her rent and was
trying everything in her power to catch up. She had been
down to the court, and they had given her thirty days
to make the payment. That deadline had passed two
days ago.

Zuri's living space was small but cozy. When she first moved in, she'd been in love with the apartment, and the vision she'd had for it used to make her smile. Zuri always took pride in the things that belonged to her. So, living in the middle of the hood didn't bother her. She would make her place look different from what surrounded it. When she had first moved into the apartment, she had spent months picking out furniture. It had taken her six months to get a couch, because she'd waited until she found the perfect one. She had laid her own tile in the bathroom as well as in the small foyer, which led to her living room. She had learned how to caulk a bathtub and how to plaster over holes in the wall so that the paint she'd picked out so carefully would go on nice.

She kept the counters in the kitchen and the bathroom pristine, and you could eat off the floors since she spent so much time cleaning them. Everything in her cabinets and closets was organized perfectly. She had hung up artsy pictures and kept bright colors in her house, but everything matched and was coordinated. Her bathroom was pink and white, including the tiles. Anyone who visited her automatically knew there was no man who resided with her. Everything she had in the place screamed girly. But more than that, everything she had screamed love and care.

That was now a memory. The apartment she had once loved was deteriorating fast, and all her hard work now seemed senseless. Walking past her bathroom, she heard the familiar sound of water running. It sounded as if her shower was on, but it was actually water falling from a busted pipe embedded in her ceiling. She had complained to the super on numerous occasions, but his lazy ass would never make it up the two flights of steps to her apartment. He would always make promises but would never show. Now her pretty floor tile was mildewed and stained from the constant water damage.

I hate this fucking place, she thought as she entered the kitchen. "I should just let this place go. I don't know why I keep trying to save it," she said out loud, tossing the eviction notice on her small kitchen table.

After Nubia's death, Zuri had come to Philly to live with her mom. It was then that she had understood why Nubia had spent so much time, had given so much of her life to create a comfortable existence for herself and Zuri. Zuri had spent so much time living with Nubia that she had forgotten that her mother's living conditions were not good. The apartment Zuri's mother lived in was a small one-bedroom in a part of Philly that had been left behind by the rest of the city. The water never ran right, and the heat always went out in the winter. There were no good grocery stores around, and the ones that were close were either badly stocked or too expensive. Zuri had felt trapped at her mother's place. Even worse, because her mother had lived there alone before Zuri got there, Zuri had had to sleep in the living room, which meant she'd never had any privacy. Zuri had got used to adapting to the different difficult situations the apartment and her mother put her in, but she'd promised herself that the minute she turned eighteen, she would never again live in a place that caused her that much pain.

Zuri hated to fail, and losing her own apartment now, no matter had bad it was, felt like failure to her. That was why she had continued to fight to keep it. Zuri walked into her bedroom to retrieve another bucket, hoping to contain the damage being done in her bathroom, but she recoiled when she saw two mice race up her bedroom curtains to the top of her dresser. She felt her heart stop in her chest.

"Oh shit!" she screamed, jumping back. "These mother-fuckas done ate through the steel wool."

Her life was spiraling downward fast: she was making petty change at the club, and her living conditions were close to those of a homeless person. Scared from what she just saw and frustrated by her reality, Zuri went into her bedroom, slid to the floor, and let the tears flow from her eyes without making a sound. She looked over at her bed and spotted mice turds on her pillow. Her stomach instantly clenched, and her disgust, anger, and frustration made her skin feel hot. She couldn't take it anymore.

"I'm not staying in this place. I got to get the fuck out of here," Zuri said aloud, panicking a little. She leaned her head against her bedroom wall and dug her hands into the dingy wall-to-wall carpet. *In and out*, she thought, reminding herself to breathe. It took a lot for Zuri to feel this overwhelmed. She hadn't felt like this since that day three years ago when she left her mom's apartment for the last time. Zuri tried not to think about that. In moments that were hard and heavy, the scar from where the bullet had gone through her head, right above her ear, seemed to act up. Right now it throbbed. She relaxed her hands and pulled her nails out of the carpet, regulating her breathing. Then she ran her fingers over the scar as she calmed down.

Even though her mother had struggled after Zuri's father had gotten locked up, she had come through for Zuri after Nubia's death in a way that Zuri almost wouldn't have believed if she hadn't seen it herself. After she had woken up from her coma, Zuri had felt fine, but the doctors had kept her in the hospital an extra two weeks and her mom had been there the whole time. They hadn't known each other too well at the time, but enough quiet hours had passed with her mom by her bedside that a love between them had developed, a love that was undeniable, even if it was complicated.

When it had come time to leave the hospital in New York, Zuri hadn't even bothered going back to the apartment that she and Nubia had shared. There was nothing there that she needed, and all it would do was cause her pain. So she had packed up what her friends had brought to the hospital for her, and she'd gone straight to Philly without looking back.

"This is where you'll sleep, baby," Zuri's mom said. Her youngest and now her only daughter had just come to stay with her, and she had bought the best bed she could with the money she had. But that didn't really say a lot.

Zuri dropped her backpack next to the skinny twin mattress that sat on top of a wobbly metal frame. There was no fitted sheet on the bed, but Zuri's mother had tried her best to make it look comfortable. Leaning against the pillow was a small teddy bear that seemed familiar to Zuri, though she couldn't figure out why. But she couldn't think then; all she knew how to be was tired and hurt.

"Thanks, Mama. It's perfect," Zuri said, reassuring her mother.

It was a weird dynamic they had going on. They had spent so much time apart, it was like they had forgotten how to be mother and daughter. The bed creaked as Zuri sat on the edge of it. There was a couch pushed against the wall next to the head of the bed, and her mom sat there, facing Zuri. The air between them was quiet. The doctors had done a lot of surgery to keep Zuri alive, but there she was. Zuri's hair was still growing back around the scar by her ear, and she kept her head wrapped up in a scarf, but in the silence of her mother's apartment, she took it off. Her mother looked at her, and it was like Zuri could hear her heart break.

"It doesn't look so bad," her mother said, but there were tears building in the bottoms of her eyes.

Zuri was trying hard not to be angry, because she knew that as hard as it was for her to lose a sister, her mother had lost a daughter. But Zuri was conflicted, because to her, her mother had lost Nubia when she left them for her addiction. "Yeah, it's whatever, I guess," Zuri muttered. She didn't really feel like conversing much with her mom, at least not yet.

Her mother sat there watching her without saying anything, and so Zuri started to unpack the one backpack of stuff she had thought worth bringing to Philly with her. A lot of the contents were a surprise to her because she had spent so long in the coma, her friends had taken over her drawers in the hospital. Mostly, it was random stuff: some deodorant, a T-shirt a nurse had given her, some of those socks with the grips. But at the bottom, wrapped in delicate tissue paper, was something Zuri hadn't expected. She pulled it out, and the expensive Gucci fabric spilled into her hands. She couldn't believe it; she couldn't explain how the skirt could have made it from that floor covered in her own and Nubia's blood to this grimy room in Philly where Zuri sat with their mother.

"Oh, that's beautiful, Z baby," Zuri's mom said happily, misunderstanding the significance of the skirt in her daughter's hands.

There was a knot building in the middle of Zuri's chest, and she felt like she couldn't breathe. She looked around the room, for what, she didn't know, but anything to take her away from the situation. But that only made things worse. Her mother's living room was small and aging. The couch sank down where her mother sat, and dust swirled from the cushions every time she adjusted her body. There were cobwebs in each corner of the ceiling, and the laminate was peeling off the floor under the coffee table. From where Zuri sat on her makeshift bed, she could see the kitchen, and it wasn't any better: the cabinets were sagging, and mold grew along the edge of the sink where water leaked from the tap.

Before any of this had happened, she and Nubia had lived in a small place, yes, but one that had been cared for and well kept. It seemed like their mother treated her apartment like she had treated her children: she tried, but it never seemed to work. Zuri clutched the Gucci skirt in her lap, holding on to the last real bit she had of her old life as she tried to make sense of her new one.

Zuri opened her eyes. She didn't know how long she had been sitting on the floor, in thought, but she pulled herself up and walked to the kitchen. She tossed the food-saver bag filled with weed onto the small kitchen table and sat down. Zuri quickly broke down the backwood like a pro, pinched some of the loud out of the bag, and spread it inside. She had been smoking for as long as she could remember, and it was one of the simple pleasures in life. Furthermore, she needed to smoke to deal with the bullshit she had going on in her life at the moment and to shove down the memories that wouldn't stop coming. She surveyed the eviction notice again. All that shit always read the same, something about rent being late and then the warning that she had thirty days to move out. Zuri double-checked the date, then tossed the paper on top of the stack of open envelopes already on the table. Each envelope contained a bill that either was due, past due, or too high for her to pay. She was drowning in them and needed to do something fast, or she would be out in the street before she could put a plan together to change her living conditions.

She took a long pull of the weed and let the smoke fill her lungs. The high was almost instant, but it did nothing to calm her worries or ease the stress she was under. She reached in her handbag and retrieved the money she had made at the club and counted it again. After grabbing the envelope beneath the eviction notice, one that read PHILADELPHIA ELECTRIC COMPANY, she stuffed the money inside. That was one bill she could pay at least. She grabbed the notebook that was under the stack of bills and started to do the math. There was no way of getting past the eviction notice; that would just have to be dealt with at the end of the thirty days. But for now, she opened up each envelope and began writing down how much she owed and to whom. She prioritized the bills based on due date, and then she put the smaller bills first.

That overwhelmed feeling that had brought her to her knees in the bedroom was back, but she forced herself to continue working. Nubia had always said that you couldn't solve a problem until you knew the situation you were in for real. She was now broke again and in search of a solution. As her high intensified, ideas raced around her mind and eventually brought her back to Scarlett's offer from earlier that night. She couldn't believe she was even considering escorting, but she was all out of ideas and options. Being self-righteous wouldn't keep the lights on or a roof over her head, morals didn't pay bills, and she needed to make money fast. She thought about everything she had done at the club that day. If Scarlett hadn't been playing her and the job really didn't involve sex, this escorting couldn't be that much different from her interactions with a lot of the men that came through the club. Zuri worked through her discomfort in her head, the weed carrying her thoughts from beginning to end, until escorting started to make more and more sense.

Couple of trips to Atlantic City with them, and I can catch up on these bills, she thought to herself. She wouldn't even have to get caught up in the game; she could just get in and out. This would be a quick fix to everything she had going on. The total amount she owed, which she had circled in her notebook, seemed to grow bigger in front of her eyes. But from everything she knew about escorting, it could be taken care of and taken care of quickly. The thought danced in her mind, mixing with the intoxicating feeling from the weed, until the idea started to make sense. Zuri picked up her cell phone, scrolled down to Scarlett's number, and pressed SEND.

Chapter 4

Zuri stood in front of the bathroom mirror, making her last-minute adjustments. Staring back at her was a flawless young beauty dressed in an all-black bodycon dress with a V cut in the back. Her hair flowed past her shoulders and was curled at the ends. Her lips were tinted red. She was perfect. She had finally come to take Scarlett up on her offer of escorting in Atlantic City. Although Zuri had apprehensions, Scarlett had assured her and reassured her that tonight there wouldn't be any sex involved. It was just an opportunity for them to look beautiful on the arms of men who paid for their company. Scarlett had explained that they did a lot more in the club for a lot less. As escorts, they would get paid to be pretty trophies. It was a perfect way to ease Zuri into the life.

"Z, hurry up, girl! Time is money," Scarlett shouted through the door while knocking. Her voice made the door shake, but she left it closed.

"I'm coming. Let me fix my mascara!" Zuri yelled back. She used her long manicured fingers to swipe under her eyes, cleaning up any black flecks that had come off when she had applied her makeup. She hated to admit it, but she was nervous.

"Bitch, these motherfuckas ain't worried about your mascara. Just make sure them titties and ass look good," Scar replied before laughing out loud.

Zuri shook her head and closed her makeup bag. She hoped Scarlett wasn't fronting about what the night would consist of. And she sure as hell hoped these men had bank the way Scarlett claimed, because she damn sure needed a come-up. If it was as sweet as Scarlett said, this would be her new hustle. She was outside of her hood too, so she could rock out freely without thinking people she knew was peeping her. Scarlett had told her up and down that Zuri would not need to have sex with the man who was paying, but the fact that she knew that and Scarlett knew that wouldn't keep people from assuming the worst about Zuri. She had never felt so blessed to be in another city.

As they rode the elevator down to the casino floor, Scarlett explained that most of the men who paid for escorts were married white men who fantasized about young black and Latina women. They thought spending a night with one on their arm would quench their appetite, but it was never enough. They wanted more of the girlfriend experience and kept calling and spending. "When the liquor flows and the dice roll in their favor, the tips are bigger," Scarlett said quietly, rubbing her fingers together, like she already had the cash in them.

Zuri didn't know much about Scarlett. They had met at the club when Zuri had first started dancing. While a lot of the other girls were misguided and undignified, Scarlett moved with purpose, and so Zuri had liked her right away. She'd thought that maybe Scarlett had kids and that was why she was so focused, but somehow in all the time they had spent together, talk about their personal lives had been quick at best.

Scarlett continued to explain how the hustle usually worked for her, emphasizing that it was all about optics. How hot the men found you, how willing you seemed to put out, even if you wouldn't. It was all about the service and charm you provided. Zuri just nodded and listened; she didn't give a fuck as long as she got paid. But she appreciated how hard Scarlett was trying to make her feel comfortable.

Finally, the ladies exited the elevator onto the casino floor, near all the blackjack tables. They spotted two white gentlemen sitting at the bar. One was stocky, and his hairline receded into the middle of his head. He kept wiping his forehead with a handkerchief but continued to drip sweat, even though the air conditioner was on full blast. The other was a tall, nicely tanned man with jet-black hair and a dreamy look. Zuri didn't dig white men, but if she had to spend the evening with one, she wouldn't mind the second guy.

"There he goes right there," Scarlett said, pointing in the direction of the two men Zuri was focused on.

"He . . . ? Ain't it two of them?" she asked. Her eyes stayed locked on the tall, tan man, but Scarlett pulled her past him. Zuri's stomach dropped.

"Oh no, it's just one, girl, the fat one. Trust me, though, he pays like he weighs," Scarlett replied nonchalantly, ignoring the fact that she had conveniently left that part out earlier.

"Bitch, we really looking like some prostitutes. Two bad bitches with a fat, greasy white man. C'mon now, Scar," Zuri mumbled, upset at her friend.

"Chill. I know what I'm doing. That greasy, fat nigga got the biggest bank in the room, and he don't have no problem spending it. So do ya thing and act like you having fun. Let's get this money, bitch," Scarlett said reassuringly. If they hadn't already been so close to their target, she would have hyped Zuri up a bit more, but the time for that had passed, and they were in it now.

Zuri adjusted her dress and put a smile on her face. She reminded herself to fuck her friend up if her night turned out horrible. But right now, it was lights, camera, and action, so just like she did in the club, she went into

Heaven mode. For her alter ego, it was all about a dollar, and she intended to get paid.

"How y'all doing tonight?" Scarlett asked the burly man sitting at the bar. He immediately turned around and smiled at the two beautiful ladies in front of him.

"I'm doing great, darling, now that you two fine ladies finally decided to show up." He turned to the guy he'd been conversing with before the women had arrived. "No matter the color, a woman is always late," he joked. Both men laughed.

"You are so funny, handsome," Scarlett said, stroking his ego, and placed a hand on his shoulder.

"Call me Bob, baby." He grabbed Scarlett by the waist and pulled her close. Scarlett laughed in a way Zuri could tell was fake, but Bob ate it up. He clearly didn't give a fuck whether they were real or not as long as they were there.

Zuri gave her friend the side-eye, but Scarlett rubbed her index finger and thumb together, reminding her about the money they were making.

After a few hours of smiling in his face and rooting for him at the craps table, Zuri was getting tired and impatient. She had had enough of his racial jokes and his liquor-laced breath in her face. He also hadn't been tipping her like her friend had claimed he would. Instead, he had been showering extras on the more outgoing Scarlett. The liquor Bob had been tossing back all night had begun to take effect, and he had become really touchy feely. A little too much for Zuri's liking.

"What you say we turn this party up a notch, sweetheart?" he said, patting Scarlett on her ass. "You ready to go upstairs for a little nightcap?" he added, his hot breath blowing in her ear.

"What did you have in mind?" Scarlett asked, encouraging him flirtatiously.

"The usual," he said with a smile.

It was starting to occur to Zuri that maybe she had been misled, and hearing the conversation between the two of them, she tugged at Scarlett's arm. The change of plans had caught her off guard. But before she could say a word, Scarlett grabbed her arm and pulled her roughly to the side. If it weren't for the fact that Zuri didn't want to cause a scene, she would have let out a howl of pain. Scarlett had the grip of a steel vise.

"Excuse us one second, baby. We'll be right back. We're gonna go to the ladies' room to freshen up. Okay?" Scarlett said to the overly excited man, still keeping her strong grip on Zuri's arm.

"Okay, sexy, but you girls hurry up now," he said with a big smile.

Zuri snatched her arm away as they walked off together. Scarlett brushed it off and pulled down the hem of her tight dress.

"Bitch, what the fuck is going on? You said no sex," Zuri said, showing her displeasure. "I'm not fucking that fat, disgusting muthafucka." Zuri was furious. She couldn't believe that she had ended up in the exact situation Scarlett had promised her they would be avoiding. Zuri felt played.

"Calm down," Scarlett said through her teeth as they entered the bathroom. "You acting like you don't need this money. And I ain't about to let you fuck up mine."

Zuri should have known that Scarlett was the kind of girl to keep going if you offered her more and more cash, but Zuri wanted to be different. "Yeah, but you said no sex," Zuri said angrily, hung up on what Scarlett had assured her about before.

"Things change. That's part of the job description, Ma. You knew what it was when you called me," Scarlett said. "You have to be able to adapt."

The part about adapting, Zuri knew to be true, and she hated to admit it, but the more she thought about what it meant to put her paper above all else, the more she convinced herself that Scarlett was right. Zuri took a deep breath.

"I do need that money," she said, shaking her head. "He's just so fat and stinking," she complained. It was one thing to fuck for cash, but thinking about Bob's body on top of hers was too much to bear.

"This ain't the movies, Zuri. That handsome mutha-fucka from *Pretty Woman* ain't out here buying pussy. In real life he don't need to. That fat bastard out there is the type of men we dealing with." Scarlett paused. Now, you with it or what?" she asked. Her tone was hard, but the expression on her face let Zuri know that she understood how hard it was to cross that line.

Zuri thought long and hard, even looking at herself in the mirror. Her hands gripped the edge of the sink counter, and she felt like her whole body would sink into the floor if she didn't hold on. If she did this, there was no going back. But she really had no choice. "Yeah, I with it," she answered.

"Cool. Now, this is easy money. Look, girl, that mutha-fucka in there is into mad shit, like kinky shit. He likes that dominatrix shit," Scarlett said, raising an eyebrow and smiling.

"What?" asked Zuri. She knew about BDSM and shit, but she had never met anyone that did it.

"Yes, he likes me to spit on him, torture him, and fuck him in the ass. You won't even have to take off your clothes. All I need you to do is tie him up while I get ready. Trust me, he's gonna love it. He wants to be watched," Scarlett explained.

Zuri was still a little skeptical. "That's it? All I gotta do is tie him up and watch?" she asked. As much as she wanted to trust Scarlett, she couldn't help but think about how she had also said that there wouldn't be sex involved at all, and now Zuri was expected to entertain Scarlett's john while she dominated him. Zuri was starting to feel overwhelmed.

"That's it, and you gonna make twenty-five hundred," Scarlett said.

"Twenty-five hundred?" Zuri asked. The number she had circled in her notebook flashed to the front of her mind. *Fuck*, Zuri thought. There was no way she could pass up the chance to make that much money, but owing to her disgust, her body seemed to be rebelling against her.

"Yes," Scarlett replied. "For smiling in a nigga's face for a few hours and laughing at his corny jokes. That's easy money, girl, and you ain't have to give up no pussy!"

Zuri thought about it for a second. She really needed the money. It wouldn't fix her money problems, but it would help. "Okay, bitch, I'm down. Fuck it. You better whip that motherfucka's ass hard too." The two of them laughed and slapped five as they headed back out to the casino floor.

"We ready, Papi," Scarlett said upon returning.

The three of them rode the elevator up to one of the luxurious suites the casino provided to high rollers. Zuri almost threw up in her mouth while watching Bob fondle and grope her friend as they both laughed and giggled. When they reached their floor and the elevator doors opened, Scarlett told Zuri to take Bob to his suite. She needed to go down to theirs and retrieve her bag of goodies. Zuri nodded and gave a fake smile, but the look on her face told a story of its own. Her eyes told her partner not to be long, as she didn't want to be left alone with the unattractive man with the active hands. Scarlett caught on and promised to be fast.

When they entered his suite, Bob immediately darted to the bathroom to relieve himself and yelled out to Zuri to make herself comfortable. She rolled her eyes and plopped on the love seat in the corner.

"I never did get your name, beautiful," Bob yelled from the bathroom.

"Chrissy," she yelled out, giving him a false name. She hated having to talk to him, but she kept thinking about the money she owed. She almost burst out laughing at how ridiculous the fake name sounded coming out of her mouth.

Zuri felt her phone vibrating in her clutch, so she got it out to see who was calling her. When she saw her mother's name flash across the screen, she quickly pressed IGNORE and dropped her phone back in her purse. *I don't have time for your shit right now, Ma. Time is money,* she thought to herself. The soft knocking sound at the door brought her out of her thoughts. "Thank God," she mumbled to herself as she walked over to open the door for Scarlett.

"Where is he?" Scarlett whispered as she entered the suite.

"In the bathroom, sounding like he's pissing for days," Zuri answered, causing both of them to laugh.

Scarlett made her way to the bathroom, knocked on the door, then turned to Zuri. "Okay, so when he comes out here, I need you to act, like, sexy and seductive while you are tying him up. Think like how you would give a dance at the club. That's it. I'm going to change, and then I'm going to come and get right to business. I'll dominate him for a while, and then we'll dip, okay?" Scarlett said, breaking down the plan.

"I'm trying to get out of here quick, okay? No funny business," warned Zuri.

"I got you, girl. It'll be quick. But, listen, you have to act interested, like, you have to be about it. The more of a show you put on, the more money he'll throw at you, okay? It's all about the show," insisted Scarlett.

Zuri agreed, trying her best to move things along. Scarlett tossed her a bag and headed toward the bathroom.

"You okay in here, big papa?" Scarlett purred after opening the door and entering the bathroom. "Hurry. I need to get ready for you."

Zuri opened the bag, and her eyes grew wide at the sight of the restraints, whips, and paddles inside. *What the fuck Scarlett really be on*? she thought to herself.

Bob exited the bathroom and sprawled across the bed in nothing but some tighty-whities. His stomach was bulging, and the hair on his chest was messy and gray. Zuri wanted to burst into laughter when she got a view of his package, but she smiled instead.

"What you got for me, baby?" he begged, full of anticipation and excitement.

"Shut up. You only speak when I tell you to," Zuri commanded, getting into character. "You've been a bad boy, and it's time to get punished," she said, holding the restraints in her hand and smiling seductively as she walked over to him. She proceeded to tie him to the bedposts. Once she got him secured, she yelled out to let Scarlett know he was ready.

To both Bob's and Zuri's surprise, Scarlett emerged from the bathroom still fully dressed and aiming a gun in Bob's direction. Zuri jumped back, letting out a small scream, and knocked the lamp off the nightstand in the process. In total shock, Zuri was caught off guard by Scarlett's actions.

"Bitch, what the fuck!" she yelled.

"What the fuck are you doing?" Bob asked, turning beet red and squirming around, trying to free himself from the restraints. "You stupid bitches! What the fuck do you think you're doing?"

"Shut the fuck up!" Scarlett shouted. "Give me the fucking code to the safe, before I blow your little dick off," she said, pointing the gun toward his crotch.

"Wait a goddamn minute. Just calm down, darling. You waving that gun a little too much. I'll give you the code. Just untie me . . . please," he begged.

"No, motherfucka! Code now!" Scarlett barked out the instructions while waving the gun around nervously.

"Yo, this ain't cool. We gonna get caught. Let's just leave," Zuri pleaded, scared of what would happen next. The energy in the room had shifted quickly, and she could hear her heart pound in her ears. She had never planned on coming to A.C. and leaving with a body on her hands, but Scarlett had flipped the script, and now Zuri was in the middle of it.

"Just pick up that bag I gave you and go over to the safe," Scarlett demanded, pointing at the closet, which housed the safe. "This fat motherfucka gonna give us the code, and then we out. I ain't leaving without the money. He spend big every time. I know he got it. So, what's it gonna be, fat man?"

Seeing no way out of the situation and not in a position to negotiate, Bob caved in. "Zero, nine, two, seven," he shouted, revealing the numbers. "Now untie me!"

"You got that?" Scarlett asked Zuri, who just nodded and then quickly kneeled by the safe, dropped the bag, and entered the numbers. Like clockwork, the door to the safe popped open, and there sat about twenty thousand in cash. Zuri's eyes lit up. She hadn't come for this, but the sight of all that cash had her all in. She reached inside the safe, grabbed all the money, and threw it in the bag. She quickly got up and walked around the bed, heading in the direction of the door. Suddenly Bob sprung up off the bed and grabbed a handful of her hair. He had gotten one of his hands loose and had her hair in a vise grip now.

Zuri screamed in agony. "Help! Get off of me!" but the heavy-handed man wouldn't let go. He busted out of the other restraint easily and fell on top of her, then tried to snatch the bag while he kept the fistful of her hair in his grip. "Shoot this motherfucka or something!" Zuri called out to her partner in crime.

Scarlett waved the gun back and forth, trying to get a clear shot, but she was unable to. She watched as her friend rolled around on the floor with Bob. Zuri held on to the bag of money with a death grip, not wanting to leave empty handed.

"You black bitch, I'm gonna kill you!" Bob grunted as he began choking her.

"Shoot him!" Zuri pleaded with Scarlett, feeling his grip on her neck tightening.

"I can't," Scarlett said. "The gun is fake," she confessed.

Bob looked up at her, having heard the words that had left her mouth, and charged at her. He was on top of her in no time and began swinging wildly as she tried to cover herself up with her arms.

Zuri staggered to her feet, dropped the bag, grabbed the lamp she had knocked onto the floor, and broke it over Bob's back. He moaned in pain as she started kicking him. She took deep breaths, trying to fill her lungs with air. She had never felt anything like this before. Every time her foot connected with his disgusting body, bruising his skin, she felt power and rage fill her. She kept kicking until she couldn't kick anymore. He had stopped moving by then and lay there, groaning. Zuri waited a few seconds before she walked over to the bag with the money and picked it up. Then she went over to where Scarlett was still lying on the floor and helped her up. In a split second Zuri had gone from unsuspecting and afraid to in control of the situation.

"Let's get outta here," Zuri said just as Bob reached up and grabbed ahold of the bag. She attempted to yank it away from him, sending all the cash and the other contents of the bag flying into the air. "Oh shit!" she screamed.

Bob reached for Zuri's leg, only to receive a swift strike to the head with Scarlett's shoe, which left a gash on his head and caused his body to go limp. He was silent as blood pooled around his head. Seeing his motionless body and the large amount of blood, Zuri once again grew nervous, but at the same time her nerves got worked up, so did her sense of power.

"Let's go," she said quietly, grabbing a dazed Scarlett by the arm and pulling her away from Bob.

"The money," Scarlett said, her voice somewhere between a whisper and a shout.

"We gotta go," Zuri insisted as she dragged her friend toward the door.

The women left the suite, rushed to the elevator, rode it down, and walked into the lobby. They headed to the main entrance doors, keeping their heads down the entire time, not wanting to have their faces caught on camera as they made their way out. Once on the street, they blended in with the crowd of people on the main strip.

"Shit, we probably was on every camera in the place tonight," Scarlett whispered to Zuri as they took quick strides up the street. "I'm sorry. I should have put you on to what was going down."

"You fucking think? Now I know why Jazz ain't come. This was so fucking stupid, bitch, I can't believe—" Zuri stopped mid-sentence upon noticing the blood on Scarlett's hands and the small trickles coming from her lip and nose. "C'mon, we need to get somewhere and get you cleaned up," Zuri told her. They crossed the street and slipped into another hotel.

"Stay here. You don't want them asking no questions," Zuri explained before approaching the desk and asked for a room for the night. She paid in the cash she had managed to hold on to, got the key, and the two of them went up to their room.

Zuri plopped down on one of the full-size beds in the room, and Scarlett headed straight for the bathroom to shower. Zuri played the night's events over and over in her mind. She didn't know if they had killed Bob, and she was full of nervous and excited energy. She turned on the TV to see if anything about it was on the news, but quickly realized that it was too soon for it to be. She got up and paced back and forth, questioning how she had even got into the situation to begin with. She wanted to fuck Scarlett up for the shit she had pulled, but she was too sore.

Ultimately, Zuri blamed herself. There had to be something that she was doing wrong as a dancer or as a person that gave bitches the understanding that she would be down for some messy-ass shit like this. Growing up the way she had, Zuri wasn't pressed about the theft or the beating. People got it like that all the time, and she was not one to pass judgment. But if Scarlett wanted to play in the big leagues, if she wanted to pull shit like the stunt she had just tried, Scarlett needed to be ready. Zuri was beyond annoyed and frustrated.

"Damn. I wanna smoke," she said out loud, looking at her reflection in the mirror on the wall. She began fixing her hair a bit. For someone who had just been through what she had, she still looked party ready. Unable to take it anymore, she knocked on the bathroom door. Scarlett didn't respond, and Zuri couldn't tell if she was purposely ignoring her or if she just couldn't hear her over the running water. *Either way*, Zuri thought, and so she yelled through the door that she was going down to the bar.

If she couldn't blow some trees, a stiff drink was the next best thing. Besides, she didn't want to be in the room with Scarlett at the moment. Zuri didn't know much about the situation like the one Scarlett had got them into, and she didn't know if going to the hotel bar was a bad idea, but she knew that if she stayed in the room, waiting to be assaulted by Scarlett's whiny voice, she would definitely be going away for murder, and would not be just suspected of it. She walked out of the room into the deserted hallway and looked both ways, like she was crossing the street, but it was empty, and she headed toward the elevator. For a moment, she was in shock as she remembered the way that her and Scarlett had left Bob possibly to die. She tried to calm her breathing as she reminded herself that it wasn't her business, because it hadn't been her idea in the first place.

Zuri entered the bar and grabbed a seat near the end. The hotel bar was semi empty, rare for an Atlantic City weekend, but she could care less, since she wasn't in need of a drinking partner. She ordered a Long Island Iced Tea, and while she was waiting on it, her phone began to ring again. Once again it was her mother calling, and just like the last time, she ignored the call and dropped her phone back into her purse. She loved her mom down, but everything was just too much right now, and she couldn't imagine dealing with her mess too. But then mess walked right on in.

When she looked up, she spotted him. How couldn't she? He was hard to miss as his tall frame glided confidently through the doors of the bar, bringing an energy into the room that she had felt only once before in her life. It was magnetic, and her eyes immediately locked on to his, and they spoke without saying a word to each other. His chinky eyes gave his handsome face a unique sexiness. After spotting her, he made a straight line over to one of the empty seats next to hers.

"Zuri? Oh my God, I haven't seen you in forever. What's up? How you been? Shit, where you been?" he said. His voice was familiar to her.

She had to stop herself from groaning. She already knew who it was. "I'm good. I been around. How you been, Trav?" she said. She couldn't believe that she hadn't recognized him right away. But of course, he was there, just where she didn't want him to be.

"I'm good, as you can see," he said, touching each piece of jewelry he wore, showing off, trying to impress her. "Damn, you look even better than I remember," he complimented her. He was waiting for her to acknowledge him. It seemed like the years that had come between them had caused Trav to forget that Zuri wasn't ever going to put out for him.

"What you think about that, Brown? I look different to you?" she said, looking directly past Trav at the man her eyes had been locked on the whole time. She would know his face anywhere, and she hadn't stopped staring at him since he walked in the bar.

He hadn't taken his eyes off her, either. He stepped around Trav and spread his arms open as she rose to her feet. Trav's face fell as he watched Zuri's attitude change. "Yeah, you've definitely grown up some, but you still ugly, no matter what this nigga say," Brown joked as the two embraced each other.

"Long time no see. What you doing here?" she asked Brown as she returned to her seat.

"Same thing everybody else is doing. Gambling and having fun," he answered.

"Oh, I got this," Brown told the bartender when the guy returned with Zuri's drink. "Let me get two Hennys on the rocks," he said, peeling off a one-hundred-dollar bill from his stack. "And keep 'em coming."

Zuri sipped her drink and smiled. "Thank you."

"No doubt," he said, taking the seat to her right, opposite where Trav sat brooding. "Where you rest at? Last I heard, you was somewhere out in Philly."

"Yeah, I'm still there," she replied. "So you was asking about me, huh?" Zuri hadn't seen Brown in so long that not only would she never think to ask about him, but she was also dumbfounded by the thought that he had asked about her. She knew he had to be lying.

"C'mon, of course," Brown replied. "Now, what you doing out here?" he inquired, taking note of the way she was dressed as he returned his money to his pocket. "You here by yourself?"

"Yes and no," she answered. "I'm out here with a friend." She paused to toy with him some, knowing he was asking if there was a man close by whom he needed to know about. "She's upstairs."

"Upstairs doing what?" He remained skeptical about her reasons for being at the bar, dressed like she was and sitting alone, but he was glad to hear the person that she was with was a female.

Zuri was quick on her toes and came up with a story. "Just had a li'l too much to drink and needed to sleep it off, but I needed another one just for my nerves," she explained, not wanting Brown to think too much about why she had left her supposedly drunk and sick friend by herself.

"Oh, okay. So what y'all doing out here?" Brown leaned closer to her.

"You ask a lot of questions," she said, not wanting to disclose her true reason for being in Atlantic City. She kept trying to remember what had happened between her and Brown the last time they had seen each other, but from what her tired mind had pulled from the recesses of her memory, their interaction had not been a positive one. Zuri wondered why Brown was suddenly showing such an interest in her behavior after not having seen her since she left New York for Philly.

"Only way to find out what you wanna know," he replied. "You sitting here drinking by yourself means it must've been a rough night in the casino."

"Something like that," Zuri muttered, her anxiety rising again.

"Yeah, Lady Luck can be a bitch sometimes," Trav said, trying to get in on the conversation.

"Tell me about it," she answered, trying her best to keep Trav out of it, thinking to herself, *If they only knew the half.*

"She work both ways, though," Brown said. "We came out here to meet with somebody about business, but he never showed." Brown leaned back in his chair and cracked his neck. Something about him seemed tense in a way that was unfamiliar to Zuri.

"I knew the nigga wouldn't show," Trav chimed in.

Zuri had to stop herself from rolling her eyes, as if to say, "How could it be unclear to him that he is not wanted here?"

"Either way, as luck would have it, we ended up right here, bumping into you," Brown said, trying to charm her.

Seeing him again brought back memories of a good time in Zuri's life, but it also opened up old wounds. Both feelings centered around Nubia. She remembered that night in the hospital when Brown vowed to get street justice for her. Now everything in her wanted to ask him if he ever did—and if he realized that even if he had gotten justice for her, he had still failed her by not keeping up with her, by letting her disappear into another city. Instead, she decided to avoid the subject all together. But it wasn't long before Brown brought up Nubia himself.

"You know that shit with NuNu still fucks with me," he said nervously, spinning his glass on the table. He waited to see how Zuri would react.

Seeing that the conversation was taking a more somber turn, and finally recognizing that he was a third wheel, Trav decided to take his drink and head back up to his room. "It was good seeing you again, Z. Hopefully, it won't be the last," he said, flirting with her, before exiting the bar.

Zuri smiled awkwardly at Trav before saying goodbye, then quickly jumped back into the conversation with Brown. "Me too," she confessed, staring down into her drink. "They say time heals all wounds, but that's not necessarily true."

"I feel you," Brown replied. "I think about her all the time. I think about you too. I always wondered if you were doing okay. It's so good to see you and see that you are."

Zuri nodded her head. Her life was in a bit of a tailspin, but she wasn't gonna let Brown think anything different than he already did.

They sat talking for a few hours, sharing stories and laughs. As time passed, a sense of comfort washed over Zuri. Being around Brown made her feel good, despite all that was going on in her life. Spending time with him also sparked the crush Zuri had had on him as a young girl, but just like then, she refused to act on it. Brown had that effect on most women, so she didn't feel bad. Still, Zuri couldn't deny his swagger was mesmerizing. He definitely had the street edge that appealed to her, and he was fine as hell, even finer than she remembered him being when they were younger. There was just something about the way he carried himself that attracted her. Brown was laid back, but everything about him screamed boss, and like everyone one else that came in contact with him, she knew it.

Throughout the night Brown caught himself staring at her. He couldn't believe how she had matured over the years. Her beauty was intoxicating. She was gorgeous, perfection in every way. Her body had filled out, and the dress she wore made it hard not to stare. He couldn't believe the stunning beauty she had grown into. Once, there had been no denying that Nubia was the better-looking sister. But now that Zuri had blossomed, she rivaled her deceased sibling in the looks department and one-upped her with a curvy body. Brown wasn't blind to any of those things, but it didn't matter to him. He was just elated to see her. He understood there was a line that shouldn't be crossed, and he was not interested in crossing it. They shared a bond, one of loss, and no matter where life took them, that would never change.

Finally, Brown looked down at his watch, noticed the time, and rose to his feet. "Damn, as much as I would love to stay here, kicking it with you all night, I gotta dip."

"Me too," she said, looking at the time on her phone. "My friend is probably buggin' out, wondering where I am."

"Give me ya math, so we can stay in contact this time." Brown smiled and nodded, happy to be back in contact with her, as she began to rattle off her digits. Once he had locked in her number, Brown reached in his pocket, pulled out a wad of cash, and counted off five hundred-dollar bills. He then placed them on the bar in front of her.

"What's all that about?" Zuri turned her face up at him. "You still giving me money? I ain't no little girl no more," she told him.

Brown chuckled. "I know, but you said you had a rough night in the casino, right? Well, I killed 'em on the dice, so I'm just trying to spread some luck. Enjoy the rest of your night, Ma," he said, then hugged her.

Zuri finished her drink, but her eyes stayed glued to him as he walked across the bar, then disappeared through the doors. She felt guilty and confused about the flutters in her stomach. From what she could remember of the last time that she and Brown had seen each other, she had not been happy with him and the role he had played in Nubia's death. In Zuri's mind, Nubia's involvement with Brown was what had gotten her killed. But tonight Zuri had forgotten that she had ever been upset with him. The charming demeanor he had exhibited, and the way he'd been ready to pay for her drinks and anything else she needed, reminded her of the Brown she'd known before Nubia died, before a bitterness had developed in Zuri's heart. She didn't know how to reconcile what she knew in her head to be true—that if it hadn't been for Brown making enemies in the street, Nubia might be alive—and the way that he had made her feel in the bar. Nonetheless, Zuri hoped it wouldn't be another five years before their paths crossed again.

Chapter 5

Zuri walked up the four flights that led to her apartment in the tenement building. After the events that had taken place in Atlantic City, she was almost happy to touch down in her beat-up apartment. After the shit that had gone down with Bob, Zuri and Scarlett had ended up staying in Atlantic City all the next day. They would have left earlier, but they had waited around in expectation of some kind of fallout from leaving a man unconscious in a hotel room more expensive than they could ever afford. But nothing had happened, and by the time night had fallen, the coast had seemed clear, and so they'd left.

Arriving to the top of the steps, she was surprised by the bolts and padlocks on her door, as well as the big orange paper taped on the peephole that read SHERIFF'S DEPARTMENT WRIT OF POSSESSION. Zuri dropped her bags instantly and felt fatigued. Her heart sank to the pit of her stomach, and tears welled up quickly.

"No, this can't be happening to me right now," she said quietly to herself as the tears began to stream down her face. Everything she owned was in that apartment. All her belongings, her memories, her whole life were in there, and the city had taken over it. The days of robbing Peter to pay Paul were over. There was no way out of this one, and nothing she could do. Zuri's hurt turned into anger quickly as she kicked the door. "Fuck!"

The loud noise caused her nosy neighbor to crack open her door slightly to get a look at who was outside her apartment. Zuri turned around to face her neighbor and shot her an evil stare. "Da fuck you looking at, you nosy-ass bitch?"

Normally, she never would've spoken to the old lady in that manner, but today she was ready to give it to anybody. She didn't care. She was convinced that everything was working against her. Flopping down on the top step, she felt a sense of hopelessness, a feeling that was becoming all too familiar to her. She tried to figure out who she should call for help right now. She needed a place to stay so that she could clear her mind and figure out how she was going to get back on her feet. After spending the weekend in Atlantic City and having to pay for the hotel room, all she had to her name was the money Brown had given her. The first person she thought about calling couldn't do much for her, but just hearing her mother's voice always made her feel better.

Zuri removed her cell phone from her purse, scrolled through her missed calls, and dialed her mother's number. The phone rang, but there was no answer. She dialed again but received the same result. She became frustrated. "Damn, Ma! Why can't you ever be available when I need you, even if it's just for fucking peace of mind!" Zuri sighed deeply before deciding to call again, and this time she left a message. "Hey, Ma. Sorry I didn't answer your calls, but my weekend was crazy. Call me back . . . please . . . I need to talk to you." She usually didn't leave messages with her mom, but she felt bad because of how many times she had avoided her calls over the weekend, and even though her mother hadn't heard her complaining about the fact that she never picked up the phone, Zuri felt bad that she had thought negative thoughts about her mom in the first place.

Zuri pressed END on her phone and just stared up at the ceiling. She didn't know what to do or whom to call. She shortly entertained the idea of calling Waheed but decided not to; she wasn't ready to play house with anyone, especially him. Waheed would see it as an opportunity to have her right where he wanted her, in his bed. She didn't have time for him and his bullshit right now. The last thing she wanted to do was put herself in a situation where she was more indebted to him and had no other way to pay him back than to put out for him. She needed to go somewhere where she felt no pressure. She needed to think, regroup, and get her shit back in order. She couldn't go to Scarlett's house; she had a million people going in and out of her spot, including some of the dancers from the club. Zuri didn't need any of those other bitches in her business. Plus, she still was pissed at Scarlett for the stunt she had pulled in Atlantic City. When Zuri had come back from her night with Brown, Scarlett had been asleep, and they hadn't really got a chance to talk about what had gone down or what their plan was if something did pop off or if Bob had died. It honestly still made her a little bit nervous to think about this, but she wasn't trying to think about that right now. There was too much shit going on.

Finally, she decided to call her best friend, Geisha. The two had been friends since back in New York, and although they didn't speak as often as they once had, they were always there for one another when they needed it. After Zuri had moved to Philly, Geisha had stayed in New York to finish high school. But having been in one place for so long, Geisha had then decided she wanted to try a change in scenery, and she'd headed toward Philly herself. Nowadays they were able to hold each other up when either of them was going through it. They would drop whatever they were doing to help each other. Zuri scrolled through her contacts until she landed on Geisha's number, and pressed CALL.

Geisha answered on the second ring. "Zuri, boo, I've been trying to call you," Geisha answered, not offering a formal greeting. "Your phone been going straight to voicemail." Her voice sounded off to Zuri. Usually, Geisha was bubbly and excited, but right now she was quieter than Zuri had ever heard her.

"Yeah, I've got a ton of voicemail notifications. For some reason, I had bad reception where I was at. What's up, though? Girl, I need a favor. My life is fucking turned upside down right now," Zuri said, almost laughing from the stress of the situation she was in. She still couldn't believe she was being evicted.

"I know, boo. That's why I was trying to call you. I'm so sorry about your mother, Zuri. I couldn't believe it when I heard it. Anything you need, Ma, I got you," Geisha reassured her friend. And that was when Zuri finally could tell that the quiet, soft tone her friend was using was a show of sympathy.

Zuri was caught off guard by her friend's mention of her mother, and instantly, she felt her nerves begin to go haywire. "What about my mother?" she said slowly, confused, but she could feel what was coming from a mile away.

It was then that Geisha realized her friend had no idea what had happened. "Oh my God! Where have you been? I thought you were trying to get away from everyone to clear your mind. That's why no one could contact you," she said quickly, rushing through all the information she had.

"Contact me about what, Gee? What the fuck is going on with my mother?" Zuri screamed into the phone, growing frustrated. She hadn't slept all night and was on edge after coming home to padlocks on her door. She felt as though the hallway was spinning around her, and she gripped the ledge of the staircase she was sitting on to keep herself from falling down the steps.

"Calm down, Zuri. Where you at? I'll come to you. I'll come get you," Geisha said, not wanting to deliver this type of news over the phone. She preferred to do it in person.

"No, tell me now. What is it?" Zuri's hand began to shake as she held her cell phone. Her palms were sweating, and nausea filled her stomach as she waited for the news.

"Zuri, they found your mother dead in her boyfriend's house Saturday night. She slit both her wrists. She committed suicide," Geisha said. She then offered her condolences as she fought back her own tears.

Zuri's mouth became dry, and no words could escape. Her hearing became temporarily impaired, and the words her friend spoke trailed off into nothingness. The whole world seemed to collapse right before her eyes. She had lost everything in a matter of seconds: her apartment, all her belongings, and her mother. The universe was seemingly against her: first, it had taken Nubia from her, and now her mother. She could hear herself scream from the inside, but for some reason, no words or sounds could escape her mouth.

"Zuri, Zuri . . . you still there?"

The once vague sound of her friend's voice was now coming in clear again as the reality of it all began to sink in for Zuri. She could feel herself gripping the phone like it was the only thing she had left, and maybe it was, because the last person in the world that was left for her was trying to talk to her.

"Zuri, are you there? Please talk to me," Geisha pleaded on the other end of the line. She needed to hear her friend, not to know if she was okay, but to let her know she would be there for her until she was.

When Geisha had come to Philly, at first, it was Zuri and her mom that had held her down, and now Geisha almost felt like it was her own mom who had done this. She had known that Zuri's mom had psychological problems, but she had never thought that it would come to this. The news had completely floored Geisha, and she couldn't imagine how Zuri was feeling. She wanted so badly to help her friend. A few seconds passed before Zuri responded.

"I'm here. Can you please come get me?" Zuri whispered into the phone. She didn't know if she had said the words out loud, but she'd tried. She was worried that her words were caught inside her throat with the scream she wanted to let out.

"Are you home?"

"Yeah."

"I'm on my way."

The line clicked off. And Zuri was left alone. Now that her friend wasn't on the phone anymore, the silence of the hallway hit her completely. She was still in shock, and everything around her felt like it wasn't real. From the writ of possession slapped across her door to the peeling linoleum that she was sitting on, she couldn't believe her life. She couldn't look at her phone, as she wasn't able to handle the voicemail notifications from her mom, who was no longer here. The phone went dark from inactivity, and the hallway fell into darkness.

With tear-filled eyes, Zuri slumped into the seat of her friend's car. She couldn't stop crying. It was like whatever well she kept in the bottom of her heart with all her pain was overflowing. And she wasn't just crying for her mom anymore. She was crying for herself. In a matter of seconds, she'd lost the only place she had left and the one and only person she had left that shared the same blood. The relationship with her mother had been far from perfect, but she'd been the only parent she had left. Her father was buried so deep in the prison system that she hadn't had any contact with him in years. After his incarceration, her mother had only been relied on to be unreliable. She had chosen to ease her pain by turning to the bottle; it had seemed like alcohol became her only coping mechanism. It had only gotten worse after Nubia got killed. As much as her mom had tried with Zuri, her addiction had always ended up winning out. And now that this had happened, she knew it hadn't been her mom's fault. The guilt was building up in her chest.

Geisha looked at her friend through sympathetic eyes. She truly felt her pain. On top of having loved Zuri's mom herself, she, too, knew what it felt like to lose a parent, as she had lost her father in a hail of bullets years prior. "I'm here for you, girl. Whatever you need. I swear I got you," was all she said as she drove Zuri to her house.

Zuri stayed silent. This was the second time she had been in a car that was heavy with silence. She thought of Waheed for a second while they waited at a light and the car filled with that red glow she had gotten so used to seeing him in. But this time it was her best friend beside her, and for that, she was grateful. She at least had Geisha to help her get through this; she didn't know what she would do without her. Her hand brushed the window, and it felt cool. She had cried so much, she had given herself a headache, so she leaned her wet cheek against the glass and closed her eyes.

Zuri refrained from speaking as they weaved through the city, but as they parked in front of Geisha's building, she broke her silence. "I can't believe she's gone," Zuri blurted. Again, she could feel the words getting caught at the back of her throat. Her mouth was so dry, and she thought she might throw up. "She called me, and I sent her to voicemail," she continued, her voice breaking.

"She needed me to talk her out of it, and I ignored her calls." Zuri's breathing sped up, and she was quiet for a moment. "I fucked up," she said hoarsely, then choked up. Tears streamed down her face. Her whole body was shaking.

"You can't blame yourself, Zuri. Sometimes people just can't handle life. Your mom was fighting a lot of personal demons. But you gotta be strong not only for her but for you too. You're still among the living, after all you have been through. And you have to keep on going." Geisha tried her best to comfort her friend, but she knew there really wasn't anything she could say to make her feel better. Because she had been there herself, she knew that Zuri was just going to have to feel her way through the situation. There was nothing the words would do; the pain was just going to be there. "Listen, I'm just gonna run up, pack a bag, and tell Biz I'm gonna stay with you for a couple of days. So you don't have to be by yourself."

Zuri put her head in her hands. She wanted to laugh. She couldn't be in a more fucked-up situation. "That's the thing, Gee. I don't have a place to stay. I just got back from Atlantic City to find my door padlocked. The sheriffs came out and evicted me. I was calling you to see if I could crash with you until I figured some shit out, but then you told me about my mother. My life is falling apart right before my eyes, and I don't know how to stop it." She had barely finished speaking before she burst into more tears. Just hearing the words out loud made everything more real for her.

Geisha reached over and put an arm around her friend. "Oh my God, Zuri. I am so sorry you are going through all of this. You know you can stay with me as long as you need, boo. I'm sure Biz won't mind. He knows what happened to your mom, and when I tell him about your living situation, I'm sure he'll feel the same way." Geisha told her. "And if he doesn't, oh well. That's my house." The lighthearted joke seemed to land with Zuri, and she cracked half a smile in between sobs. She looked at her friend, overwhelmed with gratitude.

"Thank you, Gee. I promise I'll give you some money, whatever you need, while I'm here. And it won't be long. I just need to sort some things out." Zuri was pulling it back together as best as she could. Even through all the shit that was going on, she still had such a strong supporter in Geisha.

"Don't worry, boo. You're good," Geisha said with a wave of her hand. "I just want you to be okay, that's all."

The two women hugged, then exited the car and headed upstairs. Zuri felt like she was dragging deadweight as she took each stride up the stairs. First, her sister, Nubia, and now her mother. She couldn't handle death anymore. Nubia had loved her unconditionally, and her mother had loved her the only way she knew how, and now she was forced to hang on to nothing but their memory.

After they finally got to the apartment, Geisha showed her to the bedroom in the back. Geisha had no kids and lived with her boyfriend, Biz. Biz was a hustler and was getting a little paper in the streets. Nothing major but enough to keep Geisha in a nice two-bedroom apartment in what was considered the good side of town in Philly.

"There's some clean towels up in the closet if you want to shower, boo. I'm gonna make a run to the store real quick and make sure you're all set up, but I'll be back shortly. Make yourself at home, and call me if you need anything, okay?" Geisha was truly saddened by her friend's situation and wanted to make her at least feel comfortable if she couldn't make her feel better.

"Thanks. I really appreciate you." Geisha's kindness only made Zuri want to cry more. The guilt she felt over her mom's death made her feel like she didn't deserve everything Geisha was doing for her.

"I got you. You not alone out here," Geisha reassured her before exiting the room and stepping out the front door. As she walked out, she encountered Biz walking in.

"Hey, baby," he said.

Biz was older than Geisha and Zuri. They were both around twenty-one, and he was quickly approaching thirty, but if he didn't say anything, no one would have known. He had a young face, with a bright smile. His teeth were white and flashed when he smirked, like he did to Geisha. He had light skin like Geisha's and kept his hair faded and his diamond earrings in. Geisha felt bad having to tell him all that was going on with Zuri on such short notice, but she didn't really have a choice. He had a cigarette tucked into his mouth, so he was dragging as he came inside, so she walked up to him and planted a kiss on his cheek.

"Hey back," Geisha greeted her man. "I have to tell you that Zuri is upstairs right now. It's real bad, boo. Her mom passed away, and she just got kicked out of her spot, so she's going to stay with us for a bit, okay?" She reached out her arm and grabbed his hand and gave it a squeeze.

Biz laughed. He didn't know why she thought the apartment he paid for was a halfway house, but he wasn't pressed. At least, not yet. "Yeah, that's chill," Biz said. "I'll go say hi when I get inside."

"Thank you, baby," Geisha replied, expressing her gratitude. She spent a lot of her relationship with Biz being grateful for the things he did, but how could she not when he was doing so much for her?

Zuri plopped on the bed and reached for her cell phone. Scared of what she might hear, she nevertheless decided to check her messages. Her finger was hovering above the PLAY button when she heard a knock on the door, and her heart almost jumped out of her chest for the second time that night. In the doorway stood Biz. He gave her a half-hearted kind of wave. Zuri and Biz had not spent a lot of time together, and so the fact he was here during one of the hardest moments of her life was weird to her.

"Oh shit. Hey, Biz," she muttered, still surprised by his presence.

"Hey, Z. I just wanted to come let you know that I was here, like, you know, in the crib with you. Geisha told me what happened, and I wanna say I'm sorry that happened. So if you need anything, I'ma just be in the other room," he offered. Biz was not good at condolences and was even less equipped to deal with emotions, and Zuri could tell.

"Thank you, Biz," she croaked out. "I think I'm good for now."

"Cool, cool. A'ight, well, I'ma just be over there . . ." He trailed off as he spoke and backed out of the doorway. As weird as their interaction was, it was nice that Geisha had gone out of her way to make sure that Biz wouldn't be on no dumb shit with her when he found out she was staying.

Zuri looked back down at her phone. She couldn't do it right now; she couldn't look at the messages. *I should go get a glass of water*, she thought to herself and left her phone on the bed before she walked out of the room. Because Geisha and Biz lived together, Geisha always came to Zuri's spot when they hung out. This wasn't Zuri's first time over at her friend's apartment, but it was the first time that she had spent enough time there to look around. She walked down the hallway from the room she was staying in, past the bathroom, what looked like a closet, and Biz and Geisha's room. The door to their room was closed, but she could hear Biz talking loudly on the phone.

"Man, I don't give a fuck if they letting that old motherfucker out. What's that got to do with me?" Biz said.

Zuri heard every word. She knew that he moved shit through the streets, but she couldn't imagine he was that important, so she agreed with him.

As she headed into the kitchen, she was reminded of how nice her friend's space was. Everything was clean and smelled fresh. In keeping with that generic new apartment style, the kitchen and living room were one big space at the front. The kitchen glistened, from the stainless-steel appliances to the granite countertops. And the living room was the same; everything was just so in its place. As Zuri moved from one cabinet to the next, looking for a cup, it crossed her mind that the place was too nice. There weren't pictures of Geisha or Biz anywhere. To be honest, if she didn't know anyone lived here, she would think that someone had staged the apartment for an open house. It was like everything in here was fake.

Zuri got her water and headed back to the room that Geisha had set her up in. The space was nice. Ever since everything had happened with Nubia and Zuri had had to move back in with her mom, she had been really attached to comfortable spaces. But now that feeling was mixed with guilt. She couldn't believe she had spent so many years stressing over comfort when she should have been thinking about her relationship with her mom. She had tried to call her after Atlantic City, because even though their relationship wasn't the best, she still had that very childlike instinct to call her mom when she was upset. Her phone was facedown on the bed, where she had left it. It was time. She picked up the phone and pressed PLAY on her voicemail.

"Zuri, baby, this is your mother. Call me back, okay?"
Message saved. Next message.
"Zuri! Zuri, call me back, okay? This is Mommy. I need to talk to you. This is your mother."

Zuri could tell by her mother's increasingly slurred speech that she had become heavily intoxicated throughout her last night on Earth, and it brought tears to her eyes. Her hands shook as she pressed PLAY again.

"Mommy loves you, my pretty girl. You know you always been my pretty baby girl. Nubia too. Everybody always used to say, 'Gloria, you got some pretty little girls.' And I would say, 'I know.'"

As she listened, Zuri could tell her mother was smiling and crying at the same time by the way her voice came across on the other end of the phone. She answered her mother, as if they were in a two-way conversation. "I know, Mommy. You always told us that." Zuri rocked back and forth as she listened to the rest of the voicemail.

"I'm tired, Zuri, and I'm sorry. I should have been a better mother, but I fucked up. I fucked up bad, baby. I let you down, and I let NuNu down. I miss her so much. I want to be with her. I want to be with my baby. I'll miss you. Goodbye."

"No, Ma, *I'm* sorry. *I'm* sorry, Mommy. Don't do it," she shouted after this last message ended in her ear. She began to bawl like a child. At that very point, she felt she had nothing to live for, and for a split second, Zuri felt like ending it all just like her mother did. But then she remembered all that Nubia had sacrificed for her to make it, and she just cried and cried until she fell asleep just as the sun began to rise on another day.

Chapter 6

A month had passed, and Zuri was still staying with Geisha. Biz had continued to have no problem with it, just like her friend had anticipated, but Zuri didn't know how long that would last. Waheed had managed to get her car fixed, which was a blessing, but it meant that he was on her ass again, begging for her to return the favor. If she wasn't willing to sell pussy, she most definitely was not trying to trade pussy. She was trying to stack her money as fast as possible in order to get out of Geisha's crib. Biz kept a strange schedule and Geisha didn't work, and Zuri knew that this was the lifestyle of hustlers and their women, but being in the middle of it was stressful. Hearing Geisha and Biz arguing all the time had quickly gotten old.

Zuri tried to limit the time she spent in the house. She spent most of her nights and late afternoons at Daydreams. She normally didn't stroll in the club until she knew there was money to be made. That was usually after nine o'clock, but she was desperate, and there was nothing she wasn't willing to try to keep the paper flowing in. Lately, she had started pulling up to the club as early as four o'clock in the afternoon and staying as late as four o'clock in the morning. Although Geisha had extended her welcome for as long as Zuri needed, Zuri understood that the scenario of two women under the same roof could go sour at any time. They were either going to bump heads constantly or just develop a dislike for one another for no reason. That usually was what happened, especially when you weren't blood related. There was room for only one "woman of the house," and so Zuri made herself scarce. She wanted no mishaps or confusion. She truly valued her and Geisha's friendship.

Zuri was fed up by another slow night at the club, and her mood had soured. She had been in the club for hours and had yet to crack a hundred dollars. She got off the stage and walked over to the bar, ready to cash out and call it a night. She let out a deep sigh of frustration as she sat down after deciding to order a drink. Zuri rarely drank while she worked; she always liked to remain on point, while other dancers downed drink after drink, popped pills, and even snorted a few lines to keep them going. Zuri knew plenty of horror stories about girls who got too drunk and became victims. That would never be her, she often told herself. When she got her money, she did only that, got money.

She survived by the lessons Nubia used to school her with. As she sat at the bar, she remembered again one of the last bits of advice Nubia had shared with her. *However you chose to make your paper, make it, Z, but never leave yourself open to getting violated. Watch your front and your back.* That had proven to be a valuable lesson to her in her work at the club. The bitches here were grimy, and the niggas were thirsty. Therefore, she always stayed on point.

Sipping her drink, she spun around on the barstool and surveyed the crowd. Her feet were burning, and her profits for the night were weak, a bad combination. She watched the front door, hoping some money would begin to flow in. That would determine if she stayed a little longer and dealt with the aggravation. After about ten minutes or so, however, she realized nothing was going to change. She tossed back the last of her drink, then turned to face the bartender.

"Let me get another one," she called out.

"You drinking more than usual," the female bartender said as she made the drink.

"Ain't much else to do," Zuri joked.

Out the corner of her eye, she spotted Charisma, a thick mulatto dancer she always seemed to have friction with. That bitch was just like Diamond, messy and easy. She was tucked in a corner of the club, in between some dude's legs, tongue kissing him while he groped her ass. Zuri shook her head and curled her lip in disgust.

"You see this shit?" she said, voicing her displeasure aloud as the bartender handed her the drink. "This bitch can't help but be a slut out here in front of everybody. These niggas gonna think we all get down like that for a few dollars."

"Who you talking about?" the nosy bartender asked. She always got the scoop on the dancers from the bouncers or from other dancers. Zuri's remarks piqued her interest.

"Who you think?" Zuri replied. "Young swallow over there." She pointed and snorted. It was moments like this when her gratitude for Nubia overwhelmed her. There was no way she would ever be out here looking like that.

"Oh, Charisma. Girl, she been on that nigga all night. He done busted a check on her too. He usually come through early in the day to check her. I think that's her man. I done seen them out more than a few times," the bartender said while shaking another drink.

"Her man?" Zuri giggled. "I ain't think that bitch had a man, the way she been in VIP, sucking dick."

Zuri and the bartender shared a laugh as she stood with her drink in hand. Zuri nodded goodbye and then headed toward the dressing room. As she made her way around the bar, she kept an eye on Charisma. She was dying to see who the guy was that was spending on her. Zuri was in hustle mode, and if anybody was throwing money around like the bartender had said, she wanted it. She needed it, honestly. She paused when she reached the dressing-room door and noticed the guy stand up. Zuri's heart stopped in her chest when she got a look at the guy's face. She couldn't believe her eyes. Biz flipped the hood of his jacket over his head, wrapped his arms around Charisma's waist, and kissed her before heading out the door. Charisma wiped her mouth in a trashy way and then pranced to the back of the club. A minute later she entered the dressing room from the other side of the stage.

Zuri was in shock and at a loss for words. She did an about-face and headed back to the bar, her drink still stupidly in her hands. Not only was Biz cheating on her best friend, but he was also cheating with the nastiest slut in the club. She wanted to storm straight to the door and blow Biz's spot. She wanted to walk up on Charisma and beat her ass in the middle of the club just for being a ho. Zuri balled her fist and gritted her teeth. She was enraged, but she had to think rationally and calm herself down. After her last confrontation with Diamond, the owner had pulled her into his office and warned her about her temper. He'd told her she was out of chances. She knew if she confronted Charisma, she would probably get fired. So she decided against it.

She put her drink down on the bar. It was still early, around eleven o'clock, and Zuri had definitely not raked in enough to have made the night at all worthwhile, but she at least had information she didn't have before, and that was something. So she decided she would rush home and break the news to her friend, who definitely didn't deserve this. The fact that Biz was messing around with one of the most scandalous bitches Zuri knew only made matters worse.

Geisha had given Zuri a key, and when she turned it in the lock, she could immediately hear that her friend was washing dishes in the kitchen. D'Angelo was playing quietly from Geisha's phone, and she turned when Zuri walked in.

"Hey, boo. You're home early. It's not even midnight," Geisha said, rinsing a dish and putting it on the drying rack. She grabbed another and kept washing as Zuri put her bag down by the front door and then walked straight toward her friend.

Geisha was quietly humming along to the song, and Zuri couldn't believe that she had to be the one to burst the bubble that was her friend's comfortable life. There began an internal debate in her head. What if Geisha already knew? What if there was an understanding that she was good with? It was weird, but she knew that open-relationship shit was a thing people were doing now. Zuri sighed. She wanted so badly to protect her friend from pain, the way that Geisha had tried to protect her, but Biz had made that impossible.

"Hey, girl," Zuri said quietly. "You might wanna put the dish down." She had a feeling that if she told her the news, Geisha would start throwing whatever was in her hands, and Zuri wasn't trying to start a dangerous situation. "Come sit down with me on the couch, girl."

"What? Girl, you tripping. What's the problem?" Geisha laughed at what she thought was her friend being dramatic and kept washing dishes.

Zuri drummed her fingers on her friend's immaculate counter and thought about how things had been when they met. They had both been so young. So hopeful. She remembered the days when Nubia would drive her and Geisha around, letting them in on all the grown-up business, which they weren't supposed to be a part of yet. That had been such a special time to Zuri, and she loved her friend so much. The fact that they had ended up here, with Zuri practically homeless and Geisha getting played, was just . . . She couldn't believe it.

Zuri rubbed her face. She just had to do it. So without waiting a second later, she broke it all down to Geisha about what had happened and what she had seen. About how much of a slut Charisma was, about how grimy a bitch she was. Zuri was right about how her friend would react to this news. Geisha dropped the plate she was washing, left the pieces all over the floor, and as she hyperventilated, she stumbled over to the couch. Geisha couldn't believe it when Geisha, tears running down her face, started calling Biz's cell phone. But she got no response.

It hurt Zuri to the core to deliver that news to her friend, but she could not act like what she'd seen hadn't happened or not tell her. She *had* to tell her friend. Geisha had one of the best hearts Zuri had ever stumbled across, and to witness that nigga Biz doing her friend dirty with one of the most trifling bitches set a fire in her chest. Even though Biz had done Zuri no wrong, Zuri was getting tired of the fact that these men—from the men at the club who touched her without asking to the rich motherfuckers who tried to play girls like Scarlett—were out there thinking they ran shit and could do whatever they wanted. After drinking about two empty bottles of wine, Geisha crashed on the couch.

Biz never showed up at home that night.

***

The following night, Daydreams was packed. All the hustlers had come out to play and were spending cash. Bills floated in the air and covered the floor as every stripper in the building seemed to be shaking her ass on the floor. It had been a minute since Zuri had seen the club like this, but she was happy as could be. She had already made a rack, and the night had only just begun. She was going hard tonight.

After breaking the news to Geisha, she knew things would become uncomfortable at the apartment with Biz when he finally did decide to come home. Zuri had spent all day comforting her friend as she cried and nervously paced around the house. The situation was exactly what Zuri had been concerned about when she started staying at their apartment, but she also acknowledged that Biz was the one that paid for it, and if Biz was bad with Geisha, than she and Geisha would both be out on the street. Zuri had been stacking bread in a shoe box she kept hidden in the closet of the room she stayed in, in the apartment. If tonight went right, it wouldn't be much longer before she could move out and get her own place. Nothing fancy, but something that was all hers and that no one could take this time. Something she desperately wanted to do, especially with all the drama between Geisha and Biz.

Zuri saw a few familiar faces in the club, but mostly unfamiliar ones. The party was being promoted as a coming home bash for Greg Redd, one of the biggest hustlers the city of Philly had ever seen. Redd and his crew had run the Richard Allen Homes back in the day, before the feds took them all off the streets. Zuri had only ever heard of him in passing, to be honest, but whoever he was, he had to be a person of some importance, because almost every hustler in the city was out and dancers from other clubs were even here to get some of the paper.

Zuri was next up on the stage; she was ready to put on one of her signature erotic performances. There was so much money in the club, and she was the main attraction. After her set, she knew all the ballers would want private lap dances. She could hear the sound of a cash register ringing in her head as she thought about it.

"All the money getters and big spenders, get ready to make it rain. Welcome to the stage the sexy and beautiful Heaven." The DJ laid it on thick whenever Zuri hit the stage. He didn't disappoint tonight. She was his favorite, for obvious reasons. She was one of the baddest females who worked at the club, and every man in there wanted to sample her goodies, and even some of the women did too. From the DJ to the bouncer to the promoters, Zuri was their top choice. She was used to the attention, but when the music changed, so did she. It was all business with her, never pleasure.

Zuri slowly moved her hips to the music, making eye contact with the men surrounding the stage. For an event like this, she had made sure to wear her best set. It was an all-white outfit, with a crystal-covered bustier and a white G-string that looked like angel wings across her ass. Some of the girls didn't spend time on making their outfits a part of their performance, but Zuri liked to think of dancing as an art ,and she wanted every part of her to be part of the performance. Her name was Heaven, after all. She circled the stage a few times before seductively working her way up the pole. Once she was at the top, she flipped upside down and twirled around, using only her legs. She slid down the pole, then quickly did a flip and landed on the floor in a full split. Her ass cheeks bounced in rhythm with the music as the money fell freely from the sky, as if heaven's gates had opened to her. All eyes in the spot were on her.

When her performance was done, Zuri sashayed off the stage and was immediately approached by one of the bouncers. He informed her that she was wanted in VIP. Zuri didn't hesitate and made her way through the crowd toward the private section, which was roped off and behind bloodred curtains. Purely off instinct, she expected to see a top-notch baller wanting to show off and shower her with stacks of money. To Zuri's surprise, she had been summoned by a group of beautiful, well-dressed women. They were sharing a laugh among themselves when Zuri walked through the curtain into their VIP section. They had rubber-banded stacks of money piled up on the table, and a few bottles of champagne and half-filled glasses sat in front of them. From the looks of them, Zuri assumed they had to be either some dope boys' wives or some working girls. Either way, she knew they were definitely caked up. They were sporting designer shoes and handbags that the average chick just didn't wear, especially not around there.

They can't be from around here, Zuri thought to herself.

"You did your thing onstage, Ma," one of the women said to her.

"Thank you," Zuri answered.

"What's your name, pretty gal?" another one of the women asked.

"Heaven," Zuri replied, admiring the women's thick Jamaican accent.

"Heaven," said the first woman, "what's your real name?"

"What's yours?" Zuri asked in return.

The woman smiled at Zuri and sat back, with her legs crossed. The air of confidence that surrounded the women was intoxicating to Zuri. Their attitudes were those of bosses, but with a feminine twist, which made

Zuri feel extremely comfortable dancing for them. She began to sway her hips back and forth, finding a groove in the music, while never taking her eyes off the woman who had spoken to her first. There was something about her eyes that wouldn't allow Zuri to turn away. It wasn't anything sexual, more like a silent understanding between two like souls. Zuri quietly admired the women's style. They put her in the mind of Nubia. The confidence they exuded was still such a shock to her. Usually, she could read her male customers. It was easy for her to tell the blue-collar workers from the dope boys, but with these women, she couldn't tell. They just stared at her quietly as she danced seductively, running her hands over her body. Her curiosity eventually got the best of her, and she decided to ask.

"So what y'all beautiful ladies into?" Zuri said, trying to make small talk.

"What you mean?" asked the woman with the Jamaican accent.

"You know, like, what y'all do for a living?" Zuri asked, this time more direct with her question.

"What it look like we do?" another one of the women said in a more serious tone.

Zuri scanned the women once more. "Y'all some working girls?" she asked, causing all three of the women to laugh.

"Yeah, we're definitely for hire," the Jamaican woman blurted out, causing them to laugh once more.

Zuri wasn't in on the joke, so she continued to probe. "So what's that tattoo on your wrist mean? Those two *M*s . . . Is that for your pimp or something?" she asked the woman with the serious tone.

"None of your business," the woman answered quickly, her tone just as serious, which caught Zuri off guard. Suddenly, the mood in the small section had changed, and as the song switched, the women made it clear that they were no longer interested in Zuri's services.

Zuri quickly got the message and bent over to pick up her profit. As she made her way toward the curtain, the serious woman with the tattoo called out to her, causing her to turn around.

"Hey," she said. "You see how everybody stares at you when you walk through the club?" she asked, then continued before Zuri could speak. "There is a lot of pretty women in here to look at, but they stare at you. That's because there's something special about you. Don't waste it in here, shaking your ass for these niggas."

Zuri just sucked her teeth and walked through the curtain. "Who the fuck that bitch think she is?" she mumbled to herself. "She don't know me. Them bitches ain't no better than me." She felt offended and too emotional to catch the jewel that had just been dropped on her.

Zuri stormed to the bar and took a seat at the very end. She was steaming. "How dare them bitches judge me!" she continued, speaking aloud to herself. "We all chapters in the same book, just a different page."

"What's the face for, Mama?" the curvy brown-skinned bartender asked, having noticed Zuri fuming at the end of the bar. As a result of Zuri drinking more at the club, she and the bartender had become friends. Zuri had started to think that maybe she should be worried about what was developing into a habit, but she'd decided that this was a problem for later.

"Hey, girl," Zuri said after looking up and seeing the bartender standing in front of her. "Some fancy bitches in VIP talking slick, trying to kick knowledge and shit. Fuck them. Ain't nobody trying to hear that. I'm trying to get this money."

"I hear that," the bartender agreed. "Hold up. Fancy bitches?" she questioned, on second thought. She was in the middle of stirring a drink, but her hand moved slower and slower as she processed what Zuri had said.

"Yeah," Zuri replied.

"In VIP?" the bartender asked, putting things together.

"Yeah. Why? You know them?" Zuri was getting annoyed that apparently, everyone else knew something she didn't.

"Girrrl, you don't know who they are?" the bartender said cautiously. "That's the Murder . . . Mamas," she revealed in a lower tone, then looked around to see if anyone had heard her.

"*And*?" Zuri replied, not moved by the news. "What? They a rap group or something?"

"Girrrl, just ask somebody who they are," the bartender responded. "Matter of a fact, don't," she said after giving it some thought. "Get a good look. You probably won't see them twice." The bartender wiped off the counter in front of Zuri and then walked away, but not before she gave her one last look to show how serious she was. Zuri looked at her like she was crazy. She had no idea what all that was supposed to mean.

Zuri stood up and quickly made her way into the dressing room to switch outfits. She didn't want to be off the floor too long, what with all the big spenders in the building. She opened her locker, removed another one of her favorite outfits, and was beginning to change clothes when she heard a familiar voice at her back.

"I heard you like to run your mouth, bitch. Maybe you need somebody to shut it for you," Charisma barked.

Zuri didn't turn around at first. She was so tired of these stupid-ass bitches fucking with her, but they had picked the wrong one. "And who supposed to do that, bitch? You?" Zuri said as she stood up and turned around. She immediately knew what was behind Charisma's gripe. It all had to do with Biz. She must have found out that Zuri had exposed her as a side chick.

The dressing room was getting louder and louder. Zuri turned to look and saw a group of strippers, led by Diamond, and a few others she didn't get along with.

"Hit that bitch, Charisma," one of them yelled from across the room.

Seeing her opportunity, Charisma swung and landed a blow on the side of Zuri's face. Zuri stumbled back into the lockers but came off swinging and landed swift punches to Charisma's face and head. They latched on to one another's hair and began throwing blows. Charisma swung wildly, while Zuri threw the more accurate shots, getting the best of her opponent. Suddenly Zuri felt punches raining down relentlessly on the back of her head. The group of strippers led by Diamond Eyes were jumping her. She tried her best to defend herself, but she was no match for the four of them, and she had no backup.

All the commotion in the locker room caused the bouncers to run in minutes later and begin pulling the women apart. Zuri was lifted off her feet by one of the grizzly security guards, but she still tried to get at the women, who were being pulled in the opposite direction. The group of dancers taunted Zuri, all except Charisma, who had received the brunt of Zuri's blows, and her face showed it. Her lip was swollen, and there was a cut above her eyebrow where Zuri's acrylic had caught her face.

"Yeah, bitch!" Zuri shouted, getting a glimpse of Charisma's grill.

Just then the owner rushed into the locker room, with rage and fire in his eyes. He was embarrassed by the behavior of the dancers. "What the fuck is going on in here!" he shouted, looking around at the women. Charisma was being cleaned up by Diamond and the other bitches who had tried to jump Zuri, and she was playing victim in the middle of the room. Zuri was still being held back by one of the big-ass security guards. When the owner's eyes landed on Zuri, his temper grew worse. "I should have known your ass would be in the middle of all of this," he said, shaking his head.

"That bitch came at me—" Zuri shouted, only to be cut off before she could explain what had happened.

"I don't give a fuck! I told you last time was your last time. You're fired!" he screamed.

"Fuck you and this bullshit club," Zuri said as she gathered her things from her locker and began throwing them in her bag.

"Tell your story walking," the owner said sarcastically. "Escort that bitch out of my club," he ordered two of the bouncers before walking out of the locker room.

The bouncers walked Zuri out, like the owner had asked, and she couldn't stop herself from projecting her rage onto them. She had suffered an injustice, and someone was going to have to listen to her yell.

"And fuck you, too, you big-ass bitch," Zuri screamed as one of the bouncers slammed the back door to the club in her face, then threw her bag out after her. "Fuck," she screamed again, getting all her emotions out. She was in such shock at what was happening, all she could do was yell, and she didn't notice the bartender she always chatted with leaning against the wall across from where she was throwing her fit.

"Ooh, girl," the bartender finally said, making her presence known. "Looks like you need this more than I do." The bartender was smoking a cigarette slowly, and in the bright light from the security lamp above the back door, Zuri could see that she was smiling. Zuri never smoked, but she had also never been without a job since she had been on her own, so it could be that there was a first time for everything.

"Thanks," Zuri said as she grabbed a cigarette from the pack in the bartender's outstretched hand. The bartender was a thick, beautiful woman, and Zuri was surprised that she worked behind the bar and not on the stage as a stripper.

"They fired you, huh?" she asked as she lit Zuri's cigarette for her. "They not about shit. It's not your fault."

Zuri wanted to cry at the kindness that this person, who was basically a stranger, was showing her, and she couldn't stop herself from opening up. "It just feels like everything in my life just keeps going fucking wrong. I don't get it." Zuri let out a sigh with her words. She was suddenly very tired and set her bag down on the ground.

"It's a weird night tonight, Ms. Heaven," the bartender said, referring to Zuri by her stage name.

"You can call me Zuri. Heaven died tonight," she said, upset.

"That's a little dramatic, don't you think?" the bartender joked with Zuri. But she had just lost her job, and she was having a hard time finding the humor in the situation.

"Man, whatever. I don't fucking need this," Zuri muttered. She picked up her bag and started to make her way to her car.

"Wait, Zuri. I'm sorry. You can call me Cam," she said.

Something about learning the bartender's name made Zuri feel better, but she was beyond exhausted and was starting to feel like it was time to leave. But she still had her cigarette lit, so she turned around.

"It's all good, boo. I'm just done with this shit," Zuri replied. Everything was working against her, and she just wanted to lie down. She took a drag on the cigarette. Cam was done with hers, and she threw the butt to the ground and smashed the flame out with her shoe. She walked closer to Zuri.

"What did they say to you?" she asked furtively, looking around.

"Girl, what? The owner talked about how he had warned me and—" Zuri began, but Cam cut her off.

"No, no," she said, her voice quieter. "The Murder Mamas." She had gotten so close to Zuri that Zuri could see her lash glue moving as her eyes shifted quickly from nerves.

Zuri leaned away from her. "Um, you mean those washed-up-ass bitches that had me dance for them? I don't remember. What does it matter? Why do you care?" Zuri was so confused.

"You don't know who the Murder Mamas are, do you?" Cam asked, pulling another cigarette out of the pack.

Zuri could feel herself getting more annoyed. She thought, *Bitch, obviously, I don't know who the Murder Mamas are.* But Cam had been nice to her, so Zuri would try to be nice back. She spoke as genuinely as she could when she said, "No, I don't. Who are they?"

"The Murder Mamas are assassins for hire," Cam began. She paused, waiting for Zuri to react, but she didn't. Cam continued, "They say the Murder Mamas have a reputation for being beautiful and deadly."

Zuri remained unimpressed. "Okay," she said, still wondering why this had anything to do with her.

Cam seemed frustrated. "Someone is going to die here tonight," she warned, her tone heavy.

But Zuri burst out laughing. "Girl, bye. Now who's being dramatic?" she said in between laughs.

"Believe me or don't, but you should take what they told you seriously." She looked Zuri straight in the eye. "What did they say?" Cam asked again.

Zuri took her time and thought back to that moment. If what Cam said was true, the Murder Mamas' words meant something different to her now. She gazed at her new friend with the lit cigarette and the crazy look in her eyes.

"They said I was special."

Chapter 7

Zuri rode in the back of a cab on her way to Geisha's apartment. Lately, she had been leaving her car there, because, to be honest, she didn't know how good of a fix Waheed guy's had done, and the more she had gotten into her habit of drinking at the club, the less safe it had been for her to get home on her own. She was filled with fury; her heart was racing as the adrenaline pumped through her body. Not only had she been jumped by Charisma, Diamond, and her crew, but she had gotten fired at the worst possible time. She had been stacking and was close to getting back out on her own. Her head was pounding both from overthinking and from the multiple blows she had received to the head. Those bitches might have gotten the best of her. She'd been outnumbered, but she'd made sure she spilled blood on Charisma's face. She'd held on to her for dear life, making sure that with every blow she received, she gave it to Charisma twice as hard.

A smirk creased her lips at the thought of the damage she had caused. *Them hoes knew they had to jump me*, she thought to herself as the cab pulled up to the curb in front of Geisha's crib. Zuri tossed the driver a twenty and jumped out of the car. She immediately felt her muscles aching. "Man, I need a hot tub and a massage," she said out loud while walking toward Geisha's building. It had been a while since she had been in a fight, so every muscle in her body was feeling the effects. Zuri had her house key, but her body hurt so much, and she already knew her keys had fallen to the bottom of the bag, but she just couldn't bring herself to dig them out.

Zuri rang the bell. She couldn't wait for Geisha to let her in so she could tell her what had happened. She knew Geisha would be pissed that she'd got jumped. But she also knew she would be happy to know that Zuri had whipped Charisma's ho ass. She thought back to when she and Geisha were growing up and how many times they had scrapped over bitches. As hurt as she was by the fact she had lost her job, she was excited to bond with Geisha over the story.

"Who?" Geisha's voice echoed through the intercom.

"It's me, Gee," Zuri replied. She would apologize for making Geisha get up once she reached the apartment, but right now Zuri just needed some help.

Zuri pushed the door open at the sound of the buzzer and headed up the stairs to Geisha's apartment. When she reached the top of the steps, she noticed some bags had been placed outside Geisha's apartment door. As she walked closer, she realized that the bags sitting in front of the door all belonged to her. Zuri's heart sank into her stomach. She didn't know what was going on or why all her things were sitting outside the door, like yesterday's trash, but she didn't think it was anything good.

"What the . . . ?" she uttered just as the apartment door swung open in haste. "What's going on, Gee? Why is all my stuff out here?"

Geisha had a blank look on her face and tried her best not to make eye contact with Zuri. She looked disheveled and nervous. Zuri noticed and immediately showed concern for her friend.

"Is that a bruise?" Zuri questioned, grabbing Geisha by the chin and making her face her. At the top of her cheekbone, Geisha's skin was swollen, and Zuri could see the beginnings of a deep, painful bruise.

Geisha jerked her face back roughly and leaned against the doorway.

"What happened to your face?" Zuri asked, instantly forgetting about her stuff being outside the door and about the fight at the club. At that moment all she was worried about was her friend and why her face was hurt. Zuri rattled off a series of questions. "Did he hit you? Did Biz do this to you? Did he?" She wanted to know what had happened.

Geisha wouldn't even look at her. She reached out to touch Geisha's face, but Geisha pulled back.

"What's going on, Gee? Why is all my stuff out here?"

"I'm sorry, Zuri, but you can't stay here any longer. You gotta go." Geisha spoke in a somber tone, never making eye contact with Zuri. "I took you in, and you coming over here, spreading lies about my man and shit. I ain't never take you for a person to start shit and try to break up what somebody got going on."

Zuri was in pure shock; she couldn't believe her ears. Geisha and Zuri had been friends for what seemed like forever. They knew almost everything about each other. The good and the bad. There was nothing one wouldn't do for the other. Especially having the other's back, like Zuri had Geisha's. She had taken that ass whupping in the club like a G and felt no way about it. She had got jumped, but she would gladly do it all again, because she was a loyal friend. She had just lost her job behind Geisha and Biz, which was the only thing she had going for her at the moment. And now Geisha was kicking her out.

"Gee, you buggin' the fuck out! You don't even know what I been through tonight 'cause of your so-called man. His side bitch and her little friends jumped me tonight because I told you what happened. He went back and reported it to his broad. So, who's lying? Me and that bitch Charisma got to scrappin' tonight, and I got fired.

Now you want to pull this shit. I can't believe you!" Zuri was livid. She felt the anger and pain of the multiple betrayals that night working against her as she tried to keep herself from crying.

"You heard her, Ma. You got to dip," Biz barked as he emerged from the apartment and stood in the doorway, behind Geisha, with a menacing stare.

Geisha just kept her head down and her arms folded across her chest, avoiding eye contact with Zuri. The past month that they had spent living together couldn't have prepared Zuri for this. Yeah, Biz was bogus on his good days and an asshole on his bad ones, but never had Zuri thought he would go so far as to hit her friend.

"You believe this nigga?" Zuri asked. Her blood was boiling. She wanted to swing on both of them.

She knew her friend was putting up with his shit because she didn't want to lose him. And she could see he had put his hands on her. Zuri knew Biz had filled Geisha's head with lies about her trying to destroy what they had. Biz knew how to manipulate Geisha so that she believed what he wanted her to. He had done it before on many occasions. Biz had done way more than what Zuri had revealed, and every time, Geisha had believed him and taken him back. Now he had been able to destroy a real friendship, and Zuri couldn't believe her friend would allow him to take her that far. Biz was a real snake, a true womanizer, and Geisha was blind to it. Plus, he paid all the bills, and Geisha wasn't ready to let that go.

"Watch ya fuckin' mouth. If I was you, I wouldn't waste my breath. My girl ain't trying to hear none of that," he said. He looked at Geisha. "Right?" he added. Geisha just nodded. "Yo, Ma, I'm going back in the room. Call that chick a cab or something."

"I got something in the back room I need to get," Zuri said, thinking of the money she had been stacking. She couldn't remember exactly how much it was, but the last time she had counted it, there had been about two thousand dollars. And even though it wasn't a lot in the eyes of a drug dealer like Biz, it had taken her all month to collect it.

"Everything that belongs to you is right here in these trash bags," Biz said sarcastically. "That li'l money paper you lookin' for, I'ma hold on to that for my troubles of letting you stay here. I got bills to pay and shit." Biz was smirking at her. He knew how hard she had hustled for that money, and he knew it wasn't enough to really fight her over. But he wasn't keeping it for the value: he was keeping it to fuck with her, and fuck with her specifically.

"Fuck you, nigga! Give me my money," Zuri shouted, spewing her venom toward him. She knew he wasn't shit, and she only wished she had noticed this earlier. A month of watching him and Geisha fight over nothing, and she had their script memorized, too, and she knew just what kind of rhetoric would rile him up the most. "You're a bitch, Biz. That's why you need to steal money from a bitch," Zuri yelled. "What kind of hustler steals shit from a female, you pussy-ass motherfucker!"

Biz's eyes got hard, and he moved toward her.

"What? You gonna hit me, like you hit all your bitches? I'm not one of your hoes, so you can't do shit to me," Zuri yelled, taunting him.

Biz tried to push by Geisha and enter the hallway. But Geisha stood her ground.

"Zuri, just go. I'll call you a cab if you need me to, but just go, please. I can't deal with this right now," Geisha said. It was like she had Stockholm syndrome or something. Everything she said was the opposite of what Zuri would have expected from her. How was her friend just going to stand there and let this happen to her?

"Fuck you too, Geisha. You deserve what that nigga do to you. Die slow, bitch!" Zuri spit saliva mixed with blood on the floor, the result of her busted lip. She grabbed her bags and headed down the steps, not knowing where she was headed or even giving her friend a second glance. Once again, Zuri felt completely alone in the world, with nowhere to go and no one to turn to. She stood on the curb with her bags at her feet, tears in eyes, and her cell phone in her hand. She scrolled through her contacts until she came to Waheed's name. She had truly hit rock bottom, but she was all out of options. She shook her head as she waited for him to answer.

"What up, Ma?" he said as he answered the phone. "I heard about what happened at the club tonight. You good?" She could tell he was already in the car, and wondered how far away he was. It was possible for her to have driven to him, but right now she just needed someone to care, someone to be willing to pick her up and take her home. But she didn't know what he was talking about.

"How you heard about that?" she asked, confused. There was no way news of their little-ass fight could have traveled all the way to him so fast, or at all, really.

"It's all over the news," he replied.

"What?" she asked, even more confused now, without any idea of what he could be talking about.

"The body they found in the club tonight. It's all over the news," he explained.

"Body?" Zuri asked quietly. *A body?* She thought back to what Cam had said outside the club, about how the Murder Mamas being there meant that somebody was going to die.

"Yeah, they found that OG nigga Greg Redd in the bathroom, with a bullet in his head and his tongue cut out," Waheed said matter-of-factly.

"Oh shit." It was at that moment Zuri realized why Cam had been so serious about the Murder Mamas. Shooting a man was one thing, but cutting his tongue out was a whole different scenario. "That's crazy," she said. "Why would they do that?"

"Rumor has it that Greg Redd had secretly testified against some major players on the West Coast and they sent him a welcome home present," answered Waheed.

Zuri remembered all the buzz leading up to the events of tonight, how people kept talking about some old head coming home. She never would've thought it was because anybody had snitched.

"Damn," she mused quietly, mostly to herself. She was still thinking about what she had learned about the Murder Mamas and what one of them had said to her earlier that night at the club. Now that she knew what they were capable of, she didn't know if it was a compliment or not. She hadn't seen Greg Redd at the club that night, or at least she didn't think so. The club had been packed and popping, and she had just assumed someone like that would stay in VIP. She couldn't stop thinking about how they had done it, how they could have possibly managed to get him alone and how they had managed to kill a man in a club with no one noticing.

"What's up, though?" Waheed asked, breaking her train of thought. Zuri never called him for no reason, and they both knew it.

"I need to come over. I got into it with Geisha," she confessed.

"I knew that was gonna happen. Two women can't be under the same roof for too long. I told you to come here from the jump," he said.

Zuri felt a catch in the back of her throat. She truly did not believe that Geisha was the problem. In reality, she felt bad for the things that she had said. Even though

Geisha was her own person, right now she was being controlled by a man who had taken that from her, and for that, Zuri was sympathetic, even if she was not forgiving.

"I know," she said as tears began to fall.

"I'm on my way."

Again, Zuri found herself in the passenger seat of Waheed's car. As they moved through Philly, she thought about how many times she had been here, not in this exact situation, but having called Waheed to get her out of a jam. Every time he had come. He drummed his fingers on the steering wheel as he drove. Zuri had forced herself to stop crying before he pulled up, because she didn't want him to see her in that position. She kept replaying the events of the night, trying to figure out where everything could have gone wrong.

"So," said Waheed, "you fuck up the car again, or why I have to come get you?"

He was joking around with her, but Zuri still felt shame like a hard ball in the middle of her stomach. As much as she wanted to maintain her composure, she couldn't help herself, and tears started quietly running down her face. Waheed noticed her crying and felt bad.

"Oh shit, Z, I was just playing with you."

"It's not you, Wah," Zuri choked out. "It's just everything keeps going wrong for me right now." And it was true; ever since things had gone down with Diamond in the club all those weeks ago, nothing had worked out for Zuri.

Waheed was quiet before he reached out his hand and placed it on Zuri's thigh. He rubbed his thumb back and forth. "Don't worry, Ma," he crooned at her. "We can make some things go right."

Zuri knew what he meant and knew that she didn't exactly have a choice. If he was going to be housing her, she was going to have to put out, and they both knew it. She didn't respond and just kept crying and letting him rub up on her. The situation was like something out of a bad movie. It dawned on her that this was what Geisha must feel like. With Biz paying all the bills and keeping her in her nice-ass apartment, she didn't really have a choice. If he was gonna cheat, he was gonna cheat. If he was gonna hit her, he was gonna hit her. And there was nothing Geisha or Zuri could do about it. It was horrible. Zuri started to feel bad. It was still "Fuck Biz," but she knew her friend was trapped in a bad way.

This is why Nubia always had her own hustle, Zuri thought to herself. Letting a man be in control was the most vulnerable situation a woman could be in. And here they both were, Zuri and Geisha, unable to help each other anymore.

Waheed kept driving, and Zuri kept thinking. Her mind wandered back to the Murder Mamas and how she had met them at the club. She assumed they had talked before the Murder Mamas took care of Greg Redd, but she wasn't absolutely sure. The way the club had been packed, Zuri still couldn't figure out how they had done it. Her mind took her to the night she and Scarlett had been in Atlantic City. The way they had used their sexiness to lure Bob away from the public parts of the hotel and back to his room. The way they had worked as a team, even if Zuri hadn't known it at the time, to get him in the worst position possible. The way her foot had made contact with his disgusting, sweaty body. Zuri had done her best to repress memories of that night since it had happened. The police hadn't come for them, and Zuri hadn't seen Scarlett around the club since that night, so there was nothing to remind her about it. But the buzz around the

Murder Mamas made her wonder if she and Scar had killed a man that night. Waheed broke into her reverie again.

"You good, Z?" he asked. His hand was still on her thigh and had been creeping farther up as Zuri was lost in thought. Obviously, she was not good. But she had nowhere else to go. Now, finally, she had lost everyone. So she lied to keep her spot. If this was the game she would have to play, then she would play it, and she would play it well.

"Yeah, Wah, I'm good," Zuri assured him, and she leaned over to give him a kiss.

Chapter 8

Zuri was miserable after being cooped up in Waheed's apartment for the past few weeks. She had tried to find a job, doing anything anywhere, but nothing had stuck, and no one had called her back. Without any way to make more money for herself, she was trapped. Waheed was a good guy, but he was the epitome of boring. He wasn't very spontaneous, preferring to plan even the smallest of things. And it didn't take long for Zuri to become frustrated with his unwillingness to shower her with the type of attention he normally did. He didn't bother to take her out on dates or spend much time at home with her, either. It was like he had become comfortable with the fact that she had nowhere else to go. She needed him for everything, and he kept it that way, giving Zuri only limited amounts of money at a time. Just enough to do nothing with.

The normally laid-back and timid attitude Waheed displayed toward her had slowly shifted as of late. He had started to feel a sense of superiority to Zuri, and his attitude had begun to reflect that. He finally had her exactly where and how he wanted her. Zuri cooked his meals, washed his clothes and cleaned the house from top to bottom. Waheed got sex when he wanted, fucking her on a regular. Even though Zuri didn't enjoy his performance, she felt the need to play her role. That gave him a sense of entitlement, since she needed him both emotionally and financially.

Waheed wasn't making baller money, but he had a little weed hustle that paid his bills and kept him comfortable. He wasn't the flashy type and preferred to move under the radar. He had a steady flow of loyal customers and didn't mess with everybody. Zuri not being able to get to her stash that night at Geisha's house had thrown a major monkey wrench in her game. She was flat broke and solely depended on Wah to hold her down, and he knew it. Lately, he had had no problem showing her, either. It was almost as if he was paying her back for all the times she had dissed him or used him for whatever it was she needed at the time. When those occasions had arisen, he had taken it how it came. Waheed wanted Zuri that bad. In his heart he felt he was the best thing for her, and he couldn't understand how she couldn't see it. After a while he had realized he would probably be no more than a space saver for her, someone who was easily replaced. Now he had the upper hand.

Waheed walked in his one-bedroom apartment and headed to the bedroom in the back. Zuri was lying across the bed and reading a magazine, with nothing on but an oversize T-shirt and panties.

"Get up and bag that up for me," was how he greeted her, tossing a ziplock bag filled with weed onto the bed.

"Hi to you too," Zuri snapped back as she sat up in the bed and picked up the bag.

"What up?" he responded shortly while pulling the black tee over his head and tossing it on the bed, narrowly missing the spot where Zuri was setting up his product.

"You didn't bring me anything to eat?" Zuri said, looking up at Waheed, who was getting some underwear out of the top drawer before heading to shower. She grabbed the scale out of the nightstand and broke up some of the buds, then weighed them and inserted them into the little green baggies.

"You been in the crib all day, and you couldn't take ya ass downstairs to get you nothing to eat? The chinks right across the street." Wah shook his head and walked toward the bathroom.

"I'm tired of eating Chinese food," Zuri declared with an attitude.

"I'm tired of yo' ass," he mumbled to himself, loud enough for her to make out what he said. "You ain't that hungry, then," he said sarcastically. "You spoiled." He chuckled.

"Nah, I'm hungry, nigga," she threw back. "With your selfish ass . . . I'ma 'bout to go get me something to eat," she yelled while she moved the bagged weed to the side and got up to grab her jeans and sneakers.

"Bring me back some chicken wings and fried rice," Wah yelled back, already in the shower. "And make sure they don't put no pork in my shit."

"Asshole," Zuri mumbled to herself.

She hit the door and jogged down the stairs. Her cell phone rang in her hand as she reached the bottom step. Zuri looked at the phone and smiled. The name she saw on her screen was an unexpected one, but one she was elated to see.

"Hello," she answered in a sweet tone. She had stopped at the front door to the building and waited excitedly for his response.

"What up, Ma? This Brown. How you?" His baritone voice came through the phone and sent tingles through her body. The authority in his voice spoke to his confidence and turned Zuri on. Since they had last seen each other that fateful night in Atlantic City, he hadn't reached out to her. So much had happened since then that she forgot to be mad he hadn't called sooner.

"Hey, Brown. I'm okay. How you doing? I didn't expect to hear from you. It's been so long," Zuri said, trying her best to sound regular while cheesing. She started walking toward the Chinese restaurant.

"Of course I was gonna call you, Ma. After linking back with you, I wasn't gonna let you get away from me that easy. You my peoples, so I had to check for you. You know?" She could hear him trying to make up for the fact that it had been over two months since they had exchanged information.

"Well, I have to say I am glad you did," Zuri replied. "It was definitely good catching up with you. Brought back a bunch of memories." She got to the Chinese place and swung open the door.

"No doubt," he replied. "You good, though? How are things?" His voice was quiet and measured, and she could tell that he had taken time out of his day to sit down and call her. It was a small gesture, but it meant a lot to Zuri that someone had set aside a few moments just for her.

"I'm okay. Maintaining. Things been a little crazy, but you know, I'm well. But it's good hearing from you. Can you hold on for one second please?" Zuri moved the phone from her ear and proceeded to give the Chinese man her order. Then she said into the receiver, "My bad. I'm starving."

"Yeah, I heard you ordering that cooked cat," Brown replied with a laugh.

"Nah, I'm ordering shrimp and broccoli. You can't fake that." They both laughed.

"Well, what I'm trying to say is, I'm in your city." He paused. "You should cancel that order and come link up with me. We can get some real food or something," he offered.

"You in Philly?" Zuri asked, almost blowing her cool because she was smiling so hard.

"Yeah. You gonna come hang out with me?"

"Sure," she replied. She almost dropped her phone, she was so excited.

"Okay, shoot me your address, and I'll come scoop you up," he said.

"It's cool. I'll come to you," she quickly replied, not wanting him to come pick her up from Waheed's house. She could only assume Brown had the best intentions, but if Waheed saw her getting into another man's car, it could cause a problem for her.

"You sure?" Brown asked. Zuri remembered that he had always been a gentleman to Nubia, and decided that must just be a personality trait of his.

"Yeah, this my city. It'll be easier to come to you than to explain to you how to get to me," she said, playing it smooth.

"It's cool, right? I'm not gonna get you in trouble with your man or nothing?" he said, seeing right through her excuse.

Zuri laughed. "Oh no, never that, and I don't have a man," she proclaimed, feeling the need to let that be known. She hoped that it wasn't awkward that she had said that, and as a silence grew between them, she worried that it was, but then Brown just laughed.

"Okay, I'll see you in a few," Brown said.

Zuri hung up the phone and immediately exited the Chinese spot with her food. As she walked up the steps to the apartment, her mind was racing. She was trying to think of an excuse to tell Waheed so she could go meet up with Brown. She entered the quiet apartment and called out to Waheed but received no answer. She walked in the bedroom, thinking maybe he was still in the shower, and was surprised to find that he was gone. The apartment wasn't big, and it took her no time to check it all. But he wasn't around. She went to the kitchen and put his food in the fridge, not knowing when he would be back and not wanting the food to get cold.

As she stood in the kitchen, she realized he hadn't even stayed around for her to return with his food. Zuri didn't care. She was relieved not to have to come up with a story to tell him. She looked around the apartment. It was empty, not only in the sense that Waheed wasn't home but also in the way the space was set up. It reminded her of Biz and Geisha's spot, where everything felt and was fake. Zuri upset herself by thinking about the fact that if she stayed with Waheed too long, she would end up being like Geisha. But she at least wouldn't fuck a friend over, but that was mostly because she didn't have any friends left.

She entered the closet that Waheed had let her hang her clothes up in and picked out an outfit, then quickly jumped in the shower and got dressed. She couldn't tell what the vibe was, and she didn't want to overdress and look goofy, so she wore tight jeans, heels, and a T-shirt. It was a combo between casual and sexy, which was exactly where she wanted to be.

Zuri walked into Sonny's Famous Steaks on Market Street and quickly spotted Brown's handsome face. He was sitting alone at one of the tables. He smiled, stood to his feet, greeted her with a hug, and pulled out her chair.

"Looking good," he complimented her. He winked in a way that felt more like he was joking than being flirtatious, but it still made Zuri's stomach flip. Brown's hand brushed over her waist as he helped her get seated. Zuri felt hot on the inside just from that little touch.

"You too," she replied, taking her seat. "This is one of my favorite spots," she acknowledged. Sonny's wasn't fancy or anything like what might be the norm for Brown, but the food was good, and that was what mattered. Plus, he had picked the spot.

"Mine too. I come here every time I come through Philly," he explained. He was glancing half-heartedly at the menu and handed it to her with a smile.

"Speaking of, what you doing out here?" she asked. Sonny's was so popular, and she had been so many times, she didn't actually have to look at the menu, but she hoped her question wasn't too intrusive, and she felt awkward waiting for a response, so she looked at the menu, anyway.

"I came to check on you," he admitted. "I was out in Delaware, and it was a short ride over. So I figured I'd come see you."

Zuri smiled. She liked the fact that he had made the trip to the city just for her. Brown was looking good, as usual, and he was saying all the right things.

"So tell me what's been going on. You said things been a little crazy," he said, concerned by what she had said on the phone.

Zuri looked back down at the menu. She didn't know where to start or how to say what had happened in a way that didn't make her sound crazy. "Well, since the last time I seen you . . ." She paused and took a deep breath before continuing. "My mother committed suicide, I got jumped, and I lost my job." She rattled off all the major events that had occurred, and hoped that she hadn't completely taken Brown by surprise, but when she looked up, she could tell that maybe she could have eased into things a little bit better.

"What?" Brown said, in shock. Then his mouth fell open. Zuri felt bad.

"Yeah, like I said, things been crazy." She quickly added a laugh to help break some of the tension.

"I'm sorry to hear about the loss of your mother. I couldn't imagine losing mine, so my heart goes out to you. I wish I had known. I would have come through for the funeral," he said quietly and sincerely.

Zuri hadn't thought about her mother's funeral, be-cause she hadn't planned it, and she could barely remember how it had all gone down. Between having to fight her landlord to convince him to at least let her grab a few mementos and other sentimental things and getting settled in with Geisha, she had approached her mother's funeral as just another day. Now that Brown was here, she thought about how much better that day could have felt for her if he had been around to support her.

"That's okay, Brown," Zuri said, although she deeply appreciated the sentiment. "It was nothing big. You know our family is pretty small now." It was until after she had said this that Zuri realized how that might sound. "Oh, I didn't—" she began, wanting to explain, but he stopped her.

"I get it, Z. You don't got to worry about it." He gazed at her intently. "Now who put their hands on you?" he asked, and a scowl came across his face. "You need me to send some of my young niggas through here? Cuz I will." It seemed like Brown had latched on to the part where Zuri said she had got jumped. For a man like Brown, there wasn't anything he wouldn't do to protect his people, and since the other problems in Zuri's life were out of his control, at least he could handle whoever had tried to fuck her up.

Hearing Brown offer to do something on her behalf only added to the growing crush she was developing on him by the minute. She stared at his lips as he talked and thought about how soft they looked. She watched his hands as he talked and thought about how strong they looked and how good they would feel on her body. She played it cool, but inside a fire was brewing. She hadn't been getting sex right at home, and thoughts of sexing Brown keep racing through her mind. Finally, she spoke. "No, no. It was just some chicks at my old job. It was over something with my former best friend."

"What happened with your friend?" Brown asked.

Zuri was surprised, as it wasn't like a man to show interest in women's business like that. Waheed had never asked her about what had happened with Geisha. He had just assumed the worst and had determined that their relationship had ended over something petty. "Why you ask?" she said.

"If there is something going on with you, I want to know. You're my business now," he said sincerely.

The fact that it had taken Brown months to get in contact with her after they had run into each other fell out of Zuri's mind. Now the only thing that mattered was that he was here in front of her and showing her a level of care she hadn't experienced in a long-ass time. She felt safe with Brown, and so she told him about what had happened with Geisha in great detail. About how long they had been friends, about how they had been so close and would have done anything for one another, and so when Zuri saw Biz betraying Geisha at the club by stepping out, she had felt like it was her duty to protect her girl. She explained how Biz had an unhealthy hold on Geisha, that she wasn't herself anymore and Zuri couldn't recognize her friend.

In the time that Zuri had spent explaining what happened with Geisha, their food had come, and now Brown loudly sipped the last of his lemonade through his straw. Brown being able to eat while Zuri talked made her feel good, because to her it meant that he was comfortable enough with the conversation that he could be himself.

"That's a lot, Z. I hate motherfuckers like that," Brown said when she finally finished her story.

"What do you mean?" Zuri asked.

"What's that li'l boy's name? Biz. A'ight, so Biz, for example, is a bitch," Brown explained. "If you're going to take care of a woman, you have to take care of a woman. No point in having your old girl at the house if you're going to be stepping out. If he was really a man about his paper, then he would be giving your girl enough for her to do shit on her own if she wanted to." Brown looked at Zuri. "To be with a woman is to have an equal, not a maid."

Zuri was so shocked. She could not believe that Brown had said all that. Never in her life had she met a man that thought so highly of women. She wondered if Nubia had taught him that. Nubia's sense of independence and confidence had been so strong while she was alive, Zuri wouldn't be surprised if she had changed Brown's mindset.

"Yeah, you right," Zuri said, still surprised. "It's just all so messy right now. I don't really know what to do anymore." Anytime Zuri said something that might be too much for Brown, she laughed, trying to be lighthearted, but Brown stayed serious. She laughed now.

"Damn, Ma. You been going through it. You seem like you could use a good time," he said.

Zuri was stressed, but she couldn't help but smile as nasty thoughts danced in her mind.

"Let me do something nice for you," Brown said between bites of his sandwich. "I think you need a day of pampering. I'm taking you to the spa. Then we going shopping," he announced. "All women love that. That should cheer you."

Zuri couldn't hide her happiness as a big smile spread across her face. She felt like a kid in a candy store.

Brown nodded. "There go that smile. Now, that's the Zuri I know."

"And you still the same Brown I remember," she said, referring to his charm and handsomeness.

The two of them spent the rest of the day in and out of stores at the mall and little boutiques here and there.

The day seemed to breeze by as the two of them enjoyed each other's company as they shopped and laughed. Zuri craved days like this, but Waheed had never shown any interest in spending time in this way. Truth be told, she preferred Brown's company over Wah's any day. As they went in and out of stores, and Brown paid for her to walk out with as many full shopping bags as she wanted, she was reminded of that last day she had with Nubia. What would her sister say if she saw them now? Would she be mad? Zuri was so conflicted, and she had a hard time dealing with her feelings. It seemed that the more she talked to Brown, the more she was interested in him romantically. But she couldn't look at him without seeing Nubia.

The sun had gone down a few hours earlier, and the night was upon them now. It was a beautiful fall night, and they found themselves walking down South Street. Philadelphia's famous street teemed with restaurants, galleries, and a lot more. South Street was always buzzing; residents and visitors all mixed seamlessly together on the storied street. They walked past a bar where a live band was playing music. Brown stopped and cocked his head in the direction of the music.

"You know how to play pool?" Brown asked.

Zuri smiled mischievously. "A little," she answered.

"Let's shoot and drink," he said, opening the door to the bar.

It didn't take Brown long to realize he was being hustled. Zuri was an excellent pool player. Pool was a skill she had picked up while working at the strip club. The drinks were flowing, and so was the conversation as the two of them circled the pool table.

"So I been telling you all my business all day. What's up with you? What you got going on back home?" Zuri asked as she sank another one of her balls into a side pocket of the table. She was winning, and Brown groaned every time she got another point on him.

"Same shit, Z. Don't much change with me. Trying to get money and stay free and aboveground." He was laughing and serious at the same time. He was making a fair point: in the line of work Brown was in, there wasn't much to speak of that didn't have to do with making money and avoiding arrest.

"What about your love life? No girl? No kids to speak of?" Zuri quizzed, fishing for information. These were the questions she really wanted answers to, and Brown could tell. He raised an eyebrow at her.

"Nah, none of that," Brown replied as he cued up his shot. He missed. "Damn!"

Zuri laughed. "You mean to tell me, you ain't have a bunch of females chasing after you, Brown?" she said, frowning up her face in disbelief. "I find that very hard to believe." Zuri cued up her shot and sank it in easily.

"I never said that. I said I didn't have a girl or kids," he shot back. That bright, charming smile of his stretched across his face.

Zuri rolled her eyes. *Leave it to a man to get caught up in the semantics*, she thought.

"So who's this nigga you living with, and how long you been dealing with him?" he questioned, turning the tables on the conversation.

Zuri pursed her lips from discomfort. She guessed that this was the part of the conversation where they were both going to be bold. "What makes you think I live with somebody?" she asked, unable to hide that Brown was right.

"Because you got real nervous about me coming to pick you up," he said, holding his pool stick in front of him. He raised an eyebrow, daring Zuri to lie to him.

"It's complicated," Zuri confessed. She was uncomfortable, but if Brown had given her honesty up to this point, she could be honest with him.

"How's that?" He leaned against the table, his arms open and his demeanor inviting. To Zuri, it seemed like he would listen to what she had to say.

"I'm somewhere I don't wanna be, being someone I don't wanna be. For someone who doesn't deserve it," she said quietly. She moved a pool ball back and forth under her palm nervously. It was true what she had said. She didn't want to be the person she was when she was with Waheed. She didn't want to have to be dependent, and she most certainly never wanted to turn into Geisha, who had spent so many years being kept that it had broken her.

"So why are you there?" Brown asked. He seemed to be daring Zuri to say something that he wasn't going to like or that would send him back to New York.

"Honestly . . ." Zuri trailed off as she shrugged her shoulders. "Cuz I have nowhere else to go."

"You don't have to be anywhere you don't want to be," Brown said, walking over to her and looking her directly in the eyes. "My door is always open to you."

The two of them stood face-to-face, and Zuri could feel the pace of her heart quicken. The tension between them was so heavy, she felt like she could barely move. She wanted to kiss him, but more than that, she wanted him to kiss her. Brown stepped in a bit closer.

"You gonna move so I can take my shot?" he said. "Or you just gonna stand there, trying to block me? It's bad enough you winning. You starting to cheat too."

Zuri laughed and stepped to the side. Her hopes were dashed, but she played it smooth, moving around to the other end of the table.

"I'm serious, Ma. If it every becomes too much to deal with, don't hesitate to give me a call. I mean it. My door is always open." His eyes locked on hers, and she knew he was serious.

"Thank you. That's good to know," Zuri said. It felt good to hear those words. She really appreciated the offer. It was something that stayed on her mind for the rest of the night, as they continued playing pool and drinking.

Zuri drove back to Waheed's place by herself. To his credit, he had got her car fixed enough that it turned on, but Zuri lived in fear of it breaking down on her again. It was almost a metaphor for how Waheed functioned in her life. He was there, and he was taking care of her, but it was always half-assed. Like he was barely trying. She thought about a man like Brown, about what he had said taking care of a woman would look like.

Waheed still wasn't home when she walked in. She checked the fridge to see if he had touched his food, but the bag was still where she'd left it, the plastic handles tied together at the top. He never spent this much time out when he was working, thought Zuri, so he probably had another bitch. That was fine. Zuri didn't care, after all, because she had realized that she really didn't care about Waheed. The kitchen had been neglected, with her out all day, and she started cleaning up. Like Geisha and Biz's apartment, something about Waheed's space didn't sit right with her. She thought back through all the places that she had lived, the places that she had tried to make into a home. Ever since she had come to Philly everything had failed for her. Her apartment. Her job. Her friends. And maybe even herself.

"Maybe leaving New York wasn't a good idea," Zuri said out loud. She had never let herself think that before, because even if that was what she felt, there wasn't a lot she could do about it. But spending the day with Brown had made her realize that a different life was possible if she was willing to risk it all.

As Zuri wiped down the counters, she built a pros-and-cons list in her head. On the one hand, New York held very painful memories of her sister's death. Because Nubia had died that day, there had never been a lot of attention given to the fact that Zuri had also been shot. She ran her fingers gently down her scar. Because nobody else had really focused on the fact Zuri had suffered too, she hadn't, either. But there was nobody left in her life that knew about her past other than Brown. Maybe to change her future, she had to go back to the past. Zuri continued to clean, in deep thought.

Chapter 9

Pretty Brown . . .

After he had spent time with Zuri, Brown had driven straight back to New York, and now he was lying in the bed. He was thinking about all the money that was flowing through the streets of Brooklyn and how he wasn't getting enough of it. The drug trade came with an unlimited amount of risk, but to a bravehearted lion like Brown, it was all worth it. He was ready to step it up a level, and the niggas on his team were ready to do the same.

Only thing stopping him was Dame. He was the richest nigga in the city and had the game on lock. He was a little older than Brown and his crew, and it seemed like he had come out of nowhere. He had recently turned up the heat on all the hustlers in the city. You were either working for him, copping from him, or you couldn't eat. He was taking over spots left and right, no matter how big or small, and he wanted every dollar for himself. Brown knew it was only a matter of time before they bumped heads, because there wasn't a man alive that dictated how he ate in the streets. The phone on the nightstand rang just then, grabbing his attention away from his thoughts.

"Yo," Brown answered. He was used to receiving calls at all hours from his runners.

"I need to holla at chu." The person on the other line sounded agitated and stressed.

Brown recognized the voice and looked down at the unfamiliar number on his phone, confused. "Trav?" he asked.

"Yeah, it's me, nigga. I got some shit I need to holla at you about, ASAP."

Brown's mind began to race about the reason behind Trav's call. Trav was his right-hand man, and they had each other on call for everything, but Brown had never heard him sound so anxious.

"Nigga, it's three in the morning. What's up?" he said as he sat up in the bed.

"I gotta tell you this in person," Trav said. Brown could hear the urgency and the seriousness in his tone.

"A'ight. Meet me at—" Brown began, but Trav cut him off.

"Nah. I'm already on my way to you," Trav said.

"A'ight," Brown said. He hung up and quickly put on some clothes. Brown was never the type to get caught slipping. He always looked at every angle to a situation. He never put anything past anybody, and something about Trav's call didn't feel right. He grabbed his .45, tucked it in his pants, and headed outside to his car. He parked his car on the opposite side of the street but directly across from his apartment. He wanted to see Trav before Trav saw him. Although Trav was his little nigga, Brown understood the game had no loyalty and he needed to stay two steps ahead if he wanted to survive.

Brown smoked half a blunt while he waited for Trav to pull up, the whole time keeping his gun on his lap as he paid close attention to every passing car. Finally, a Camry pulled up on the opposite side of the street and parked. It was Trav. Brown surveyed the scene, seeing if Trav had come alone and if he could detect any change in his behavior. After a few seconds he rolled down the window and called his name.

"Trav!"

Trav jogged across the street, over to the car, and got in. "My nigga," he said, sounding stressed.

"What the fuck is so important you had to holla at me right now?" Brown asked, still keeping a close eye on his young comrade.

The two paused when they noticed a car creeping slowly up the block. Brown gripped his gun in his hand; he was ready for whatever. But they both relaxed once the car drove past and they realized it was a gypsy cab.

"What's up?" Brown asked.

"The nigga Dame turning up the heat on everybody in the streets right now. He just sent them Queens niggas through Shine's block and murked all them niggas," the young hustler said, shaking his head back and forth. There was no love in the game, and a hustler getting taken down was nothing new, but to air out a whole crew was some shit that neither Brown nor Trav had seen in all their years of running the streets.

"For real?" Brown asked, shocked by the news he had just received. Shine was his coke connect, and if what Trav was saying was the truth, his death put a major glitch in Brown's hustle. "What about Shine?" he questioned.

But Trav confirmed it by just making a slashing motion across his throat.

"This nigga Dame really tightening the screws. He on some real get down or lay down shit," Brown continued with a big sigh, shaking his head.

"We need to grip up and go at that nigga before he come at us. You know we ready to go," Trav said, referring to the group of young Bloods that followed Brown. "We ain't having that shit. Fuck that nigga."

Brown smiled at his young hitta; he had groomed him well. He was all heart and balls and was ready for war. But Brown knew better. He wasn't strong enough in the streets to go head up with Dame. He would be signing his own death certificate by doing that, and he wasn't the reckless type. If he was to go to war, he would need to outsmart Dame instead of outmuscling him. But that was the furthest thing from his mind at the moment. He needed a new connect fast.

"We low on work. I need a new connect ASAP." Brown thought for a moment. "What's up wit ya man out in Southside?" he inquired. He was willing to go out farther if it meant that he was able to pick up. But he had never been in this situation before, and he was trying to strategize.

"He ain't got that butter no more. Straight garbage," Trav explained. Trav was a jumpy dude, and he kept moving around, ready to get going.

"Fuck," Brown muttered, voicing his frustration. "Just rock everything up until I can find something. It's dry as fuck out here."

"A'ight. I'ma holla at you later," Trav said before giving Brown a pound and getting out of the car.

Brown went back upstairs and lit up the other half of the blunt. He smoked as he got himself situated to rest.

He had been having trouble sleeping lately, and having seen Zuri was weighing on him. He had a plan building in his head, and as he pulled on the blunt, he could see things unfolding in his mind just the way he wanted them to. He was nervous, but he was going to find a way to make it work.

Dame moved slowly around the room, watching on the camera's small screen as the two beautifully built women coiled their bodies around each other. He was turned on from watching the two of them explore one another intimately and began stroking himself until he was fully erect. The two Latina video models were feeling the effects of the lines of coke that they had been snorting all night, and their shackles of inhibition had been removed. They seemed to relish their roles as the stars of Dame's private show. One of the women made eye contact with the camera as she seductively licked and kissed the other's breasts before she moved south on her body. The other woman's face displayed her pleasure, and she bit down on her bottom lip and spread her legs wide when she felt the woman's tongue circling her love button.

Dame had a perfect view behind the woman perform-ing cunnilingus. Her plump, round ass was up in the air, inviting him in. He returned the camera to the tripod and made sure it was still capturing it all. Then he approached the women on the bed and joined in on the fun. Dame rubbed his rock-hard manhood against one of the women and slid into her wetness. She welcomed him in a like vac-uum, using her vaginal muscles to grip him. Dame gave her powerful strokes as he fingered her asshole, and she screamed in ecstasy. He took his turn with each woman, fucking every hole possible before spilling his seed all over both of them.

As the women lay spent and sprawled out on the bed, Dame sat on the side of the bed and sparked up a cigarette. He took a few puffs, then exhaled and watched as the smoke danced in the air around him. He looked back over his shoulder at his two conquests and immediately felt annoyed by their presence.

"This ain't no slumber party," he announced rudely, signaling to them that it was time for them to go. They clucked at him in annoyance like a pair of chickens and collected themselves.

He slid on a pair shorts, draped his mink blanket over his shoulders, and followed the naked women out the double French doors of his bedroom. He watched as they descended the spiral staircase into a living room filled with half-dressed women, empty champagne bottles, coke, and weed residue. Dame's crew moved all throughout the house, their weapons visible, bottles in hand, partying. This was a normal occurrence: Dame partied hard every night. It was nothing for him to hit the clubs in Manhattan and have carloads of women follow him and his crew back to his rental home in the Whitestone section of Queens. These were the perks of being one of the biggest drug dealers in Kings County.

Dame never rested where he ate, he made his money in Brooklyn, and he laid his head out in Queens. He leaned against the railing on the landing now and surveyed his kingdom. He was older than a lot of his crew, but he wasn't an old head. He had gotten locked up as a teenager back in the day, but after he had gotten out, he had gotten back in the game, and now that he was older and smarter, he was untouchable. His time in prison had developed his body, and his face was handsome and tight. He kept his lineup clean and his beard trimmed, and he had tattoos over his entire upper body. Dame had spent too many years of his life behind bars, and he would never go back again, which meant he ran a tight and ruthless ship.

As the women neared the bottom of the stairs, they were passed by a handsome gangster by the name of Cuba, who was heading in the opposite direction. Cuba was actually from Panama and had moved to Queens, New York, with his family when he was eight years old, but despite being Panamanian, the street name had stuck. After reaching the top of the steps, he approached Dame, and they greeted each other with a half handshake, half hug. While Dame was the hustler and businessman, Cuba was the muscle. He was a killer who had killers who had killers. He never said much, a trait he had developed as a child to deal with the language barrier, nor did he show much emotion. He viewed murder as a necessary part of doing business and never hesitated when it came to pulling the trigger. He was even older than Dame and a lot less flashy than his partner, but together they had taken over and gotten plenty of paper.

"What's the word on that little problem we talked about?" Dame asked.

"It's no longer a problem," Cuba replied, emotionless. "We went through there tonight and took care of it." Shine had been the last connect in Brooklyn that had refused to work for Dame. But now that he was done, Dame would be able to corner that part of the market.

"There's one more thing I need you to take care of," Dame said, directing Cuba's attention over the balcony and down into the living room, to one of the crew members who was surrounded by a group of females.

"What's the deal with that?" Cuba asked, interested in why Dame suddenly wanted to kill one of his own. The young man under discussion had his head back as he laughed and drank straight from a bottle of Cîroc. He couldn't have been more than twenty.

"Snakes gonna slither, but you gotta get the serpents out ya yard before they can snake you," Dame responded. The younger members of his crew were misguided and were having some difficulty adjusting to the high standards of loyalty and secrecy that Dame required of the people that ran with him. He needed to make an example of someone, and Cuba would know just the way to do it.

Cuba just nodded his head while twirling the toothpick in his mouth. Nothing else needed to be said; Dame had just sealed his crew member's fate.

Almost three weeks had passed since Shine's crew had been taken out, and Brown had run through the last of his supply over a week ago and was starting to get desperate. He had been making small wholesale buys off of other dealers just to keep his clientele fed. That was the thing about the drug game: addicts' only loyalty was to themselves and good product. If you had it, they would return around the clock to continue to buy. But they would easily spend with whoever had it if you didn't. They had the need to get high regardless. Once you opened the door for them to find another source, they rarely returned. Brown needed to find a new connect, but until then he had to survive the best way he knew how.

Brown gripped his .45 as he sat low in the passenger seat of the Camry as Trav followed a black Ford F-150 with dark tints through the streets of Queens. The driver of the truck was a local dope boy that moved weight in Baisley Projects. He wasn't a big fish, but he was big enough. The two had been laying on him for a couple of days and had been following him now for about fifteen minutes, waiting for the perfect time to snatch him and make him take them to his stash. It had gotten that real for Brown, and desperate times meant niggas had to feel it. He was smart enough to do his dirt out in Queens, where nobody really knew him. Robbing hustlers around his way could lead to more trouble than it was worth. Plus, he never felt them Queens niggas like that to begin with. That was part of the reason he didn't respect Dame: he used goons from Queens to take over in Brooklyn. That was the ultimate violation in Brown's eyes.

After racing through a couple of green lights, the truck pulled into a parking lot of a strip mall. The driver quickly parked and hopped out. Trav followed him into the parking lot. The two finally had their shot. The pickup truck just sat there. But Brown could feel something was wrong.

"Hold up, son," Brown said, putting his hand on Trav's chest, stopping him from making a move. "Nigga got his seed wit 'im," Brown said, pointing. They both watched a toddler exit the truck. She stood next to her father and played on a phone as he collected what looked like a diaper bag.

Trav laughed. "Why the fuck this nigga got his daughter out here this late? Fuck that. She ain't my baby," he said, cocking his gun and rolling his mask down over his face. "He'll definitely hand over his shit now."

"Nah, nigga. Chill," Brown demanded, surveying the situation. "Be easy for a second. Let's just see how it play out. We got the drop on this nigga. No need to be reckless." Brown's father had a legacy of respect, and Brown wasn't about to fuck it up because one of his boys was trigger happy. Killing a rival was one thing, but doing it in front of his child was a situation that wouldn't let Brown sleep at night.

Trav didn't like it, but he followed Brown's instructions and lifted the mask from his face and leaned back in the driver's seat. After Shine had been taken out, the streets had been quiet, as people moved with caution and he was missing the action.

"Look, nigga, see?" Brown said, tapping him and pointing in the direction of their target.

They watched a car pull up and a short, thick redbone female emerge from the driver's side. Immediately, they could tell she was the little girl's mother.

"See? The nigga dropping his shorty off to his baby mom," Brown said. "As soon as they make the exchange and she pull off, we snatching the nigga." Brown wasn't too much older than Trav, but he used moments like this to put him up on game. He wanted his crew to move like him and not have him looking stupid.

"Word," Trav said and nodded in agreement. Brown had a point. Killing a baby and a female for no reason didn't seem like it was in a good taste. "That bitch bad. I would have gone raw too," he joked.

The baby mom picked the toddler up and strapped her into a car seat. She and the hustler that they had been following talked for a bit before she got in the driver's seat and pulled away. Trav and Brown expected this dude to get back in his car, but instead, he locked his car and started walking away.

"Hold up, son. Where the fuck this nigga going?" Trav barked as they watched the hustler disappear into one of the storefront doors.

They waited to see if he would reemerge from the same door, but he never did. Half an hour passed while they waited, with their guns at the ready. He had basically vanished into thin air, leaving the two would-be jackers in a state of confusion.

"Where the fuck is this nigga at?" Brown spoke through a tightened jaw. It was one thing for him to have held back because there was a baby involved, but now he just felt stupid that his would-be hit had evaded them.

"You think he spotted us?" Trav asked. "I knew I shouldn't have stayed that close to him—"

"Nah, he ain't see us," Brown said, cutting Trav off in mid-rant. He turned his head back and forth a few times, assessing the situation. He started to put two and two together. "Yo, ain't this the spot where they be having them dice games on the late night?" he said, noticing their surroundings.

"Oh shit, yeah," Trav replied, realizing where they were at as well.

"That's where he at. C'mon. We going inside," Brown said, then hopped out of the car before Trav could say a word. He had tried to move with dignity ever since Dame took down Shine, but he was starting to get frustrated and to think that his plan had been derailed because his target liked to gamble. This was too much for Brown to walk away from.

"Nigga, you trying to rob the dice game?" Trav said as he hopped out behind him. He was in disbelief since this was one of those reckless-ass plans that Trav would come up with himself, but not Brown.

"By any schemes necessary," Brown stated, looking back over his shoulder, his eyes filled with anger and determination.

Trav followed closely behind as Brown headed to the storefront door their target had used, stepped inside, then navigated the dimly light hallway that led to the basement of the establishment, which was where the dice games took place. They took the steps down to the basement and then entered a room that was filled with about twelve or so people. They were all players in the dope game around the city, and all of them were big-time gamblers. There were just enough people that Brown and Trav were in a bad position numbers-wise, but the crowd was small enough that if they got a drop on a good number of the gamblers, they might make it out alive.

Brown instantly spotted their target in the crowd. Crouched down, he was placing his money on the wood as an old head shook the dice in one hand and held cash in the other, all while talking cash shit to everybody and taking side bets. Brown looked over at Trav, who had an intense look on his face. He gave him a head nod and a look to signal him to loosen up. They didn't want to tip their hand. Trav looked around. He couldn't believe what Brown was thinking. They were outnumbered, and he knew a high percentage of those in the room were strapped, if not all. But Brown was his man, so he was all in.

Brown moved around the room, trying to get in a position where he could have his eyes on every part of it. He wanted to see everything coming and going as he blended in with everybody.

"Tracy!" one man shouted as the man holding the dice finally decided to roll them.

"He gonna ace," another gambler yelled out as the dice hit the wall and began to roll back.

The room grew silent for a split second, as the dice came to a stop.

"Four, five, six. C-low!" called the old head who had tossed the dice, reading them out loud.

The crowd erupted. Their target had a hot hand and was breaking them.

"Pay up," he shouted, cocky as ever.

Brown watched Trav's eyes light up as all the money began to get exchanged and passed around the room. The once intense look on his face was now a look of excitement, and he was just waiting for Brown to make his move. But the energy of the game itself was intoxicating, and they both mingled with the crowd, placed bets, and enjoyed laughs. Brown even ended up standing directly next to the hustler they had trailed to the spot.

About forty minutes had passed when Brown looked over at Trav and gave him a nod. Their target had been drinking and was relaxed and fully focused on the game in front of him, and as matter of fact, so was everyone else in the room. It was a go; they were going to pretend to leave the game, only to return minutes later, masked up and with guns drawn. It wasn't even about kidnapping for the drugs anymore. They had stumbled upon a bigger lick. The amount of money, drugs, and weapons in this spot was too good to pass up.

As the two of them made their way toward the door, Brown heard someone call his name from behind. After turning to see who it was, he spotted Cuba emerging from the shadows along one of the basement room's walls. He moved confidently in the space as he headed toward Brown, and as unfortunate as it was to see someone he knew when he was in such a messy position, Brown was happy to see Cuba.

"Pretty Brown," Cuba said, walking up on him and extending his ring-covered hand. Cuba never smiled, but

Brown did. He had known the old gangster for his whole life.

"Cuba," he said, dapping him up.

"I thought that was you," Cuba said, nodding his head. "Long time no see. How's your mom?"

Cuba and Brown's dad had been in the same crew back in the day, and even though Roman was no longer here to see the hustler his son had turned into, Cuba was at least there to hold down his friend's child. But Brown was nervous. It had been many years since he had seen Cuba. He thought very highly of Cuba and almost felt embarrassed that they had run into each other in this way.

"She good," Brown said apprehensively. "What you doing in here?" He cut a furtive glance around the room to make sure it wasn't a setup. Seeing Cuba out and about could go badly.

"This is my spot. This is my game," Cuba explained, to Brown's surprise. "Let me talk to you," he said, motioning for Brown to follow him.

Brown looked over at Trav, then stepped away with Cuba.

"I see the play you and your man was about to make. So I figured I'd put a stop to it before it got ugly," Cuba declared. "That can't happen here, you feel me? Because I know you didn't know, and out of respect for your pops is the only reason I'ma give you a pass."

Brown swallowed hard. He couldn't believe that he had got caught up, but he was grateful that it had come from Cuba, and not from someone who would have been a lot less forgiving. Cuba looked at Brown with a hard expression but kind eyes. He knew that his friend's son must be going through it, because nothing else could explain the stupid move he and his boy were about to make.

Brown just nodded, without confirming or denying.

"You know your pops was my OG. He raised me in these streets. First nigga to put a gun in my hand and money in my pocket. I heard you out in Brooklyn, doing your thing. Why you ain't come see me?" Cuba said in a sober tone. "We family. You need to be rollin' under the umbrella."

"No disrespect, Cuba, but I ain't the worker bee type," Brown said honestly. He respected Cuba, probably more than he respected anyone else in the streets. But he just couldn't fold for not running his own enterprise. He had been up on his paper for too long, and he wasn't going to give that up because he felt sentimental as he looked at his dad's friend.

"Yeah, you definitely Roman's boy. I can respect that," Cuba said, then chuckled at the comment from the brash young lion. "You were spending with Shine, right?" he asked. He continued, without allowing Brown to answer. "Look like you in need of a new connect now, though," he said, basically confirming what the street had already figured out, that he was responsible for Shine's untimely demise. "And since you family, you should be doing business with me. Whatever he was giving it to you for, I can beat it, and the product is three times better than that bullshit he had."

Brown needed a coke connect bad, but he still wasn't sure about fucking with Cuba. Although he was one of his dad's old peoples, that was a while ago. Cuba was in business with Dame now, and Brown wasn't interested in doing business with him.

"It's something to think about," Brown said, not willing to sign himself up for anything without giving it proper thought.

"It's really not," Cuba answered, somewhat annoyed by the stubbornness of his mentor's son.

"It's not you. It's ya boy Dame I'm not really feeling like that. He just a little too loud and cocky for me," Brown confessed.

Cuba nodded in understanding. For Cuba, the streets were never where he wanted to take the lead. He allowed himself to be in business with louder and cockier people like Dame because when the heat came down, he could always avoid getting caught up. But Roman hadn't been like that, and that's exactly how he had died, in a firestorm of bullets. He wished that Brown could understand that, but he was too old now for Cuba to change his proud and defiant attitude. He could tell that Brown would die for pride, the same way his dad had.

"You wouldn't have to deal with him, just me," Cuba explained. "Here. Take my number, and when you ready, give me a call," he said, ending their back-and-forth. "Good seeing you again."

"You too," Brown said, then gave him a pound and a hug before leaving up out of the spot. Cuba watched the young man walk out of his function and worried.

As soon as they got outside, Trav started talking. "Damn, Brown. That was Cuba? *The* Cuba? That crazy-ass Panamanian motherfucker that be taking people out left and right? Yo, I can't believe it. What the fuck is he doing here, running a dice game?" Trav ranted. He was excited and confused. There was something going on that he didn't understand, but maybe Brown did. He looked at his boss, but Brown remained quiet. "You all good, bro?" he asked, but Brown stayed silent.

Brown thought about what Trav had said. What the fuck was Cuba doing here, running a dice game? He didn't need bread like that, and he most certainly wasn't the kind of motherfucker that liked to gamble just to gamble. Trav and Brown made it to the car, and Trav clicked open the doors, but Brown was still processing what had happened, and he stood next to the passenger side, absentmindedly holding his gun. Trav thought about bothering him again, but something about Brown's demeanor concerned him. His eyebrows were tight, and his jaw was clenched. Finally, Brown opened the door and got in the car, and Trav followed suit.

"Dame is up to something," Brown said seriously. "I don't know what it is, but I don't like it."

Trav tapped the dashboard with his index finger, thinking. This was the first time he had heard Brown say that he didn't know what someone was up to. It seemed to Trav and to the rest of Brown's crew, they were always the first to know when something was up. He didn't like thinking that someone had the jump on Brown and his team.

"What you want to do, boss?" Trav asked. He was willing to go to the ends of the earth if Brown asked him to.

But Brown didn't respond. It looked like his mind was running a mile a minute, and any conversation that Trav expected was outside the realm of possibility.

"Let's go," Brown finally said, ignoring Trav's question.

But Trav got the hint, and he turned on the car, and they took off.

Chapter 10

Four days had passed since Brown had crossed paths with Cuba, and the opportunity offered to him still weighed heavily on his mind. He had spent the last hour staring at the number in his phone as he spun it around on the counter. Everything in him knew he needed to make that call and get back on properly, but his stubbornness kept getting in the way. The hustler in him eventually won out. He figured doing business with Cuba had its advantages. He would be getting the best work and would be able to keep Dame at bay while he himself got strong. He could keep Cuba close, learn all he could about Dame, and eventual convince Cuba that they should be in business together. It was a risky plan, but he was counting on the fact that Cuba and his late father had been tight, and he was hoping that this bond extended to him some.

Brown had never got to meet his father, well, not really, but throughout his whole childhood, he had observed Cuba, and his memories of Cuba were vivid. As a kid, Brown would see him at block parties, or sometimes Cuba would drop off flowers for Brown's mom on Mother's Day. Even though they hadn't had a deep relationship, Cuba had been around in the way that only family was. He'd been here and there, but he had always somehow found his way back to Brown and his mom. He couldn't remember when Cuba had stopped coming around. It felt more like he had backed out of their lives slowly, in phases, so as not to cause a problem. But now that Brown thought about it, it felt like when he had first started coming up in the streets, Cuba had lost contact.

He picked up the phone now and dialed Cuba's number. The phone rang twice before Cuba picked up on the other end.

"Yo." To Brown, Cuba's voice was turning back into a familiar one after all those years of not talking.

"What up, Cube? This Brown," he said awkwardly. Finesse and charm weren't usually problems for him, but in this situation, he was struggling. There was a complexity to their relationship that Brown didn't like when it came to doing business. Connections like his and Cuba's, even though they had been abandoned or were more relevant to another generation, could fuck shit up if people started moving funny. He didn't know if he could trust Cuba completely, but for now he had to make it move, just from the perspective of making sure his money stayed good.

"Brown, my nigga," Cuba said in a monotone voice. "You hit my line, so that mean we on, right?"

There was silence on the line, and Cuba waited.

Brown rubbed his hand over his head before answering. "Yeah, I decided to take you up on ya offer." He was still nervous, and the conversation that they were having made it all too real for him. But he needed to pick up; there was no other way around it.

"Cool, cool. When you trying to get up?" Cuba said.

"ASAP."

"Bet. Meet me at the gambling spot in thirty minutes. And come dolo. Don't bring your little man from the other night. There's something about him I don't like," Cuba told him.

"Nah, he cool," Brown said. "But I understand." Inside, he thought it was funny. He had been telling Trav for years that he was moving with the wrong energy, and to hear Cuba make a comment on that very thing was unsurprising.

"Your cool and my cool two different things, fam," Cuba joked.

Brown laughed and then hung up the phone. He rubbed his hands together, happy that he was back on. He dialed Trav's number and put him onto the situation. He told him to meet him at their spot in the Gowanus Houses in a few hours.

He had just put his phone down when it rang again. Brown picked up the phone without thinking to check who it was. "Boy, we just got off the phone. What you need?" he greeted, getting up from where he sat at the kitchen island. He had a little wiggle room in terms of the time because the dice spot was nearby, but he wanted to get there early to make sure Cuba wasn't going to try anything. He didn't think he would, but if Brown did anything, he always tried to stay ready.

"Hello?" came a female's questioning voice.

Oh shit, Brown thought, and he checked the caller ID to see Zuri's name displayed across his phone. He was embarrassed. It had been about a month since they had met up in Philly, and they had talked on the phone a couple of times, but he hadn't heard from her in a few days, so he was surprised.

"Hey, Z. That's my bad. I was just talking to Trav right now," Brown explained.

"That's okay," Zuri said. Her voice was lower than usual, and she sounded like she was nervous. Brown got worried.

"What's going on?" he asked hurriedly. "Are you okay?" The last time he had left Zuri alone for too long, her mom had died, and she had gotten jumped and fired from her job.

"Oh yeah, everything is fine," Zuri assured Brown. "Or at least I hope everything will be fine. I've been thinking a lot about what you said the last time we saw each other, and I know you said you were serious, and I'm just going to believe you not playing with me." She was quiet for a second, and the phone amplified both her and Brown's breathing. "I think it's time I came back to New York."

"Really?" Brown was shocked. His offer to Zuri had been serious when he made it. He looked around his house and imagined Zuri there with him. He smiled as he walked out the door, hating to rush the conversation, but needing to keep his appointment.

"Yeah," Zuri said. "I think it could be really good for me, and I just don't know that there is anything left for me in this bum-ass city." Brown knew she didn't mean it. She had talked to him about how much she loved Philly, but he understood that the past few months had been hard for her.

"I get it, Ma. A change of scenery might be just the thing you need," he said. The vibe on the call changed, and he swore he could hear her smile through the receiver.

"You think so?" Zuri asked, but she wasn't really asking. Brown could tell that she was glad to have gotten the go-ahead from him.

"Honestly, Zuri . . . ," Brown began. He didn't use her entire first name often, so she knew that whatever he said next, he was serious. "I don't know why you're not already here."

Zuri laughed. "Boy, if you don't!" she teased, but he could tell she was happy.

"Pack your bags, Ma. I'm buying you a ticket back," Brown promised before he hung up the phone and rushed to his meetup with Cuba.

Now that he had Zuri to worry about, he needed a new connect more than ever.

Things were finally back running smooth for Brown and his crew; he had the projects on lockdown and had a few other spots too. The relationship with Cuba was definitely turning out to be a good one. Brown went from seeing him once to re-upping every few days. He had his young crew of Bloods in the street, going hard, getting money, and causing mayhem. Gowanus was on fire: there were nightly shoot-outs between rival gangs and bodies dropping left and right. It was to the point that Brown wore a bulletproof vest wherever he went. There was so much jealousy in the streets aimed at him and his crew for the money they were making, he had to stay on point at all times. He knew he had a target on him. He was a stripe for rival gang members, which meant killing him would boost their status in the streets, but he wasn't having it.

Brown cruised through the block with Trav and Grease, another one of his gang members. They were passing weed back and forth in the smoke-filled car. Even in the midst of beef, Brown moved wherever he wanted. In his mind, there was no point in running the streets if he couldn't do what he wanted. He was strapped and was sure both Trav and Grease were, in case anything popped off.

"Yo, I gotta hit this nigga Cuba. Time to re-up again," he said with a smile on his face.

"Damn, we can't keep that shit," Grease said.

"That's a good thing, nigga," Trav joked, causing them all to laugh. "But on another note, when we gonna make a move on the bitch-ass nigga Dame? We need more than just the projects."

"In due time. A move like that takes time. We rock 'im to sleep, and then we bury him," Brown said. If his dad had left him with anything, it was the understanding that you didn't move on an opponent who wasn't attacking you straight up until you were ready. Hitting Dame before Brown was ready would mean certain death for him and his crew, and as much as Brown wanted his borough back, territory wasn't worth the lives of all his boys.

"You really think Cuba gonna go along with it?" Trav asked.

"Let me worry about Cuba," Brown told him. "Matter of fact, let me give this nigga a call," he said before he blew smoke from his mouth and grabbed his phone.

Cuba answered on the second ring. "Brown, what up, fam?"

"What up, my nigga? I need to come check you."

"I'm OT right now," Cuba explained. "But you could go see my man and he'll take care of you until I get back." It seemed weird to Brown that Cuba had decided that now was a good time to leave the city, and he wondered what was going on. It was bad etiquette to ask a hustler, especially an old head and a killer like Cuba, what he was up to, and so Brown controlled his urge to interrogate him about the situation.

"Yeah, man, who?" Brown asked. He was nervous that this was going to go in a direction he didn't like, and he was worried that he would have to push back on a man he had a lot of respect for.

"Dame," Cuba replied.

Brown quickly objected. "Nah, I already told you, I wasn't feeling that."

He couldn't believe that Cuba would suggest that to him. Brown had thought he had made it abundantly clear that he wasn't fucking with Dame like that. Trav and Grease looked at him, hearing only one end of the phone call. Brown could feel his blood pressure rise. If Cuba was so trusting of Dame that he was willing to send Brown to see him, maybe Cuba couldn't be turned as easily as he had originally thought.

"I know, but it'll be a one-time thing. Just this time only. I'm taking care of something, so I'm out of reach right now. You gonna sit still till I'm back, or you gonna handle ya biz? I can make that call, and it'll be just like you was dealing with me, or you can wait till I get back. It's on you."

Silence fell on the line as Brown gave some thought to what Cuba had said. Trav and Grease were still looking at him, and he could feel the pressure from all sides. But this was his deal and his crew, and he was going to think through his options.

"Time is money," Cuba said, pressing Brown for a speedier response.

Never one to be rushed or pressed, Brown continued giving it some thought for a few more seconds before answering. On one hand, he could say no and try to figure out an alternative to working with Cuba, though he didn't know where or who he would go to for the kind of product Cuba had. And on the other, he could just swallow his pride and go to the meetup with Dame and see what he was working with, how many men he had with him. This information might help him plan his next move. *Fuck it*, Brown thought.

"Make it happen," he told Cuba.

"Say no more."

Brown pulled his car into the half-circle driveway of the two-story mini-mansion. It sat on about a half acre of land, atop a hill, among a dozen beautiful homes in the upscale residential community. Rows of manicured trees lined both sides of the property. An all-window, high-ceilinged sunroom was attached to one side of the house, and a two-car garage was on another. A white Maserati was parked in one of the bays, and a maroon Porsche truck sat in the driveway. There must have been other cars around the way, because the number of shadows they could see moving on the curtains was double the number of people who could fit in the two cars.

Trav immediately was impressed by the size and beauty of the residence. He had only heard about niggas living like that or seen it on TV. He had never actually witnessed it firsthand. He was impressed, but Brown was nervous. They were isolated out here, and if anything went down, there was no good way for them to get out or for help to get in.

"Damn, this nigga living. This some fly MTV cribs–type shit. I see why Cuba play this nigga so close. He eating hard," Trav observed.

After Brown had got off the phone with Cuba, he had explained to Trav and Grease exactly what it was they were going to do and why they were doing it. They hadn't come here to kiss ass, and they hadn't come to get strong-armed into working for Dame. Brown moved on his own terms, and he needed Trav to get with the program.

Brown cut his eyes at Trav and shot him a glare out of the corner of his eye. He was unmoved by the luxurious home. He just wanted to get what he came for, handle his business, and get back to the money. Brown could hear the money machine in his mind ringing as he thought about all the dollars he could make if he knocked Dame out of the way. He was glad that Trav and Grease had come along to hold him down in case shit went left. It was always good to have an extra trigger with you when dealing with niggas like Dame. He was just a little stressed that the trigger he had with him was so jumpy. Trav was already crawling out of his seat, ready to get to the action.

Brown parked in the driveway but didn't turn the car off. He just reached in the back and grabbed a diaper bag off the seat back there. He didn't have any kids; the diaper bag was only for the look, in case he got stopped by the cops. Trav had always suggested that they get a child's car seat to really complete the look, but Brown thought that it would fuck with his image and thus would not be worth the protection it offered.

"Keep this muthafucka runnin', son. You never know," Brown instructed Grease.

Trav offered a nod, showing he agreed, then exited the car with Brown and walked to the front door. Brown looked at his protégé as they stood there. He thought about the relationship between Cuba and his dad, and he put himself in Cuba's shoes. If in twenty years Trav's son came to him for help, would he set him up under the guise of offering assistance? Brown wouldn't, and from what he'd been told, his dad wouldn't, either, but at this point it was too late to think about whether Cuba would or wouldn't set him up. He was already here.

Brown knocked twice, then looked up at the camera above the door. Dame had his crib tightly secured and clearly wasn't taking any chances. The door opened, and to both of their surprise, a stockily built, butch-looking female with dreads answered the door. She stepped aside, allowing them to enter. That was when Brown noticed the large contingent of Dame's crew chilling in the living-room area. He raised his arms, and the female bodyguard patted him down first, then Trav. She wasn't as thorough as she should have been, missing the small gun he had tucked in his Timberland boot. She led them through the living room toward the kitchen. As they passed the large group of Dame's crew members, Brown could see that most, if not all, were strapped. He gave Trav a look and could tell he had noticed the same thing.

The two men entered the kitchen behind the bodyguard. Dame stood in the middle of the room, behind the island, dressed in a white Louis V polo shirt, shades with a diamond-encrusted chain hanging from his neck. He was entertaining the men in the room with a story about a weekend tryst in Miami with the female R & B singer whose video was playing on the TV. The men seemed to be enjoying the blow-by-blow details, as no one in the room acknowledged Brown's or Trav's presence. They stood in the crowd with everyone else. Brown wasn't one to interrupt, especially when he didn't have the upper hand, so he waited for Dame to acknowledge them.

Dame finally finished his story, then looked over at the two newcomers standing in his kitchen. "What up? Which one of y'all is Brown?" he asked as he poured himself a shot of Patrón.

Brown chuckled slightly to himself. Dame knew exactly who he was, since the two of them had come up in the streets around the same time. They had had dealings only in passing but knew one another's name and face. Only because of a chance encounter with the stepdaughter of a major plug had Dame risen in the game faster than Brown.

Still, for the sake of the deal going smooth, Brown decided to play along.

"I'm Brown," he said, stepping forward to differentiate himself from the others. But everyone had already identified him and Trav as the strangers in the crowd.

"Oh, okay. My man Cuba really vouches for you. That says a lot." Dame looked at him with one eyebrow up. They were sizing each other up, and the tension spread through the room as the men around them grew quiet.

Brown didn't respond. He was going to maintain his stoic nature as long as possible. He chose to listen instead of speak. He just nodded as Dame continued.

"Cuba said your pops used to run the city back in the day, that's what's up." He paused. "You wanna drink or something?" Dame asked, gesturing to the bottles in front of him. There was everything from Henny to Cîroc to the Patrón Dame was drinking himself, and Brown could tell he was trying to subtly flex on him.

"Nah, I'm good. I rather just take care of this little business and be on my way," Brown responded, breaking the illusion that Dame was trying to build a friendship. He was here for his product, and he was going to leave. That was it, and he meant it.

Dame looked over at his men with a smirk on his face. "I like that, straight business. So what's up?"

Recognizing this as his cue, Brown walked over and placed the diaper bag on the counter.

Dame looked down and couldn't contain his laughter at the sight of the baby bag. "Man, the fuck? What? You run a day care or something?" He roared with laughter.

Brown gritted his teeth; Dame was working his nerve, but he kept his cool. He hated being the butt of the joke, but Dame not being up on game was not his business, and he wasn't going to waste time explaining himself. "Nah," he said without participating in the joke.

Dame unzipped the bag and peeked inside. When he saw the stacks of money packed in the bag, he stopped laughing. He looked over at one of the men and barked out instructions. "Yo, go take care of my man here." The man sprung from his seat and disappeared into another part of the house.

Dame looked past Brown at Trav, whose head was on a constant swivel as he took in his surroundings. He looked out of place, or at least over his head, to Dame. "You good, li'l man? You look nervous. You want a drink or something?"

Trav looked like he was about to answer, and Brown didn't want any distractions or for Dame to get further in his boy's head.

"He good," Brown said, answering for Trav.

"Yeah, everything good. Y'all Cuba's people, so ain't nothing to worry about," Dame said, holding Brown's eyes for longer than casual conversation usually called for. It was like watching two lions on the savannah stare each other down, or two sharks circling when they smelled blood in the water.

"Exactly," Brown replied, staring Dame in the face, letting him know he wasn't afraid at all, even with the odds stacked clearly against him.

"So you getting a lot of money in Gowanus, huh?" Dame asked.

Brown knew that he was making fun of him. There wasn't no pride in Gowanus. It was just a hustle, and they both knew it. If they had been anywhere else, in any other situation, Brown would have handled this differently, but they were on Dame's turf, and he had only Trav as backup, which, given how jumpy his right-hand man was, wasn't saying a lot.

"I'm doing a'ight," Brown said.

"Yeah," Dame answered with a smirk. "Brown, Brown, Brown," he repeated aloud, snapping his fingers, trying to recall from where he knew the name. "I remember you now. You used to fuck with that bad light-skinned chick with the freckles and fat ass. What was her name? Nubia," he said. "Yeah, that was it. Fucked up what happened to shorty." Dame was mocking Brown. If Brown couldn't keep his own bitch safe, how was he supposed to run the streets? It was an insult.

Brown gritted his teeth and nodded his head but didn't offer a response. Just then, the man Dame had given instructions to returned with a medium-sized duffel bag and placed it on the counter, next to the diaper bag. Dame motioned for Brown to check out the bricks. Brown stepped closer to the counter and unzipped the bag.

Wrinkles formed in his forehead from confusion when he saw the large number of bricks inside the bag. He was a little taken back. "What's all this? I only wanted three."

"Yeah, and I gave you four more on the arm. What you complaining about? You bought three at the price Cuba quoted you off the love, and I fronted you the rest at my price. Which is slightly higher than Cuba's, of course," Dame informed him, with no give in his facial expression.

"No thanks. I'm good on the consignment. I'll just take the three I paid for," Brown said as he began removing the extra bricks from the bag and stacking them on the counter.

"Nah, you gonna take what I give you. The terms are non-negotiable," Dame said as he folded his arms in front of him.

Brown felt Dame was trying to little dog him. He was trying to turn him into an employee, and Brown wasn't having that. The volume of his voice increased, and his tone was as serious as it could be, when he said, "What! You got me fucked up, my nigga. I don't know who you think you is or what Cuba told you, but I don't get down like that. I ain't for none of this." He was trying to keep his cool as much as possible, because he knew that Dame would take him out then and there if he thought Brown was fucking with the hierarchy he had built or the way he moved things.

Brown reached for the diaper bag containing his sixty thousand dollars in cash, but Dame snatched it off the counter and stepped around the island. The tension had just tripled, and everyone could feel it as the two alpha males jockeyed for the position of power. Trav attempted to step up but was quickly aborted by the boyish female when he felt the cold steel of her gun pressed under his chin. Brown gave a quick glance over his shoulder and saw that every member of Dame's entourage who was in the kitchen had his gun drawn and pointing at his back.

"You ain't for none of what?" Dame questioned, grilling Brown as they stood face-to-face. "I know exactly who you are, nigga. I didn't feel you then, and I don't feel you now." They were the same height, and so they stood eye to eye, almost like distorted reflections of each other.

Brown refused to back down. "The feeling is mutual, my nigga. But this some sucker shit you trying to pull, and you know it." Brown kept thinking about Cuba. He wondered if he knew that this was the shit he had let Brown walk into.

"Sucker moves get sucker results. You know about that, right?" Dame laughed as he took a step back and looked at his henchmen. All it would take was a nod from him, and Brown and Trav would cease to exist. There was no more jockeying; it was clear who had the power. Brown knew it, even if he didn't want to accept it. Dame had seen it in his eyes, and at that moment, that was enough for him.

"Here, nigga," he said, tossing the diaper bag at Brown's feet. "Get the fuck out my house."

Brown was burning up on the inside as he bent over and picked up the bag off the floor. He wanted to put a bullet in Dame's head, and it took everything in him not to reach in his boot and pull out his gun and die for pride, but he understood this wasn't the time or the place. Any move other than retreating would be pure suicide. He turned to leave as the room parted, allowing him and Trav to walk out. A group of Dame's henchmen followed them out to the driveway and made sure they got in their car and left. Brown no longer gave a fuck about bricks or hustling; he wanted only to kill Dame, and he wouldn't rest until he did.

Grease unlocked the doors to the car, and Brown was glad he had had the foresight to tell him to keep the engine running. He and Trav jumped in, and Grease started driving away.

"What the fuck was that?" Trav yelled. "We gon' kill him. Nah, fuck him." He was in the backseat, cocking his gun, and Brown didn't know what to say to him. He was silent with rage.

"What happened?" Grease asked nervously. He was less scared of Dame pulling up on them and more scared of Brown yelling at him for asking stupid questions.

Trav continued to yell angry nonsense, but Brown remained quiet. He was thinking.

Brown's father, Roman, had run the streets; that much was a known fact in New York. And Brown had trusted Cuba off the strength of the relationship he had had with his father. He couldn't determine if Cuba had known what Dame had up his sleeve and had sent him in as a way of strong-arming him into working for Dame. Working for Dame was basically working for Cuba after a certain point, and Cuba hadn't tried it with Brown before. He was just

so confused. Nothing that had happened with Dame and
his crew made sense. Nothing about Cuba running a dice
game made sense to him, either. Brown felt himself growing paranoid and jumpy.

"There is something bigger at play here," he said quietly.
Trav stopped his grumbling in order to listen to what
Brown was going to say next, but he stopped there.

Grease was feeling left out and wanted to understand
what was going on, so he decided it would be on him to
break the silence. "What do you think is going on?" he
asked, keeping his eyes on the road. Brown didn't look
at him, either. His eyes remained focused on the air in
front of him, but Grease and Trav knew he wasn't seeing
anything outside the scenarios he was painting in his
own mind.

"I don't know yet," said Brown honestly.

Grease was shocked. He had never heard their boss say
he didn't know something. For years, Brown had been
the head hustler in the streets. He had so many bodies
under his belt, he rivaled Cuba. He had the legacy of his
father and numbers in the streets, but for the first time,
he would have to work for his power.

Trav started muttering to himself in the backseat again,
talking shit about Dame and his crew, and talking about
what he would do when they finally got the drop on him.
Brown thought about Cuba again and the original question he had had in his head. If the roles were reversed
and it was Trav's son coming to him for help, would he
snake him? Brown realized he had made a mistake. The
equivalent scenario wasn't Trav's son coming to ask him
for help. It was if Brown's son went to Trav in the future.
Would Trav protect him and help him, or would he step
on him to get ahead?

As he looked into the little mirror on his visor and
watched his hyped-up young protégé in the backseat

continue to have imagined conversations with all the targets he was going to take out, Brown realized he didn't know the answer, but he didn't trust the depth of the relationship across that many generations. He decided he was done with Cuba. This was a slight he couldn't forgive, his father's name be damned. As they sped down the streets into Brooklyn, the wheels in Brown's brain were already spinning and plotting the ultimate revenge.

Chapter 11

Zuri . . .

A foul smell smacked Zuri in the nose as she boarded the bus and made her way to an empty seat. Once she was seated, she reached into her handbag and removed her phone. She placed her earplugs in and began to scroll through her music list on her phone as she prepared for the ride to New York. She stared out the window and zoned out as Beyoncé played in her ears. She was a bundle of nervous energy. She had long left New York in her rearview and had never planned to return, but here she was, making the trip up I-95. She hoped she was making the right decision, but she still wasn't sure. Brown's offer was too good to resist; more importantly, so was he. Just the thought of him made her smile and bite down on the tip of her fingernail as she squeezed her legs together from the sensation shooting through her panties.

It had been a weird couple of weeks for Zuri. After they had spent the day together and Brown had wined and dined her and taken her shopping, Waheed had caught on pretty quickly that there was something going on with her. And maybe it was because of the amount of time they had spent together already, but he didn't seem to care and let her keep doing what she was doing. He had been spending less and less time in the house and had shown less of a sexual interest in Zuri. After months of chasing her with no success and then suddenly having access to her whenever he wanted, Waheed had lost the fire that kept him thirsty. That was all good for Zuri, though, because he wasn't laying it down right in the bedroom, and he wasn't really paying attention to her in any other way, either.

She had thought long and hard that first night about what Brown had proposed she do, but it had taken her a month to make a decision. She had kept going back and forth between whether or not she would go stay with Brown, because she didn't know what staying with him would look like. When she had told Waheed she was leaving, he hadn't even tried to stop her. He had just asked her for the date of her departure and had told her to make sure he left her copy of the key. She didn't feel any kind of way about him anymore, but it still stung a bit to think that he cared so little about the fact that she was leaving forever.

As the bus rolled through the empty space between Philadelphia and New York, Zuri couldn't help but think about Nubia. She hadn't been to New York since Nubia was killed and she was shot, and she had repressed so many of those memories that she didn't know how she would react when she got there. Beyond that, though, she wondered how Nubia would feel about the fact that she had romantic feelings for Brown. Zuri hadn't developed them on purpose, and really, she had tried her best to talk herself out of feeling the way that she did. It was her dedication to Nubia that had kept Zuri from calling Brown for a month after he had taken her on their shopping excursion. But as the days with Waheed had started to add up, and there was no way out that Zuri could find, she had decided that as much as she loved Nubia, she was sure Nubia loved her enough to want her to be safe and happy. As the bus got nearer to New York,

Zuri continued to think about her feelings and tried her best to process her decisions. She took some time to pray that she was making good choices and that her life would move only forward from there on out, but mostly, she was lost in thought for the rest of the bus ride.

The bus finally arrived at the Port Authority terminal in Manhattan. Zuri wasted no time exiting the bus, trying to escape the repulsive odor. As soon as her feet touch the pavement and she walked into the New York night, she spotted Brown and Trav posted up, waiting for her. Brown smiled as they made eye contact, and the way he eyed her up and down sent tingles through her body. The affect he had on her was like nothing she had experienced before. She felt like a schoolgirl with a crush, and she could only hope she didn't look like one. She knew that Brown still saw her as Nubia's little sister.

"How was your trip?" Brown asked as he leaned in and hugged her. Then he took one of her bags out of her hand and nodded to Trav, who immediately walked over and relieved her of her other bag.

Trav didn't say anything to Zuri, and she wondered if it was because of how dismissive she had been with him before. She felt kind of bad, but she was too tired to think about his feelings, and so she didn't bring it up.

"It felt like I rode here in a bathroom stall," she admitted. "That bus stank," she added, turning up her nose. It had been over a week since Zuri had called Brown and told him she had made her decision. She would have traveled to New York then, but Brown had asked for time to finish up some business, and with all he was doing for her, she couldn't deny him whatever he wanted.

"I'm sorry, Ma." Brown chuckled. "It was last minute, but I'll make it up, I promise."

The three of them drove over the bridge to Brooklyn. Zuri sat in the front passenger seat, taking in all the familiar sites, as Brown and Trav talked. Trav was still ignoring her, which she thought was weird, but she figured that maybe Brown had said something about not bothering her, and she let that idea put her mind at ease. Her heart began to race as they entered her old neighborhood. The last time that she had driven down these streets was the day that she and Nubia were shot. She couldn't believe that on that day they were on their way to meet Brown and now here she sat with Brown himself, while her sister lay in a grave somewhere in the outer borough. Her emotions were getting the best of her, and she kept her face turned, hoping to prevent Brown or Trav from seeing the tears forming in her eyes.

As they drove through the part of Brooklyn in which she had grown up, Zuri wondered why she had ever left. *Running away from the problem doesn't solve it*, she thought to herself, *because if you ever have to go back, the problem will still be there, waiting for you.* That was how she felt about the memories of Nubia: she had run from them after her death, but now that she was back, it was like she was seeing her sister on every street corner. The phantom pain that assaulted her scar when she thought too hard about that night Nubia was taken from her came back full force while she was in the car. She winced visibly and put her hand over her hair, on the spot where she could swear the scar was pulsating. Worried that she was causing a scene, she shifted her tear-filled eyes over to Brown and Trav, but they were still in deep discussion over some street affairs she had no business knowing about.

"Yo, I need you to go check on some shit for me," Brown said, looking in the rearview at Trav. Trav had been talking to Brown readily, but he was doing his best to avoid Zuri, so he was sitting all the way back now, a very different position from the one in which he usually rode, which was with his head obnoxiously pushed in between the driver's seat and the front passenger seat.

"Wassup?" Trav asked aggressively. After years spent trying to stay in Zuri's good graces, and maybe one day achieving something even better than that, and having her dub him the whole time, he was tired of dealing with her. Therefore, he would do anything if it meant that he could get out of the car, away from her, and back to work.

"The nigga Grease ain't re-up in, like, a week. Go see that nigga and find out what's good. Why he moving so slow." Brown pulled behind Trav's car, which was parked in front of the Gowanus Houses.

Zuri hadn't realized that they had actually made it to the Gowanus Houses, the last part of Brooklyn she and Nubia had been together in. She turned her body toward the car's interior, as she didn't want to look out the window anymore, but she kept her face down and pretended to scroll on her phone.

"Be safe, my G," Trav said as he gave him a pound. He cut his eyes at Zuri without saying anything. This was her opportunity, she thought, to see what was good with him. Maybe he was just in a bad mood overall.

"Good seeing you again, Trav," Zuri said, looking up for a second, trying to test the waters and make a show of politeness and civility in front of Brown.

"Yeah," Trav answered in a very dismissive tone, and Zuri realized her plan had backfired. "I'ma hit you later, son," he said to Brown with a half-cocked smile. Then he hopped out.

"No doubt," Brown said as the door closed. He then turned his attention to Zuri, who remained with her head turned. He had seen the look on her face as they entered the neighborhood, no matter how much she had tried to hide it from him.

He put his hand under her chin and turned her face up toward him. Tears were dancing down her face. "I'm sorry for bringing you over here. I know the old hood hold a lot of memories, not all good, either. This where I get my money, though," he said, pointing to the buildings that made up the projects. "Right here on these blocks, all these niggas you see work for me. I don't say that to brag. I'm telling you that to ease any fears you may have. Whatever happened in the past will never happen again. And whatever stresses you had in Philly are behind you now," he assured her as he ran his warm thumbs under her eyes, collecting her tears and wiping up her smeared mascara.

Zuri felt flutters in her heart when those words left Brown's lips, and they got even worse as he took his hands away from her face. She knew she was taking a risk by coming to New York at Brown's request, but after all she had been through, the thought of him made her feel a sense of peace coming back to her heart. She felt safe. Brown was the closest person to her and her sister outside of family, not that she had any family left, anyway.

Being around him brought vivid memories of Nubia to her mind. A small part of her still felt wrong for having romantic feelings for Brown, but she couldn't help herself, and she reminded herself of the conclusion she had come to back in Philly. Nubia would have wanted her to be happy. And the heart wanted what it wanted. She remembered how he used to treat Nubia, which was like a queen. She craved the same treatment, and she was a grown woman, and no longer a naïve little girl, and she understood how rare a guy like Brown was. Life had dealt her a bad hand, but Brown was looking like the change she needed, and she wasn't about to pass up the opportunity.

"What wrong with Trav? Why was he acting funny?" she asked as they cruised the old neighborhood. She knew why he had been acting funny, but she didn't want Brown to know she knew, so she pretended to be baffled.

"You know that nigga been feeling you since back in the day." Brown chuckled a bit.

"I ain't never gave him no kick it, so I don't know why he acting like that," Zuri replied, continuing her charade but with honesty. She felt her stomach flip as she realized how many times she had said the same thing to Nubia all those years ago.

They drove for about thirty minutes, until they reached a three-story brownstone. The area looked cleaner than the streets they were just riding through. The small bushes along the sidewalk were manicured, and the houses were well kept.

"This is where you live?" Zuri asked, breaking the long silence.

Brown parallel parked into a spot and looked over at her. "Yeah, this is my spot."

Zuri was impressed. The block was different than the ones that she had lived on when she stayed in New York, and she wondered what Brown got into in such a nice little area. They both exited the vehicle, and Brown hit the button on the alarm to secure the car.

"It don't look like you need that over here," Zuri said, commenting on how nice the neighborhood seemed, as she looked around her.

"This is still New York," Brown joked as they reached the top of the steps. He held the first door for her and then walked in behind her. "I'll come back down and get your bags in a minute. Let's get you upstairs, so you can make yourself at home," he said with a smile as he opened the second door. Zuri returned the smile as she walked past him. "Excuse the mess. I ain't have time to straighten up before I dipped out to pick you up," he said as he followed behind her.

"Don't make excuses 'cause you keep a nasty house," she teased.

"Oh, you tryin'a play me," Brown said with fake horror.

They shared a laugh as they climbed the stairs. Brown watched Zuri as she purposely swayed her hips as she walked up the steps. He would have to be blind not to notice or admire the woman she had grown into.

"It's open. Just turn the knob," he directed her when they reached his front door.

Zuri looked around, confused. "You just leave your door open? What about the people that live downstairs?" she asked.

"What people? All this is me, Ma. Nobody live here but me and now you," he replied.

Zuri was impressed. It was one thing to own a house; it was a whole other level for Brown to have a brownstone all to himself. Zuri opened the door, stepped inside, and was surprised to see how neat his place was. Clearly, he was either kidding or exaggerating about it being messy. Not only was it neat, but the furniture wasn't all black, like that in most guys' bachelor pads. He had red leather couches in his living room, where there was lots of sunlight coming through the windows. Brown leaned up against the wall that separated the kitchen and the living room and smiled as Zuri plopped down on the couch, making herself at home.

"Your place is nice, Brown, but you always had style," she complimented. "Thank you for letting me stay here." She grabbed a pillow and hugged it in her lap like a little girl. After all the places she had stayed in the past months, this was one that finally felt like a home to her.

Brown smoothly walked over and took a seat next to her. "No thank-you needed. I told you that day in the hospital that I would always look out. This is me keeping my word. When that shit went down back in the day, a piece of me was broken . . ." Brown lowered his head as his voice trailed off. He didn't want to bring up Nubia's murder, hoping to keep the smile on Zuri's face there. But he felt the need to explain himself and how much he had been affected by their shared past. He needed her to know how much it had destroyed him and how having her back in his life was so important to him. He looked at her, and she was staring at him, with a hope in her eyes that was so strong, he almost didn't say anything, but he had to.

"I loved your sister, Zuri. I never want you to feel like I didn't. When you bounced, I didn't come looking for you, because I thought you wanted to leave all this shit behind you. Start new. You know what I'm saying? But if I had known you were out there by yourself, not on some peace shit, I would have definitely come for you, Ma."

Zuri replied quickly, "I know you would've, Brown, and before you continue, I want you to know that I don't feel a way about you, and I don't blame you. I chose to leave. I created my path, and I made my own decisions. I am just happy that I am here now and finally around someone who cares about me. I know Nubia would want me to be happy. She would want me to be safe with someone who is truly looking out for me." Zuri's face lit up as she spoke. She felt comfortable in Brown's presence, like she finally was where she belonged.

"I definitely care about you, and I promise to keep you safe," Brown assured her.

"I know you do. That's why I am here," Zuri said sincerely, maintaining eye contact with him. He stared back at her intensely. She thought this was it.

Brown placed his hand on her neck and ran his four fingers up through her hair before kissing her gently on the forehead. For a second, she was worried he would run his hands over her scar, and she didn't want to remind him of all the bad that had happened to her that night too. But he just missed it. "I want you to feel at home, Ma. I'm gonna go get your bags out of the car," he said, jumping to his feet. "I know you want to shower and get that stinking bus smell off you."

Zuri laughed, but she honestly felt a little disappointed by the kiss on the forehead. She had thought that Brown would place his soft lips on hers, but she understood his trepidation. She leaned back on the couch, letting out a small sigh, then proceeded to play it off. "You ain't never lie. I feel like I got every person on that bus's breath on me."

Brown laughed as he headed for the door. "There's a shower in my bedroom. If you go straight through that door, you can't miss it," he explained, pointing down the hall. "There's towels and washcloths in the linen closet."

"Brown," Zuri shouted before the door closed behind him, stopping him in his tracks. "You said no one lives downstairs. Why you need all this space?"

A charming smile creased his face. "A nigga like his privacy. Plus, I want a family one day, you know, a wife and some seeds. Make this crib feel like a home."

Zuri waited until the door closed, then cracked a big smile. It felt dumb, but she started to imagine that life for herself, being here with him, raising two badass sons that looked just like their daddy. The thought alone was enough to make her forget about the pain of the memories that had brought her to tears earlier that night. She headed down the hallway and through the bedroom, but not before noticing how organized Brown's dresser was, with his jewelry lined up side by side perfectly, his colognes looking like they had been purposely lined up in order of their size. Zuri couldn't help but wonder if he had a touch of OCD.

Damn. He's neater than me, she thought. The smell of his cologne lingered in the room. She inhaled a deep whiff while walking to the bathroom. When she opened the bathroom door, she was in shock again. "Shit," she said out loud to herself, "is everything about this man pretty?" The bathroom was all white, and there were amenities everywhere she looked, everything from lotion to an aromatherapy diffuser. She couldn't help but feel like she was in a spa. Impressed, she began to take off her clothes, and as she pulled off each garment, it felt like she was shedding the stress of the past months along with it.

The steaming hot water was relaxing and soothing to her body and mind as Zuri let the shower rain down on her. She rubbed the soap on her body and closed her eyes, thankful for the fresh start in her life. It was a chance to be happy, something she had always longed for. She wanted total happiness, and the thought of Brown made her feel like that was possible. He was playing things so cool, but she could see in his eyes that there was something more there. She knew he saw how she stared at him; he would turn away when their eyes locked. The kiss on the forehead was such a tease, and it only made her want him more. *Maybe he knows that,* she thought to herself. *Well, if he does know that, then that would mean that he wants me, too, right?* She continued her internal monologue, posing questions to herself, but she had no good answers and no better understanding of what Brown wanted from her.

Either way, he had stirred up feelings in her body, and if he wasn't going to scratch her itch, she had no problem serving herself. She brushed up against her throbbing clit with her washcloth and felt a tingling sensation. She continued to rub it, dropping her washcloth in the tub. Her senses were heightened, and her heart began to palpitate. Zuri inserted two fingers inside herself while rubbing her clit vigorously with the middle finger of her other hand until her legs became like Jell-O. Her soft moans grew slightly louder as she leaned up against the shower wall. She lifted one leg up on the edge of the shower and went to work on herself. After removing her fingers from her love spot, she squeezed her breasts. As her nipples hardened, she tried to control her moans. Her breaths quickened.

She hoped Brown couldn't hear her, but at that moment of climax, she didn't care. She imagined his thick lips sucking on her clit as she gyrated her hips on her own finger faster and faster. Zuri orgasmed hard until her breath was caught in her throat. She cracked a smile and exhaled before washing up one last time and exiting the shower. Zuri grabbed the white towel off the back of the toilet and wrapped it around her body. She opened the bathroom door and screamed in surprise when she found Brown sitting on the edge of the bed, waiting for her. Her two bags sat at the foot of the bed.

"Oh my God," she yelled. "You scared me. Why you just sitting there?"

"I wanted to make sure you were good. I wanted to be able to hear you if you needed me for anything," he said with a sheepish smirk on his face, letting her know he had heard her pleasuring herself in the shower. "Did you enjoy your shower?" he asked.

"Very much," she replied with no shame, then laughed.

"Damn. You had it harder than I thought out in Philly," he teased, staring at her as the sexual tension in the room built. After a brief pause Brown rose to his feet. "Your bags are at the foot of the bed. I'll be in the living room if you need me." He started to walk toward the door, and just before he went to turn the knob, Zuri stopped him.

"Wait," Zuri said. He was just far enough away now that she couldn't touch him, but she couldn't control herself either way. "Now that you mention it, there is something I need." Zuri's pleasure in the shower had given her more confidence than she maybe normally had, but she could still feel her heart pounding in her ears. Once she crossed this line, there was no going back, but she couldn't stop imagining Brown's body on hers, and she couldn't help herself anymore.

Brown turned around just as Zuri let her towel fall to the floor, and he was greeted by her naked frame. There was no denying how beautiful her body was. Her pretty brown skin glistened from the beads of water that remained from the shower, and her hair was wet and wavy. He stood there in silence, but Zuri could sense his breath quicken. Even though there couldn't be more than four feet between them, it felt like there were so many years and memories worth of space separating them. She knew that Brown was too respectful of her, and it would have to be she who made the first move. The towel had made a circle around her legs when she dropped it, and she stepped out of that circle to move toward Brown. He said nothing as she got close to him. She pressed herself into him, the water on her body getting his shirt and pants wet. Brown still didn't utter a word or move a muscle.

Zuri kissed his bottom lip, then sucked on it a little, and Brown finally broke. He grabbed her by the waist and kissed her passionately as the sexual tension between them bubbled over. Their tongues danced in a synchronized movement as Zuri closed her eyes and Brown engulfed her in his embrace. Brown's hands explored her body until they landed on her butt, and he scooped her off her feet effortlessly, then carried her over to the bed. Brown pulled his shirt over his head as Zuri simultaneously unbuckled and removed his pants. Zuri reached inside his boxers, stroked his erect manhood. Holding his length in her hand made Zuri desperately want to feel him inside of her. She lay back on the bed and spread her legs, inviting him in.

After staring at her pretty flower, Brown placed his lips on her clit, then licked and sucked until he brought her to an orgasmic state. Zuri's mouth fell open as Brown pleased her body with his oral skills. She threw her head back and gasped while arching her back as Brown entered her. His thick girth filled her like no one had before. Zuri wrapped her legs tightly around his waist as he passionately stroked her. On many nights she had imagined what sex with him would be like, but the reality was more than she could have dreamed. It was like nothing she had ever felt before. Brown could feel her body tremble with every thrust. He grabbed the back of her neck and kissed her as they stared into one another's eyes. This was more than just sex. The connection was so strong between them. They both felt it. He continued to work her, quickening the pace, as her moans became louder, echoing off the walls in the room.

"Ooh," she cried out as she exploded, creaming all over his shaft. Zuri gripped the sheets as Brown's thrusts became more powerful. She could feel him throbbing inside of her and knew he was close to climaxing.

Brown let out a loud grunt as he released his seed inside of her. He collapsed on the bed next to her. The room fell silent, except for the sound of heavy breathing as they tried to catch their breath. Zuri stared up at the ceiling; she was in ecstasy. She felt so many emotions racing through her body and mind, and she let a single tear escape from her eye.

Brown ran his fingers through her hair, then pulled her into his chest and kissed her forehead. Neither of them spoke a word—there was no need to—and after a while, Zuri heard Brown begin to snore. As she watched him sleep, she thought about all the things that had gone wrong in her life up until this moment, and she wondered if maybe all those things had happened for a reason, namely, to bring her to this moment with this person. It was a corny way to think about it, but she couldn't help herself, as she had never felt a contentment so complete.

She smiled to herself, and before she knew it, she slipped off into a slumber of her own.

Chapter 12

"Mmm . . . mmm," Zuri moaned as she began to stir from her sleep. She opened her eyes and immediately realized the source of the pleasing feeling she felt. She could see the top of Brown's head peeking out from under the white sheet as he kissed and licked her inner thighs.

"Well, good morning to you too," she said with a seductive smirk on her face.

"Good morning, Ma." He trailed kisses up her stomach and breasts until he reached her lips.

Zuri could feel his rock-hard manhood up against her and spread her legs to let him know she was thinking the same thing he was. Brown rubbed the head of his shaft against her, then entered her opening. Her wetness welcomed him in as he found his rhythm, and Zuri's hips joined in the lovemaking dance. Brown had her by the back of her neck and was pulling her into him intimately. It felt like they were in their own world.

The sound of the doorbell ringing uncontrollably caught both of them by surprise.

"Who the fuck?" Brown asked rhetorically as he jumped up from the bed, grabbed his jeans off the floor, and quickly slipped them on.

Zuri pulled the sheet up over her naked body, disappointed by the interruption of their early morning session. She hadn't been at Brown's long enough to know what the norm was at his spot, but she didn't know anybody that had early morning callers who weren't bad news.

Brown marched down the hallway and over to the intercom. "Who is it?"

"It's me. Trav," came a voice up through the intercom.

Zuri groaned and was glad that Brown was too far away to hear her. She knew it wasn't anybody's fault that Trav had that crush on her, but it did make things awkward, and it did mean that her being in Brown's bed was mortifying. She debated getting up and getting dressed, but she was too tense to move, and so she just lay there, listening intently.

Brown quickly buzzed him in. Zuri could hear him running up the stairs, his footfalls heavy and ominous. Brown had the door open before Trav could even knock.

"What up?" he said, greeting Trav with a pound. Brown could see in his eyes that something was up.

"Yo, the jects on fire right now. We had to bang out with some niggas last night," Trav said, full of excitement. "I had to lay a few niggas down, but Grease got hit up bad," he added as his voice dipped.

"Damn," Brown said. He put his hands on top of his head and closed his eyes after receiving the bad news. Brown wasn't much older than his guys, like Trav and Grease, but he felt responsible for them, anyway, and the fact that Grease had gotten shot up on his watch was killing him. "Was it Dame's crew?" Brown asked, confused. He couldn't imagine that anyone else in Brooklyn would have been reckless enough to try him and his people.

"I don't know, but whoever it was, we need to get the team together and smash on them niggas," Trav said, one foot already out the door.

Brown wondered why he had come, but he quickly realized that if Trav had called him, he wouldn't have picked up, and for the first time he was grateful for his protégé's eagerness.

"No doubt. Give me a few minutes to get dressed," Brown said, then disappeared down the hall and into the bedroom. Zuri could tell that Trav had stayed waiting by the door, as every so often she would hear a footstep as he fidgeted anxiously.

"Everything all right?" Zuri asked as she sat up in the bed. She had overheard everything Trav had told Brown, but she didn't want him to know that.

"Yeah, Ma. Nothing you need to worry about. I gotta go take care of some business. I'll be back in a few. Then we can pick up where we left off," he said, trying to ease her worry. Brown felt bad playing things down the way he did, and he didn't know how much of the conversation she had heard, but he also knew that just being back in Brooklyn made her nervous, and he was trying his best to make sure she felt protected.

Zuri stood up and slipped on a pair of sweats and one of Brown's T-shirts without thinking.

"See you feeling at home already," he joked at the sight of her in his shirt.

Zuri blushed and pulled on the hem of the shirt and shook out the wrinkles. It had been a long time since she had worn a man's shirt and been comforted by the smell. But if Brown was going to play it cool, so was she.

"What you got in here to eat?" she questioned, following him down the hallway to the front of the house, where Trav was waiting. She had completely forgotten that he was there and suddenly felt very self-conscious about what she was wearing.

"There should be something in there. If not, I'll bring you back something," Brown replied. He was walking quicker than someone would normally walk in their house, and as much as he had tried to tell Zuri that things were cool, she could tell that something was up.

As they entered the living room, Zuri decided that if she really wanted to avoid any awkwardness, she would have to be the one to take the plunge and say something to Trav.

"Hey, what up, Trav?" Zuri said upon seeing him. The expression on his face in response to her greeting was so discouraging that she regretted having said anything at all.

"Wassup?" he said shortly. "Yo, I'll be downstairs," he said to Brown, with a visible look of disdain on his face upon seeing Zuri in Brown's T-shirt. Trav did an about-face and walked out the door without saying anything else, and Zuri wondered how long they could realistically go on like this.

"I gotta go, Ma," Brown said, turning to Zuri. "I'll bring you back something, okay?"

"Don't forget," she said with a nervous smile, then kissed him before he left out the door.

Zuri walked into the kitchen and headed straight for the fridge. Even though she had a feeling something was up, and it was nothing good, there was nothing that she could do about it but wait to see what happened. She pulled open the refrigerator door, and staring back at her was an expired gallon of milk, some old Chinese food, and a half-empty sixteen-ounce bottle of Sprite.

"I should've known," she said out loud as she laughed to herself. Brown was a bachelor, and his fridge reflected just that. Zuri decided she would just get some water and go lie back down and wait for Brown to return with some food. As she looked through his cabinets for a clean water glass, she couldn't help but compare where she was with where she had been. She had gone from the apartment that she had got evicted from, which was covered in mold, to Geisha's tension-filled spot, to Waheed's empty one, and so Zuri hadn't had a home in the true sense of the word in a long time.

But as she looked around at the way that Brown had decorate his space, she felt connected to him. This was someone who had spent time putting his heart and soul into his living space. His red couches matched the pot of a plant that lived on the windowsill of one of the big windows. Like Zuri had once had, Brown had art everywhere, and it was clear he had spent a long time selecting pieces. She leaned against the kitchen counter, taking in her surroundings. Even though the counter was hard against her back and the floor was cool against her feet, she was having a hard time believing that this was her real life. As she finished her water and walked back to the bedroom, she felt very blessed. She already missed Brown, and she knew that her body was still feeling the effects of the passionate sex the night before and she could use some more sleep.

Zuri was jolted from her sleep when she felt a hand cover her mouth and squeeze her face tight. She opened her eyes to see the nose of a pistol inches from her face. She tried screaming, but the intruder's giant hand muffled the sound. Her breath came quick and hard as she realized what was happening. She tried to quickly take stock of what was going on. The intruder's fingers pushed farther into the corners of her mouth, and she could taste sweat and cigarettes. She knew it was still daytime by the way the sun broke through the curtains, and she prayed that that meant whatever was going to happen wasn't going to kill her. She hadn't realized it, but she had been screaming into the intruder's palm.

"Bitch, if you want to live, you better shut the fuck up," he threatened as his grip on her face grew tighter and tighter.

Zuri tried her best to stop herself from yelling, but she was so scared, she could only lower her voice to a pained groan. The fear in Zuri's eyes was evident, and it seemed only to feed the intruder's ill intentions.

"I came to kill Brown, but look at what I found," he said. "If you make a sound, I'll kill you," he warned before he removed his hand from over her mouth.

Zuri fell silent, her voice caught in her throat.

The intruder was wearing a mask over his face, one of those generic ski ones that they sold at Walmart. It wasn't that cold outside yet, but he had on a big green puffy jacket, and her years of living in Brooklyn had taught her that when a man wore a coat that much bigger than his body when the weather didn't call for it, it meant he was strapped. Sure enough as he leaned his body over hers and his hands pulled the covers off of her, she could feel the shape of a gun in the part of the man's waistband that was pushing into her side.

Zuri started to cry as his hand began to roam her body and found its way into her panties. She knew what was going to happen next, and she felt like she was going to throw up. The covers were off her now, her last barrier of protection crumpled on the floor. Before she had climbed back in bed, she hadn't thought twice about removing the sweatpants and T-shirt she was wearing, but she was grateful at least that there was another layer for the man to get through . . . until the panties slid off so easily.

"Please don't," Zuri begged as she trembled in fear, but he forcefully pried her legs apart, leaving finger bruises on her thighs. "No please!" she cried out as tears raced down her face. Her hands were free, but with the cold steel of the gun so close to where she had already been shot once before, she couldn't bring herself to fight back physically. "Help!" she screamed as loud as she could, but no one was there to rescue her. The brownstone was occupied only by Brown. She thought about making a run for it, but the apartment was so big, there was no way that she would get to the door without being caught. All the things that had seemed like blessings before were turning into problems.

"Bitch, didn't I say shut up?" the goon barked as he came across her face with a backhanded slap. Zuri thought that she was seeing stars, as the pain from his heavy hand caused an explosion of light in front of her eyes. He wrapped his hand around her throat to ensure that she wouldn't yell again.

Straddling her, he quickly unbuckled his pants, revealing his erect penis. Zuri tried to scream, anyway, as he forced himself inside her. She could feel his hot breath on her skin with every painful thrust as he made disgusting grunting sounds. Every time he breathed, she could taste cigarettes. Zuri lay crying in silence as he violated her body, brutally having his way with her, until he was finished.

"I bet that nigga Brown don't do you like that, huh?" he quipped as he stood up and he fixed his pants. He had let go of her and had a loose, casual grip on the gun, so if Zuri was going to fight back or try to run, there was no better time. But she couldn't.

Zuri just sobbed in a ball on the bed. She felt disgusted, violated, and scared all at the same time. Not even six hours ago she had been in the same place, feeling more loved than she had ever before, and the fact that her feeling of safety and trust had been ripped from her so quickly made it impossible for her to push forward and try to fight. The intruder stood by the side of the bed and looked down at her, taking pleasure in his conquest.

"I know Brown don't know what to do with all that good pussy, but I do," he said as he snatched Zuri up off the bed by her arm. It felt like he dislocated her shoulder as he threw her to the floor. She screamed in agony, and her body's natural reflexes kicked in, and she tried to stand up. The goon hit her in the head with the butt of the gun the minute he saw her try to get up, and the room went black, as he had knocked her unconscious.

Zuri opened her eyes. She felt lost and disoriented. She didn't know where she was as she tried to focus her eyes and adjust to the darkness in the room. She thought for a second that maybe she had had a bad dream and if she pinched herself hard enough, she would wake up and Brown would be there, lying next to her, and she would be safe still. But as Zuri came to, she realized she couldn't even pinch herself, because her hands were bound. She was sitting on a cold floor, shivering, and the shock she was experiencing from being snatched from Brown's apartment made her feel like she was having flu-like symptoms. Her skin was hot, but she was freezing on the inside. Her head was aching, and her eyes hurt from trying to make out her surroundings. There were no windows in the room. The only light that seeped into the dark space came from underneath the door. Zuri heard the slow drip of water coming from a leaking faucet, but she couldn't make out where exactly in the room it was coming from.

Zuri could faintly hear voices in the distance; most belonged to men, but occasionally, she would hear the voice of a female. Minutes seemed like hours, and hours like days, for Zuri. She had been captured and had no clue why or where she had been taken. Her abductors had removed her clothes and had left her with nothing on except for her torn panties and a bra. Her right ankle was chained to a wall, and her hands were taped together at the wrists. Zuri pulled at the chain, trying to free herself but had no luck. All she wound up doing was creating a huge gash on her ankle, with bruises to accompany it.

She had lost track of time and didn't know how long she had been in this room. For the first few hours, she had screamed for help at the top of her lungs, and when that hadn't worked, she had screamed obscenities in hopes of grabbing the attention of her abductors, thinking they would at least come to shut her up. Neither tactic had been successful. Zuri began to talk to herself now while she stared blankly into the dark, thinking of what could have possibly gotten her to this predicament.

"God, if you're there, if you're listening, please help me. Why is this happening to me?" she cried out. Then she prayed silently.

Zuri had never really believed in a higher power. After what life had shown her, she didn't think God cared for people like her, but today she was willing to put her faith into anything if it would help her get out of this situation. Zuri felt like this was the end, and if it was, she thought it was fitting. Family members had met with a horrible end—her sister had been murdered, and her mother had committed suicide—so why would Zuri's end be any different? Maybe this was supposed to be her demise. Maybe this was how her story was supposed to go. Her end was supposed to be tragic. It was her destiny. All Zuri could do was cry silent tears at this point and accept her fate.

She closed her eyes tight and tried to imagine what her life could have been like if she had been able to live a normal one. If her father had never been sent to jail for life, would her mother have turned to alcohol to console herself? She and Nubia may have never needed to fend for themselves. Nubia would have never felt the need to turn to the streets for their survival. Maybe then her sister would still have her life. If she had grown up in a two-parent household, how different would life be? Zuri imagined herself graduating and becoming a nurse, and Nubia would have been a lawyer, like they used to talk about as little girls. They would have met up twice a week for lunch to talk about work and their kids and to plan their parent's fiftieth-anniversary party.

Instead, Nubia was gone, and so were her mother and her father, so to speak, and now it was her turn. She would die alone, with no one around her. Not even Brown. Nobody would miss her. The thought of Brown made her cries become louder. He had just come back into her life, and just that fast it was over. She hoped he would save her; she prayed he would find her. But in her heart, she just knew it wasn't in the cards for her. Her luck had run out, but when she thought about it, all she had ever had was bad luck. Even the past few months had proved that to Zuri, from the way that she had been fired from the club to the moment that Geisha had decided to kick her out. It seemed that everything in her life was an example of what not to do. Zuri lay on the cold floor and cried herself to sleep.

The sounds of the locks and the bolts on the door moving woke Zuri from her sleep, and she sat up and pressed her back against the wall. A shadowy figure held a construction lamp in his hand as he entered the room. The bright light blinded Zuri, causing her to shield her eyes with her bound hands. There had been a gush of air as the man had swung the door open, and she realized just how cold she was. From the light of his lamp, the things around her started to come into focus, but even then, she couldn't determine what kind of room she was in. There was a table a few feet from where she was tied up, and a long utility sink hugged the wall farthest from her. If she had to take a guess, she would say she was in the garage or the boiler room of a big house. But that still didn't tell her location on a map or who had taken her there.

"Where am I?" she asked. "And why are you doing this to me?" She tried to shout, but after all the hours she had spent screaming earlier, her voice had nothing left in it, and it didn't matter, anyway, because her questions fell on deaf ears, as the man holding the lamp didn't respond. The man let the room get quiet, and Zuri couldn't take it anymore.

"Please let me go," she said quietly, but she was begging.

"This bitch don't ever shut up," the man finally said as he closed the door. Zuri immediately recognized his voice as that of the man who had raped her.

She scooted farther back against the wall, in fear. She could see a bit of his face from the bright light he had brought in with him, and she knew that she would never be able to forget the eyes that watched her now.

Her reaction made the goon laugh, and she would never forget that sound, either. "Yo, come in here and listen to the bitch beg for her life," he shouted to whoever was on the other side of the closed door. The knob turned, and Zuri could see another figure enter the room. She still couldn't make out faces, due to the brightness of the lamp and the fact that her eyes were still adjusting.

"This bitch got some good pussy. I can see why that nigga Brown had her all up in his crib," her rapist said to the other man before he lit a cigarette, the lighter further illuminating his disgusting face, and took a drag to get the tip to burn.

"Yeah, I bet," the other man said.

Zuri's heart jumped in her chest as she instantly realized she recognized that second voice. "Oh my God," she said in a loud whisper, then looked up as the man moved the light, allowing her to see the faces of both men who were in the room. The man with the familiar voice walked over and crouched down in front of her. Zuri couldn't believe her eyes.

Trav's face was inches from her own, and he perched there in front of her, with a devilish grin on his face. "You surprised to see me?" he asked sarcastically. "Never seen this coming, huh? Neither does Brown's bitch ass."

"Brown is gonna kill you when he finds out what you've done," she said, sounding confident and sure of her statement. Although seeing Trav had completely blown her mind, it had also made her feel better, because as sure as Trav was that Brown had no idea what was going on, Zuri knew that it was impossible. Even when she was growing up, it had always been Brown and Trav together. Brown had always run the streets and devised the plans, but Trav had been a part of the pair for so long, Zuri couldn't imagine a world where Trav betrayed Brown, and Brown didn't know about it—even if that was the world she was living in right now.

"That nigga is too wrapped up in you to even see what's happening," he bragged. "He's heartbroken over you. He just can't understand why this type of shit keeps happening to him. You know, like, Nubia," Trav said jokingly, making light of Brown's lost loves. "I'm right there playing the concerned friend."

Zuri was horrified by what she was hearing. She thought about all the times that she had seen Trav and Brown together, about how deeply Brown cared for Trav, even if he didn't show it. And Trav could talk shit to her face all he wanted, but the minute he brought Nubia into the conversation was where Zuri drew the line. She was willing to die to keep her sister's name out of Trav's dirty-ass mouth. "He will find me!" she yelled.

"I don't think so, Ma," Trav retorted. "My man here said the pussy is right, so by this time tomorrow, your ass will be en route to Las Vegas, where you'll be in a sex-trafficking ring, and from there, only God knows where you'll end up. And as for Brown, it'll be all over for him soon too. I made a deal with the nigga Dame. I'll be running the set in a minute."

Zuri dug deep down in the pit of her stomach, hawked up a glob of spit, and spit it right in Trav's face. He immediately wiped his face, then smacked her, causing blood to trickle from her lip. Even though he had hit her, the fact that Zuri knew her assailant and had begun to understand why what was happening was happening made her feel strong and bold.

"Are you fucking serious, Trav?" Zuri asked. "You did all this just because I wouldn't give you some pussy? You're pathetic, and you're disgusting. And Brown is going to figure it out, and he is going to find you and me, and he is going to kill you while I watch. And the last thing you're going to see is my face above yours, because I will have won, you stupid, spineless, bitch-made motherfucker," Zuri hissed.

She had never experienced pain and anger so deep that it was quiet. When someone said something as cruel and as heartfelt as what Zuri had just spit at Trav, it was never said loudly. For the first time in her life, she was not yelling, even though she was mad. Instead, she was speaking matter-of-factly. Trav was going to die; Brown would make sure of that. She was absolutely certain. Even thought Trav was still taller than her while he was crouched down, Zuri had raised her eyes to meet his, and they were having a stare down to rival Dame's and Brown's.

"Fuck you, bitch. You ain't as bad as your sister, no way. You'll always be the runner-up, even to her ghost.

It should've been you who died that night," he snarled, taking verbal jabs at her. "You ain't worth me wasting the energy and seed to fuck you, you ran-through piece of stripper shit. You still think you're too good for me? By the time they're done with you, you won't be good enough for anything. No one will want to touch you."

What he was saying didn't shake Zuri. He was right. She was a stripper, and so she was used to men talking to her crazy, but what came next, she wasn't ready for.

"Y'all niggas, gon' and break that bitch in," Trav yelled, and two young bloods walked in the room with smirks on their faces. Trav walked out, leaving them to violate Zuri.

Zuri left the room. At least mentally. The two young men that Trav had sent in to assault her wasted no time getting down to business, and something in her spirit broke as they took turns smacking her face. She wasn't even putting up a fight, and after a while she could tell that they were hitting her just for fun. They took turns penetrating her, switching before either of them finished so they could go longer than they normally would. But Zuri didn't feel any of this. While her body was on the cold concrete floor of some random drug runner's house, Zuri herself was back in the apartment that her and Nubia had shared. She didn't know why her mind had brought her back there. But there she was.

In her memory, Nubia was alive and more beautiful than Zuri had ever seen her. Her mind had done Nubia the kindness of keeping her young and gorgeous, in a way that real life would have never let her be. Nubia looked up at her as Zuri walked up to her. Zuri couldn't tell where they were; anytime she tried to make sense of what surrounded them, the shape and color of things seemed to shift.

"Hi, boo," Nubia said, putting her hand up to her baby sister's face. "You okay?"

Zuri realized that she wasn't revisiting a memory. Instead, whatever part of her brain that was keeping Nubia alive had opened itself up to her to provide her emotional safety during the assault. And safety for Zuri could only ever look like Nubia. She tried to speak, but she didn't know how, not like this. The image of Nubia nodded her head.

"I understand, girl," she said. "I'm sorry for you more, though. Because this isn't the first time you've been here." Nubia's face was sad, and Zuri could feel her heartbreak.

How many times would life kick her down? Why was it worth holding on? Even though Zuri had said none of this out loud, Nubia responded.

"Those are good questions, Z. I don't know that anybody on God's green earth could tell you why the things that happen, happen. They just do. I know you keep thinking about what life would be like if our father had never gone to jail, but he did, girl. That was the hand we were dealt. And as much as I hate to watch you in pain now, I know that you will be better than I was. I made so many mistakes, Zuri. It took me years to figure out what I was doing, and even then, I might have been doing things wrong. But I kept going. When I died, I know that that was hard for you, and at that time you also thought about whether or not it was worth it to hold on. But you did. I know that when our mother killed herself, that question came to your mind again. And again, you held on, anyway, even when things seemed to get worse and worse. I know that you think that this is where it stops, that you won't make it out of this one, that it's not worth holding on. But it is. You've done it so many times before. Do it one more time."

Zuri cried in real life as her spirit talked to her sister. The two men laughed at her. They were finishing up now, finding different and creative ways to humiliate her. But Zuri had the strength of her sister in her mental, and as much as they beat her, she was going to hold on until she made it to the other side.

Chapter 13

Zuri lay on the cold, dirty floor, in pain from the young gang members taking their turns on her. She had detached her mind from her body in order to deal with the gang rape, but at that moment she wished she could just die. She thought back to her memories of Nubia, the way her smile lit up a room and the way her laughter transformed her whole face. Such a beautiful person and she was gone. She then thought about all the people that had betrayed her. Trav, to start, had committed the worst sin possible. He had double-crossed not only his friend but his mentor, boss, and partner too. If Zuri was going to die, it wasn't a far stretch to think that so was he.

This was the first time she truly understood what her mother might have been feeling in her last moments of life. Death had to have been a better option. She kept going back and forth in her mind, trying to decide whether, be it here or in Vegas or wherever she ended up, she would take her life. Taking her own life would let her control her own destiny; no one else would dictate her fate but her. Zuri was broken, and at her lowest point, she just wanted it all to end. The only thing that kept her going was thoughts of Brown and the time they had spent together. Even though it had been short, it had been so special to her. She was starving, and her throat was dry from not having anything to drink in almost thirty-six hours. Or at least that was how long she thought that she had been with her kidnappers. Her thirst was made worse by the fact that during the entire time she had been there, the sink has not stopped dripping.

Zuri heard what sounded like male voices in the distance. It was the first noise she had heard in hours, and she immediately assumed it was a new day. She sat up and leaned her back against the wall. Zuri was prepared for the worst, not knowing if Trav was sending in more guys to have sex with her or if she was about to be shipped off to a sex-trafficking ring. She could hear the voices become louder and louder, and she realized that they were arguing. Then she heard a brief commotion, followed by a series of gunshots. And then there was silence. She didn't want to make any noise yet, because there was no way for her to know if the people that had fired the shots were on her side or Trav's. Or maybe they were on neither side and Zuri was about to enter a new level of hell. She shook from fear and cold as she waited, holding her breath.

"Zuri! Zuri!" She heard someone call her name. "Zuri! Zuri!" the voice called again, and even though in her heart, she knew who it was undeniably, she thought she was hallucinating at first. But as she continued to hear her name being called, she knew that it was Brown's voice calling her.

"Brown! I'm in here," she screamed.

After a few seconds the bolts and locks on the door to the room started to move, and then Brown stood in the doorway, holding keys in one hand and a gun in the other. He was illuminated by the light from a TV, which must have been on mute in the other room, and once his eyes adjusted to the darkness, he gasped.

"Zuri!" he shouted, with a look of concern in his eyes, as he had seen the condition she was in. Brown raced over to her and unlocked the chain on her ankle, then tore off the tape on her wrists. "I'm sorry, Ma. I'm so sorry," he kept repeating as he freed her from her restraints. "C'mon. Let's get you outta here," he said, helping her to her feet.

Zuri felt weak and struggled to get to her feet. "Hold on! Where is Trav? Trav is the one who did this to me!" she cried out. She didn't want to waste any time, in case Brown was still being played by him, and she wanted to make sure they were safe.

"I know, Ma. You don't have to worry about him no more. Trav tried setting me up last night, but I got the drop on him. I taught that nigga everything he knew about these streets. He could never outsmart me," Brown said. "Once that happened, I put two and two together. The nigga had been acting jealous ever since we saw you in the casino that night. I knew this was one of his low-key stash spots, so I came here to look for you."

Zuri was too weak to stand, and so Brown picked her up in his arms and held her the way a parent holds their newborn child or the way a husband carries his new wife over the threshold of their home. As they left the room and headed to the front door, Zuri took in where she had been tortured the past few days. It was disgusting, and it looked like it wasn't a home but instead a place for transient members of the gang to fuck bitches and do drugs. On the other side of the door she had been locked behind, there was a collection of dingy couches forced close together in the tightest way possible. Sprawled across a particularly dirty one was a man who was bleeding out from a bullet Brown had apparently shot through his head. His friend, or backup, must have failed, because a dead body lay on the floor, blocking the way out of the room filled with couches. But Brown stepped over the corpse that was bleeding out onto the floor. He had come to get Zuri, and now it was time to go.

"I knew you would come," Zuri said as he carried her out of the abandoned house and to his car. It would have taken too much to put her in the passenger seat, so he laid her across the backseat like she was a child, and she looked grateful for the comfort of the soft leather on her naked skin.

Brown drove straight to his house and parked in front. He turned off the car, and as he began to climb out, he noticed Zuri didn't move. She had sat up through the course of the ride here, and he realized she was shivering in fear at the sight of his brownstone. Brown immediately understood her fright. Zuri refused to move out of the car or go into Brown's house after she had been assaulted and raped there. Brown didn't hesitate for a second. Without even getting out of the car, he started the engine back up and drove them to a nice hotel in Manhattan.

Brown ran Zuri a hot bubble bath in the deep jetted tub of the five-star hotel. He sat on the side of the tub as she soaked and relaxed. He knew she had been through things he wouldn't dare to imagine. He felt sorry for her and felt rage that he hadn't been able to prevent the brutal attack. Another woman in his life had been harmed on his watch, and it didn't sit right on his heart or mind. It hadn't hit him how terrible she looked until he had walked her into the hotel in her ripped underwear, covered only by his oversize leather jacket. But the way that people had stared—the kind of people who went out late and had seen much and thus were rather impervious to violence—let Brown know that whatever harm and damage he had imagined being done to Zuri, it was probably worse. He bathed Zuri from head to toe now, scrubbing her body, trying to help her get the filth of the past few days off her body. He knew it would be a long time before it was off her mind. As he watched Zuri cry her eyes out, he rubbed her back. He remained strong for her, but inside, it was killing him.

Even as Zuri sat in the warm water, she could still feel the cold of the bare floor at Trav's spot on her skin. She didn't know if there was a way to wash off the memory of a feeling, but if there was, she wanted to do it so badly. In between the trauma of having been shot the same night her sister had died and then having been kidnapped and raped, Zuri honestly didn't know how much more her body could take, let alone her mind. She felt so blessed to have Brown with her, as he was the last person in the world to make her feel safe.

"Brown." Zuri spoke his name softly. "Can you hold me?" she asked.

He quickly obliged by getting in the tub fully clothed and sitting behind her, wrapping her in his embrace.

Zuri cracked a brief smile at him. "Thank you," she whispered. She could feel Brown's jeans sinking his legs to the bottom of the tub, and even though the moment was serious, she giggled.

"No doubt," he said awkwardly.

If Zuri had to guess, Brown had left his pants on because after the trauma that Zuri had been through the past few days, his male body, even if it touched her only casually, might be too much for her. She was so shocked to learn how sensitive Brown was, as evidenced by the fact that first, he had gotten the hotel suite they were in and then he had helped her bathe. Her heart swelled. Before Brown had allowed her to relax, he had cleaned and bandaged all her wounds. As they sat in the tub, her leg was raised up and hung out of the water, as Brown had wrapped in gauze the gash on her ankle from where she had been chained up. On her face there were multiple cuts. Her lips were busted, and so was the bridge of her nose. She hadn't spent a lot of time looking at herself in the mirror before she got in the tub, but she knew that she could not look good. And yet Brown was still with her, by her side, and that meant more to her than anything else.

"Trav said he made a deal with someone named Dame," Zuri revealed, breaking what had been a happy silence. "I don't know what that means to you, but I figured you should know."

"Word," Brown said, caught slightly off guard by her revelation. "Dame is a nigga I've had issues with in the past. He don't like me, and I don't like him. Shit like that can be deadly on these streets," Brown confessed. "It's only a matter of time before I go to war with the nigga, but now that I know that he got Trav to cross me, I don't know who to trust."

Zuri felt good that Brown was confiding in her. It made her feel a deeper connection to him. Of all the men that she had been with before, Waheed was the only one she had connected with, but the connection that she and Brown were building was unlike anything she had ever experienced. It dawned on her as she sat in the cooling water that Brown hadn't just saved her from getting assaulted more. He had saved her life.

"You can trust me," she said.

"Yeah, I know, Ma. I don't mean you. I'm talking about out in the streets," Brown explained. "I'm gonna have to kill this nigga before it goes any further." Murder wasn't a crime that was foreign to Brown; he had killed two men earlier that night in his fight to get Zuri away from her kidnappers. But trying to kill Dame would be like trying to kill the president or something. Even if Brown did manage to do it, dominoes would fall all over New York, and he had to be ready.

"So kill him, and kill Trav for crossing you." Zuri couldn't believe the words that had left her mouth, but she had been through so much, and Brown had saved her, and she didn't want anything or anybody to bring harm to him, the last lifeline she had. And she wanted Trav dead for personal reasons.

"Ha-ha. If it was that easy, Ma, I would've done it already," Brown said jokingly. But then he was quiet, as he had realized just how deep of a hole he was in. If Trav had truly betrayed him and gone to work for Dame, then there was no secret that Brown had left, no space that felt safe. He and Trav had shared everything; he had given Trav everything he had. He continued in a more somber tone. "Dame ain't the type of nigga you can just roll up on at the corner store, pull your gun out, and murk. He will see that coming."

"But he won't see *me* coming," Zuri declared.

In the three days she had spent chained up in that dark, cold room, alone and in pain and unprotected, she had thought a lot about what the Murder Mamas had told her at the club when she danced for them. When Trav's boys had been breaking her in, she hadn't felt special, and when those other men had slapped her and kicked her, she hadn't felt special, but when Brown had come to save her, she had understood that she had always been meant for more than what she was doing.

"Huh? What you talking about?" Brown asked. He couldn't imagine Zuri strapped up and rolling up on Dame and his crew, although she was right when she said no one would see that coming, because the thought of Zuri killing anybody was absurd.

"Use me. I wanna help you. I really care about you, Brown, and I want you to know I'm down for you all the way. When them niggas in the street start acting shiesty,

I want you to know I always got your back. Just like you told me that day in the hospital," she said.

"Nah, no way," Brown said, refusing to entertain this idea.

"Please, I can do it," she pleaded. "Let me be your Murder Mama." Zuri said the words confidently. After her conversation with Cam, she had assumed that she was the only one left out of the loop, and so now she was sure that Brown would know what she was talking about. And even though she couldn't see his face, given where he sat, holding her, she could tell she had confused him.

"Murder what? What are you talking about?" he asked, completely bewildered.

"Never mind. Just let me help you," Zuri pleaded.

"I'm sorry, but I just can't risk it. You've never been in a situation like that before, and I just can't have you in a vulnerable spot."

She thought back to that night all those months ago when she and Brown had run into each other in Atlantic City, and she realized that he was wrong.

"I've done it before," Zuri said quietly.

Brown tensed up as he held her. "What?" he asked. "What have you done before?"

Zuri realized that she was going to have to lie. She had never found out if they had actually killed Bob or only beaten him up. But how was Brown going to know the difference? She hated lying to him now that they had established such a deep trust, but this was a lie for his protection, which made it worth it.

"Well, you remember that night that we ran into each other and you asked me what I was doing in Atlantic City and I said I was there with a friend?" Zuri proceeded with caution; she didn't know how Brown would react to all this. "I was technically there with a friend, but the reason that we were there is that she had been trying to scam this rich motherfucker that was trying to pay for her to fuck him."

This was where Zuri had to deviate from the truth. She couldn't let Brown know that it had been an accident, that she hadn't been in on the plan and had almost lost it when shit started to go down. "Me and her seduced him and he took us to his hotel suite. Once we were there, we tied him up, because he thought it was sexy to do that, and then we beat him until he gave us the code for his safe." Again, a slight deviation, but how could things with Dame be that much different? "Before we left, we killed him to keep him from trying to track us down, and it was after this that you saw me at the bar," Zuri said, finishing her story awkwardly and without a flourish. She only hoped that her tale was enough for Brown to consider bringing her in as a partner in his revenge scheme. It was as much her fight as his at this point.

Brown sat silent, considering what Zuri had said to plead her case. He began to consider it in his mind. *He won't see her coming. I can tell her exactly what to do, and everything could go smooth*, he thought to himself, blocking her out as she talked quietly about something else because she felt awkward. Finally, he said, "Okay," to her delight and surprise.

"Really?" she asked. She splashed water on the floor as she turned around excitedly.

"Yeah, I got a plan I think will work," he said, laughing at how eager she was to get into the business.

The next two weeks or so felt like they flew by for Zuri. She continued to stay in the hotel that Brown was paying for in Manhattan, because she still refused to go back to the brownstone in Brooklyn, and he understood. The men he still had left that he trusted, he trusted with a grain of salt, but they had been kind enough to get Zuri's stuff and give it to Brown at a park a couple of blocks away. Until both Dame and Trav were dead, Brown wanted Zuri to be unfindable.

Brown was doing his best to figure out how to deal with Trav, but the problem was that Brown had been the one to bust Zuri out, so Trav knew that Brown knew that he had been the one to double-cross him. With that knowledge moving through the streets like wildfire, there was no way that Trav was going to make himself easily accessible to anyone whom he hadn't hand selected himself. Until he could get Trav one-on-one, Brown would focus on prepping Zuri for what would have to go down with Dame.

A couple of days before Brown planned for the hit to go down, he and Zuri were in the bathroom of the hotel suite and he was inspecting her face. He couldn't put her in the club as bait if she looked like she was getting beaten by some other crew. She needed to look pristine. Zuri winced as Brown pulled the Band-Aid off the cut on her nose.

"It's healing up nice, Ma. You look good," Brown assured her.

Zuri looked in the mirror for herself, and he was right. What had last week been a split in her skin that oozed blood was now a scab, and she could see a healthy pink color under it. Once the scab came off, she would probably have a scar for a bit, but she could cover that with makeup. But it was another scar to add to the catalog of injuries she had sustained on the streets of New York. She gently touched the side of her own face, where there was still a bruise radiating a dark purple color on her cheekbone.

"What do you think?" she asked Brown. "We could just get me some makeup, and we could be good to go, right?"

Zuri smiled at her man. That was what she had decided he was. They had been living and loving together for two weeks now, and she couldn't imagine her life with anybody else, or him with anybody else.

"I think you gonna make it work, but you know I think you're beautiful even with the scars and bruises," Brown said, hugging her from behind. Zuri had gone through so much and would be doing so much in the coming days that she savored these moments she had with Brown. She put her arms around his where they crossed on her chest, and they rocked back and forth.

"My ankle, though," Zuri said jokingly, "is a whole different story." Looking down at her leg, where the shackle had left her with a gash, she knew that she probably should have got stitches. The scene was too hot for her and Brown, and he wouldn't dare put her in the line of fire before the time was right. On the other hand, the gash had scabbed over okay, and if she just didn't bring attention to the scab, maybe she could get away with it.

"Don't sweat it, Ma. Ain't no man out here looking at ankles. Well, maybe they look at yours, with your fine ass," Brown said. He was flirting with her, and it felt good to be desired by him instead of coddled.

In the first nights that she was in the hotel with him, she would wake up screaming from memories of what had happened while she was at the brownstone and then later on at Trav's. Her mindset was close to how she had first felt when Nubia died. Everything around her made her feel jumpy and overwhelmed. But before, she had only had her mother around to help, and as much as she had loved her, that hadn't been enough for Zuri. But Brown was able to provide in ways that no one had ever before.

Zuri turned her head back to kiss him. Then, having made the decision that while she was still beat up, she was presentable, they headed back out into the hotel suite's sitting room, where their plans to lure Dame and kill him were out on full display.

For Brown, this situation felt like something out of a movie. He had never tried something so slick before. Usually for hits in their circle, someone would pull up on someone else, air out the clip, and keep it moving. But given Dame and all his power, Brown's plan would require finesse, and he was grateful that Zuri was around to provide it.

Laid out across the coffee table were the floor plans to every major club the hustlers liked to hit in the city, and to all the hotels the high rollers used to hit up afterward. It was a lot of information for Zuri to keep in mind, but if she was going to do the job and get away with it, she would have to.

"Okay, so look here," Brown said, holding up the plans for one of the clubs. "You need to remember to keep an eye on the exits. I don't think that you could do anything that could cause shit to pop off, but when you fucking with a player like Dame, you have to have an exit plan." He handed the plans to Zuri so that she could get a close look at what he was talking about.

"Bet," Zuri said. "So then I'm going to want to post up right about here." She used a highlighter to carefully mark up the plans, indicating where the bar was, where the VIP section was, and where it was best for her to stand. She had never focused or worked so hard on something in her life. But that night with Scarlett had fucked with her mental, and they had cut it way too close and hadn't even made it out with all the money. She was not about to have that happen again. If she was going to kill Dame, she was going to kill him. "I'm happy we're doing this," she told Brown. "It's critical to have a plan in place. Can't be caught slipping."

Zuri's remark caught Brown off guard, and he thought back to when he had tried to do the pickup with Dame that Cuba had set up, and how grateful he had been that Grease was ready to go. That he was there as backup. He paced the room, moving away from Zuri, deep in thought.

A wave of sadness hit Brown as he reflected on his old crew. Grease had passed from his bullet wounds a few days after Trav had taken Zuri and the funeral was supposed to be happening the next day. He and Trav had pulled up on the scene, but by the time they had got there to light the block up, the men that had taken out Grease were gone. He sat with that realization. Trav would not miss Grease's funeral, not for nothing. If Brown wanted a shot at taking Trav out, that was the way to do it. He looked at Zuri, who was very focused on learning every part of the plans that Brown had got his hands on. His sadness quickly turned to anger as he realized that despite the respect and care he felt for Grease, the only place he would be able to catch up with Trav, without Trav catching him first, was at Grease's funeral.

"Hey, Zuri, chill a sec. I got to talk to you," Brown said seriously. He rarely used her first name, so Zuri knew that he was serious, and put down the paper she was study-ing. One of the first things that Zuri had asked Brown to do was take out Trav, and he knew that she was coming at this from a personal place of pain, and it was important to Brown to let her know that he had heard her and he was going to do it.

They sat down next to each other on the edge of the bed. He broke down his plan to her, how he was going to show up at Grease's funeral and confront Trav after the service. She was quiet as he spoke. In all honesty, she didn't care what happened to Trav specifically, as long as he got what was coming to him, which was a quick and painful death.

"I hear ya, Brown," she said, using his real name to make sure he understood that she was serious too. She could tell that he was giving her all the details to make her feel better about the fact that it had been a minute since Brown had found out Trav had double-crossed him and he was still out walking the streets.

"Tomorrow, Z, I promise it will happen," Brown said. His eyebrows came together, but Zuri couldn't tell if the expression on his face was one of anger or pain. Having been betrayed before by the people not only around her but closest to her, she did her best to comfort Brown in the face of what she knew was a very painful decision for him to make.

The next day Zuri watched Brown get ready for the funeral. Even on a sad day like this, he still managed to look incredibly fine. He was in an all-black Tom Ford suit, and Zuri watched him fix his tie in the mirror by the closet. Brown called this his funeral suit. He hated that he had one, but it was true. He had gone to so many funerals in his life, he didn't have a good recollection of all the times that he had worn the ensemble out. But it was always the same clean-cut, bespoke look. The jacket was a mixture of cashmere and wool and felt like butter on the skin. The pants hit him in all the right places, and when he had his jacket off, with his shirt tucked in, Zuri couldn't stop her passion from rising. His shoes had been shined perfectly, and he looked like he was worth more than the thousands of dollars that all the pieces put together cost.

There was only one problem. When wearing a suit like this, it was hard for Brown to stay strapped. But he had spent years perfecting his craft, and the best way for him to keep his piece on him and maintain his style was to slide a clean 22 mm into the breast pocket of his jacket.

He felt like a bitch, keeping a pistol that small on him, but for the purposes of what he had to do, it made the most sense, and he wasn't going to let his ego get in the way of his success.

"A'ight, it's time," he said, brushing his lapels and patting down the front of his suit jacket to make sure nothing looked suspect.

"You look good," Zuri said. In any other circumstance, she would have taken the opportunity to flirt with him and make him feel good, but there was tension in the room, and she was trying to respect the somber energy Brown was putting out.

"Thank you, Ma," Brown said and gave her a hug. He kissed her on the forehead and left out the door.

Zuri watched him leave in silence. She didn't know what was appropriate to say for a moment like that. *Good luck? Be safe?* Nothing made sense to her, and so she said nothing. As the early morning sun entered the room through the curtains, she looked at all the plans laid out on the coffee table. She felt ready mentally. She was nervous, but she felt ready. The cuts on her face were healing, and her former beauty was returning. There was only one thing that still concerned her.

She and Brown hadn't been together in that way since she had been assaulted at Trav's spot. He had been kind and had tried not to touch her, and excited as he made her, the fire in her stopped at her mental. As much as she hated to admit it, Trav had meant it when he told his boys to break her, and it had worked. She felt herself recovering and was able to push herself forward out of anger, but she didn't know how she was supposed to handle sex. Zuri left her spot by the coffee table and did a study of her body in front of the mirror that Brown had just left unoccupied. There were still the shadows of bruises on her thighs and finger marks on her wrists. It was one thing to feel powerful; it was another to feel sexy.

Seducing Dame was a critical part of her and Brown's plan. Her method of murder wouldn't work if they were at the club. She would have to get him back to a hotel room. To do that, she would have to feel sexy again. She was wearing a big T-shirt and sweatpants. Usually, she donned a big T-shirt and panties, but with the number of bruises that had covered her body when Brown first rescued her from Trav's, she had got used to covering everything up. With Brown gone, however, it was the perfect opportunity for her to practice her seduction without having to worry about the follow-through. She swayed her hips from side to side and slowly removed the baggy sweatpants. They fell around her ankles, and she stepped out of them, continuing to move her body, and even though there was no music, she hummed Beyoncé under her breath. She tried to channel her inner stripper, to remind herself of how talented she was, about how enticing she could be if she tried.

Zuri bounced around the room in the T-shirt and her panties, shaking her bruised body out and letting her hair down. Before she got used to stripping, this was what she would do to loosen herself up. After finding her way back to the mirror, she rubbed her hands up her chest, pulling her T-shirt up with them. She flashed herself and the mirror and giggled. Like she had promised herself, she was making it work. And she was having fun. She practiced her smile in the mirror, and once she was finally happy with her performance, she returned to the papers on the coffee table. She was trying to learn as much as she could about the places Dame haunted, and no matter how much time she spent, it was never enough in her eyes.

It was late at night before Brown came back. Zuri was lying in bed, not quite sleeping. Her nerves were heightened because of what she knew Brown was attempting to do. Her body tensed when she heard the door to the hotel room open, and she prayed it was Brown and not someone coming to kill her. But it was him, and he came and sat down next to where Zuri lay. His suit jacket was off and draped over his shoulder. The gun he had taken with him was nowhere to be seen. He brushed his thumb across Zuri's chin and held her face in a way that made her feel loved and cared for. And at that moment, she knew what had happened. But Brown confirmed it for her, anyway.

"It's done," he said. "Sleep easy."

Chapter 14

Life was the hottest nightclub in the city; it was where everybody who was somebody went to party. Hustlers, hoopers, and hoes all hung out there, and on any given night, it was the place to be. It was only natural that Dame and his crew would be in the spot, popping bottles and spending money. The club's sound system was banging. The DJ had the dance floor packed by playing all the latest hits.

Zuri maneuvered her way through the crowd and could feel all eyes on her as she made her way toward the bar. She was wearing a skintight pitch-black bandage dress with a V-neck plunge so deep that it exposed her belly button. Her outfit accentuated every curve she had and absorbed the light that flashed around the club, making her look like an optical illusion. Men stared and even some of the women turned their heads, as Zuri stood out in the sea of people. She posted by the bar after ordering a drink and swayed her hips to the music as she sang along. It had been a long time since she had been in a club, and an even longer time since she had been at one where she wasn't working. But from what she remembered, she never had a problem getting attention when she wanted it. She remained cool and unbothered on the outside, but inside she was a nervous wreck. She wished the bartender would hurry up with her drink, and she hoped the alcohol would help to settle her nerves. From her spot at the bar, she could see Dame and his crew.

Brown had described him to a tee, but even without his description, Dame was easy to pick out among the crew in VIP. He sported the biggest chain and the brightest watch, thanks to the diamonds on its face, which danced as the lights hit them. He was definitely a fly nigga, Zuri had to admit to herself. She could tell by all the bottles and jewelry that he was moving heavy in the streets. Having worked in a strip club, she could easily spot a fraud. It was important not to spend your whole night dancing for a fronting-ass nigga with shallow pockets. Her experience in the strip game also made it easy to catch the eye of any guy she wanted, and she wasted no time putting herself in Dame's line of sight.

She sipped her drink slowly as hustler after hustler stepped to her, attempting to get a moment of her time. She turned each one down. It seemed like the more she dismissed them, the more she noticed Dame staring. She was playing on his pride. A man like him took pleasure in having things most men couldn't obtain. And seeing nigga after nigga strike out only piqued his interest that much more. Out of the corner of her eye, Zuri could see Dame whispering something to one of his underlings and nodding in her direction. She pretended not to pay attention but noticed the member of his crew heading her way.

"What up, Ma?" said the young, handsome dark-skinned goon as he walked up on her. "My manz seen you over here being real antisocial and thought you should come rock with us over at our table." Zuri looked him up and down. She had only been twenty-one for a little while herself, but this boy looked so young, she wondered how Dame had even got him in the club.

"Well, if your 'manz' feel like that, he should've came and told me that himself," she replied, playing hard to get while she mocked Dame's runner, not wanting to appear as if she was thirsty to join them.

"He would've, but he ain't really the type to have everybody all in his business," he explained.

"Is that right?" Zuri stated, unfazed by his explanation.

"Damn. Ma. It's like that?" he asked.

Zuri didn't even bother to answer. She just gave him a look that caused him to walk away, defeated. She smiled on the inside. If she had played her cards right, Dame would come right to her. She took a peek over her shoulder and watched as the young goon reported back to him. Just as she thought he would, Dame rose to his feet and began making his way over to where she was. She had read him right.

"What's going on, beautiful?" he said smoothly. His charm was evident, and his smile was perfect. She had watched him as he had made his way over to her, and as much as Brown would hate to hear it, Dame was fine.

Zuri smiled back. He was even finer close up. He was neatly groomed and smelled extremely good. He exuded a boss aura that was even stronger than Brown's. His crew appeared more organized than the niggas that ran under Brown, and she could tell that he was more powerful in the streets as well. She could see why Brown couldn't war with him in the streets, but that only made her want to help Brown more. She wanted to see him on top, the way Dame was, and if that meant killing him to do it, she was all in. Brown had proven he would do anything for her, and she was willing to do the same.

"Now, I done watched you shut every dude in here down tonight, and I'm trying to figure out, is niggas' game really that bad, or are you getting a kick out of saying no?" he asked.

"A little of both. I just came to have a good time, that's all. I'm not really for all the extra, and you looking real extra," she said, looking at his flashy jewelry.

Dame laughed, and Zuri knew it was because most women would never talk to him like that, but that was all part of the game, because Zuri also knew that men like Dame didn't like most women. "You shouldn't judge a book by its cover. How can you fairly assess something from the outside, looking in?" he said. "The majority of the time you'll be wrong."

Zuri debated arguing with him a bit, but she didn't want to waste any time caught up in flirting, so she let it go. "True," she said, and she hoped she hadn't given in too easily.

"So, come to my section and let me prove you wrong . . . or right," he joked.

Zuri laughed and agreed to go back to VIP with him. As he walked through the club with her, he knew that other men were looking and other women were jealous, and there was nothing he loved more than that feeling. Dame liked her whole style, and she was by far the baddest chick in the club. He admired her body as well as he walked behind her through VIP before stopping at his table. He grabbed a bottle of Dom Pérignon out of the ice bucket, snatched an unused flute off the table, and poured her a glass. He handed it to her and raised his glass for a toast.

"What we celebrating?" Zuri asked.

"I'll let you decide," he answered.

"Friendship," she said.

"But you don't even know my name," he said.

"You don't know mine, either." She winked, then sipped her champagne.

Dame smiled. He was definitely digging her style.

The two of them sat talking with one another while the rest of his crew met and mingled. Zuri had been taking baby sips of the bubble in her glass. She had the same drink the entire time they sat talking. That was something Brown had schooled her on when putting together the plan. He had told her to fill her glass one time and sip light. She watched as Dame keep refilling his glass over and over. Zuri played her role like an Oscar-winning actress. It came easy and natural to her, partly because a small part of her was really feeling Dame. Maybe a little too much, as she started to have second thoughts about going through with the plan. She had expected him to be some asshole drug dealer that treated all women like shit, but he was turning out to be the exact opposite. She was having an inner conflict, but she reminded herself it was more about her nerves and not actually about Dame. She started to question whether she could actually kill someone. Her heart began to beat fast, and she could feel herself begin to sweat.

"Excuse me for a second. I need to go to the bathroom," she said, standing to her feet. She wanted to be able to pull herself together out of the line of sight of the most important target of her life.

"I'll walk you," Dame offered, standing up. She hated that he was a gentleman.

"I'm good. I think I can handle that," she teased, trailing her hand across Dame's shoulder to show him that she meant no disrespect by turning down his offer.

Zuri made her way through the crowd as fast as she could. She felt like she was beginning to hyperventilate. She entered the bathroom, walked into an empty stall, and closed the door behind her in haste. She stood in the stall, questioning herself. She was trying to talk herself out of going through with the plan, but she felt obligated to Brown. He deserved her loyalty, and Dame was in his way and had tried to have Trav kill him. And when Trav had failed at that, Trav had targeted Zuri. She tried to remind herself that it was personal, but she was afraid. *What if this nigga is on to me?* she thought to herself. She was thinking and overthinking, which was something she never did when it came to the decisions she had already made, but this was deeper than anything she had ever been a part of. Zuri took a deep breath, trying to calm her jittery nerves, then flushed the toilet and opened the stall door.

As Zuri exited the bathroom, she felt somebody grab her from behind and pull her into a dark corner. She tried to scream, but a hand was quickly over her mouth.

"Ssh. It's me," a voice said in her ear, and then hands let her go.

Zuri relaxed when she realized it was Brown being dramatic, but she also grew more nervous upon realizing that if Dame or any of his men saw Brown here, it would blow up their spot. She turned around, and Brown was standing in front of her. "What are you doing? Why did you scare me like that?" she said, slightly angry.

"My fault, Ma," he said. Brown looked nervous and kept looking around them to keep an eye on their surroundings. Zuri had never seen him do that before.

"What are you doing? I thought it was important that he doesn't see you or see you talking to me. What are you even doing in here?" she asked. She loved Brown, but she was frustrated. She had been putting in so much work to make sure their plan went off without a hitch, and here was Brown, putting everything at risk.

"I just wanted to keep a close eye on you. Just in case," he said, rubbing her hands. "You okay?" he asked, noticing her jumpiness. "You not having second thoughts, are you?"

"Well . . . ," she said. That was the last question she had wanted him to ask her and the last thing that she wanted to talk about. But now that Brown was here, she may as well take advantage of his wisdom and support.

"I knew this wasn't a good idea," Brown said. "I don't know what I was thinking, asking you to do this. I shouldn't even have you involved in this shit."

"No, it's not that. I just never did anything like this before. That's all." Zuri was trying her best to be honest. She was nervous, and she was upset by the fact that she had to get to know Dame first. The plan had seemed a lot easier when she was able to pretend that he was a dude that was in the streets, causing damage and mayhem. But now that she had met him, he reminded her so much of Brown, it was hard to wrap her head around what she was going to have to do.

Brown lowered his head; he truly understood her fear. He felt ashamed of himself. He wanted Dame dead, and he wanted it bad. Maybe too bad. His lust for revenge had begun to cloud his judgment.

Zuri saw the sadness in his eyes and felt she had let him down. "I'm sorry . . . I don't want you to think—"

"Nah, Ma," he said, quickly cutting her off. "It's not that at all. I could never feel a way about you," he assured her. He had never said the words that were about to come out of his mouth to anybody. He had only let the thoughts replay over and over in his mind, but he needed her to know why he hated the nigga Dame so much. "Look, Ma, I ain't never told nobody this, but if me and you gonna be together, I gotta keep it a buck with you. Back in the day, I put in a lot of work, gun work. It was how I got my name up in the street. Supposedly, one of the niggas I laid down was real tight with the nigga Dame. Now, I'm ninety-nine percent he was behind that shit that happened to you and Nubia. I think he sent them niggas to send a message to me. On some 'You take one of mine, I take one of yours' shit. Now, I don't care if it's tonight, tomorrow, or a year from now, but I'm not gonna rest until that nigga is dead."

Brown's revelation hit Zuri like a ton of bricks. She instantly was taken back to that fateful night at the apartment. She saw the flash of the gun and traced her hand over the scar that hid beneath her long hair. She remembered seeing Nubia lying with a hole in her head and remembered there was blood everywhere. She remembered waking up in the hospital from her coma and receiving the news that she had missed Nubia's funeral. But most of all, she remembered the hurt and pain it had caused her. She was so mad, she couldn't even cry. Brown recognized the look in her eyes, as it was the same one he had every time he thought about Dame and what went down in that apartment years ago.

"I'm gonna kill him, Brown," she said in a cold, emotionless tone. "Not for you, but for me. He took everything from me, and I'm gonna do the same to him. I'll call you when it's done."

Brown didn't say a word; he just watched her walk away.

"Damn, Ma. I thought I was gonna have to come looking for you," Dame said when Zuri returned to the VIP. He was surrounded by his crew still, an array of scantily dressed women interspersed between them. They talked vapidly, and she did her best to match their affect and cadence.

"It was a line. You know how the women's bathroom be in a club," she said, snapping right back into character. She was flirty and mischievous again, exactly how Dame seemed to like it.

"We about to slide," he informed her. "But I don't want our night to end," he said.

"Me either," she replied. "And it doesn't have to," she added, flirting seductively to feed his ego.

"So you riding with me?" he asked. He bit his lip in a way she knew he thought was sexy, but now that Brown had told her that it was Dame who was responsible for her sister's death, she found everything he did disgusting. But she was here to play the game.

"No doubt," she said with a smile.

Zuri rode in the passenger seat of Dame's Benz as he cruised through the city. His system was knocking as he dipped in and out of New York City traffic. He reached over and lowered the volume.

"You hungry?" he asked.

"Not really," she answered, reaching over, placing her hand on his thigh, and rubbing it. "But I'm sure I will be in the morning," she said as she moved her hand from his thigh to his shaft and rubbed it until it started to swell in his pants.

"Say no more," he answered.

They were all over one another as soon as they entered the plush room at the hotel. Dame had two handfuls of her ass, palming and squeezing, as they kissed aggressively. Zuri pulled Dame's shirt over his head and tossed it on the floor as he did the same to her skintight dress. Zuri wore black lace panties and a matching bra. She began to step out of her shoes, only to be interrupted by him.

"Keep 'em on," he requested, and she obliged.

When she and Brown had been coming up with this plan all those days before, she had worried about this part, the part where she would have to seduce him to make him more vulnerable. But now that she was here, looking at him half-naked and desperate for her, she realized that the events of the past months had made her the perfect person for the job. After Trav's boys had broken her in, she was able to separate herself from what her body was doing almost on command. And that was what she did now with the man who, she'd been told, was responsible for attacking her and her sister all those years ago.

Zuri tugged at his belt, then pushed him back on the bed. She got on her knees between his legs and unbuckled his pants, then pulled them and his boxer briefs down around his ankles. He was fully erect, and she quickly took him into her mouth and glided her wet mouth up and down on his shaft. She flicked her tongue around his mushroom-shaped tip as she rubbed his balls.

"Mmm," Dame moaned in pleasure as she traced her tongue down his rock-hard manhood, then took his balls in her mouth.

Her oral skills had his head spinning. Her mouth was so wet, he pleaded for her not to stop. Zuri began to use her hands, twisting them counterclockwise, as she sucked faster and faster. She felt his shaft begin to throb and knew he was nearing his climax. Zuri moaned as she took him across the threshold of ecstasy and he spilled in her mouth.

"Ooh." Dame closed his eyes and grunted as every muscle in his body tensed up. His heart was pounding, and his chest heaved up and down as he tried to catch his breath. He lay back on the bed and closed his eyes, still breathing heavy.

Zuri rose from her knees, climbed up on the bed, and straddled him. Without thinking or wasting time to worry about how she felt, Zuri smoothly removed the straight razor from her bra. Dame never open his eyes, remaining wrapped in the bliss of the moment. Zuri slid open the razor silently and swiftly came down with a swipe across his windpipe.

Blood splattered on the bedsheets and headboard, and small specks covered Zuri's face. Dame's eyes sprung open, and his mouth made a wide O from shock, and as he reached for the gash across his neck and throat, Zuri leaned over him and spit his seed in his face.

"By the way, my name is Zuri, and that was for my sister, Nubia," she stated with an ice-cold stare that matched the tone of her voice.

Dame's eyes grew wider. Zuri couldn't tell if it was from realizing who she was or from the fact that he was quickly running out of air. Blood was pouring uncontrollably out of his neck and through his hands. He tried to open his mouth to speak or gasp for a breath of air, but blood began to bubble up and out of his mouth. She watched him for a moment, and she thought of Bob, the rich man Scarlett had tried to stick up the first night that she had taken Zuri to try escorting. That night Zuri had been nervous and anxious and had rushed them out of the hotel room, but this time she waited. She wanted to see for herself the moment the life of a man, especially a bad man, left his eyes. Dame gurgled for a few more seconds. And then his heavy breathing stopped; his hands fell down, no longer trying to hold together his slit-open throat; and his eyelids flickered before his eyes became unfocused. Suddenly Zuri felt nauseated, and nothing about the situation felt real.

Zuri got off the bed and wiped the blood off her face with her hand. She just stared at her hand as the reality set in as to what she had just done. She raced into the bathroom and ran her hands under hot water as she scrubbed her skin, trying to get rid of the blood. She turned off the water and watched as the crimson pool swirled down the drain. She walked back in the room and picked her dress up off the floor and pulled it over her head. Dame lay dead on the bed.

Zuri quickly located her cell phone in her handbag and dialed Brown's number. The phone rang once before he picked up on the other end. Zuri didn't say anything at first; she could only do her best to regulate her breathing and make sure she didn't hyperventilate.

"What's up, Ma?" he said, his voice filled with concern. "You good?"

"Yeah, I'm good," she said as her voice cracked a bit. "It's done. I did it," she informed him.

"Okay, where you at? I need to get you somewhere safe, so you can lay low."

"I'm at the W downtown."

"I'm on my way ASAP," he said. "I love you, Ma. I'll be there in a few."

"I love you too," she replied, then found comfort in his words as they hung up.

She walked over and sat down in a chair in the corner of the room. She glanced at Dame's dead body on the bed and quickly turned away. His blood had continued to soak into the mattress, and Zuri could only think about the horror of the poor hotel maid who would find the body. Zuri jumped in fright at the sound of her phone ringing. Her nerves were shot, and her hands shook as she answered the call from Brown.

"You here already? That was fast," she said into the phone but received no direct response. She could hear Brown talking. "Hello?" she said but still received no direct answer.

Brown just kept talking, and she could hear music playing low in the background. It was then that Zuri realized that Brown's phone had accidentally called her back. Zuri went to hang up but paused when she heard another voice besides Brown's join the conversation.

"It took me a minute, but I finally got that nigga," Brown said proudly, with a sinister look on his face. He was on his way to get Zuri, and he could not believe the bitch had actually pulled through.

"Yeah, my nigga, and you killed three birds with one stone. That was some smooth shit," Trav proclaimed as he showered Brown with praise.

"It took long enough, but that plan came together nice," he confessed. "That bitch Nubia thought she was slick. She thought I didn't know she was fucking that nigga Dame on the low and she got my spot robbed." The slight from Nubia had occurred years ago and had been handled, but Brown was clearly still fucked up about it.

"Nothing worse than a bitch scorned," Trav joked.

"It didn't matter what I was doing. She should've never given my pussy away or fucked with my paper. That's why I murked her ass. Thought I killed Zuri's li'l ass too, but that bitch had the nerve to live. I can't front. I'm glad she did, though," he said, grabbing his crotch. "That's the best pussy a nigga ever had."

"Better than Nubia?" Trav asked. Even though he truly used to have a thing for Zuri, being his boss's hype man was more important.

"Hell yeah," Brown declared. "And she was so easy to manipulate. That dick got me in that bitch's mind. Got her to kill the nigga Dame for me. You should have seen it when I hit her with the 'I'm ninety-nine percent sure it was him.' Her face killed me," Brown said, causing them both to laugh.

"Fuck them and that nigga," Trav said.

"No doubt," Brown said. "And this keep shit with the nigga Cuba running smooth too. I was worried about him for a second, but I didn't want to fuck with anyone my pops kept close, and I'm glad now I won't have to."

"You a cold nigga, son," Trav said.

Brown smiled. "Yo, she at the W downtown. Go scoop her and make sure nobody ever find that bitch's body. And maybe you can finally get her to give you some pussy," Brown instructed jokingly.

Zuri sat in the chair, with tears racing down her face. She couldn't believe her ears. She had never felt so dumb in her life. Everything that had happened up until then had been a lie. "How didn't I see it?" she said aloud as she cried hysterically. All she had seen was red; she had been blinded by fury and rage. She had slept with the man who had killed her sister and had tried to murder her. She felt disgusting.

She jumped from the chair and raced into the bathroom and began vomiting in the sink. All that she had been through—Nubia's death, being kidnapped and raped—was all a part of Brown's plan. How could one person be so evil and hell-bent on destroying someone's life? she wondered. She looked at herself in the bathroom mirror, on the edge of a nervous breakdown. She took a deep breath and wiped her face of the tears she had been shedding. Zuri took another look at herself in the mirror and realized that no matter what life had thrown her way, she always found a way to survive, and she would do the same this time too. Brown wouldn't win. He could not and would not break her. She was done being a victim.

In that moment in that mirror, Zuri found herself. She walked out of the bathroom and stood by the door to the hotel room. She used a tissue to wipe Dame's blood off the razor. If Trav was going to show up to finish the job, she was going to get him first. Because of everything else Brown had revealed on the accidental call, the fact that he had lied about killing Trav didn't feel as horrifying as it should have. She thought back to her last interaction with Trav, and she had meant what she'd said. She would watch him die one day, and that day was today.

Zuri didn't know how long she had waited, but a jiggle of the door handle broke her concentration. She didn't remember hearing Trav knock; he was stupid if he thought the door would be unlocked. She took a breath and put on a voice like she was scared and crying.

"Brown, is that you?" She had almost slipped up and said Trav, but they both knew that for all she knew, he was dead. She laughed to herself as Trav, on the other side of the door, debated how to manipulate his voice so he sounded more like Brown. He was struggling.

"Yeah, Ma," Trav said quietly, and maybe it was because of all the years they had spent together, but Zuri was impressed at how close he was able to come to impersonating Brown. Now it was Zuri's turn to perform.

"Oh, thank God," she said, in fake tears, and she put her hand on the doorknob. "I was so scared."

She opened the door and let Trav tackle her, just like she had expected him to. He truly lacked any sort of criminal finesse, and she giggled from where she landed on the floor, under him. He may have knocked the wind out of her, but just like Dame, he was gurgling because Zuri had stabbed him in the neck. He stared into her eyes as he sputtered, and then did the same thing Dame had done: he he put his hands on his neck, letting Zuri's arms go free. The razor was still sticking out of his jugular, and Zuri smacked his hands away as he reached for it.

"Are you dumb or what?" she asked. "You know if you take a knife out of a wound, it only makes you bleed faster. Brown really gave you no training, huh?"

Trav was trying to choke something out, but his throat was filling with blood too fast.

"Why, Trav?" Zuri asked sincerely. She suddenly wished there had maybe been another way. It was looking like she would never get answers for why Brown was so dedicated to destroying not only her sister but the memory of her that lived in Zuri too.

Maybe it was because Zuri had left the razor in Trav's neck, but he was finally able to spit out what he wanted to say. "Because," he gurgled, "Brown said so." And just like it was with Dame, his eyes lost focus and his body fell farther into Zuri's as the tension of life left it.

She lay there with his dead body on top of her for longer than she should have, but she was thinking. What a life Trav must have lived, where all his decisions, all his choices were made by someone else. As she moved his body off of her, she thought about them as teenagers, about how much he had said that he cared for her, about how in love with her he'd been, even if it was in a puppy-dog way, and she was deeply saddened. Imagine kidnapping and setting up the girl you once loved to be raped just because your boy had told you to? The lifestyle of the streets had broken Zuri for the last time, she thought as she pulled the razor out of Trav's neck. There was a final spurt of blood, and a stain started to spread on the carpet to match the one that had been drying on the bed.

Zuri looked at the two dead men, taking in all that she had done. Was it enough? Was this bloodshed enough revenge for her life and the life of her sister? Nubia was the only one who had died, but Zuri realized that she had never had her life back after that fateful night, either. She decided that it wasn't enough revenge. She didn't know what she was supposed to do next, but she was going to learn.

Trav and Dame both had guns on them, and she took a pillowcase off the part of the bed that had no blood on it, and dropped both weapons into her makeshift bag and took both of their wallets and cell phones. Trav had hundreds stuffed in his wallet, and as she frisked Dame's body, she could feel stacks in his pockets and in his jacket. She grabbed all the cash. She debated dumping the wallets in the first sewer she found until she realized she was going about things all wrong. She definitely needed the cash, but as she thought about it, she realized that taking their IDs and phones somewhere else would make the scene look too suspicious. At first, she had thought getting rid of their personal items might mean slowing down the investigation process when the cops inevitably got involved, but then she had realized that her DNA was all over the room, or at least her saliva was definitely all over Dame's crotch. From all the crime shows that she had seen, she decided it was better to lie and say that she was in the hotel room, hooking up with Dame, when Trav rolled up to take him out. Yes, if anyone ever caught up with her, that was what she would say.

Girls that sell pussy steal money off guys all the time, Zuri thought to herself. It would work out, but it was time to go. With everything stuffed into her makeshift bag and her hands cleaned up, she got dressed, took one final look around the room, and spoke so that the spirits of Trav and Dame could hear her.

"I won."

Chapter 15

Zuri had never visited the cemetery where her sister Nubia had been laid to rest. The violence surrounding her death, and the injuries that Zuri had been left with, had made it an impossibility when she was first buried, and as time had gone on and Zuri had sworn off New York, she had never gotten around to it. Zuri knew that a big part of her avoidance of her sister's grave site was the fact that since Nubia died, she had been avoiding the reality of her sister. She stood in front of her grave site now, brushing back the grass that had grown over it. Dressed in a baggy black sweat suit, the hoodie over her head, and with big shades covering her face, she held one single rose in her hand and had a duffel bag slung across her chest.

It had been a few days since the cops had discovered the bodies of two gangsters in the W Hotel in Manhattan. The way the news was reporting it, drug king Damon Ward and rival gangbanger Travis Smith had been killed in an altercation as part of a drug deal gone bad. Zuri thought that was stupid. It didn't surprise her that the news had misreported what had gone down, but the drug part was especially dumb, as she had cleaned out both those motherfuckers before she left. But this news was good for her, because it had given her some time.

After she had left the W in Times Square, Zuri's mind had moved quickly. The days she spent planning Dame's murder with Brown had been especially helpful to her, because it meant she already had a plan in place, except for instead of avoiding Dame's goons, she had to avoid Brown. Emptying Trav's and Dame's wallets had left her with about fifteen thousand dollars in cash between them, and she was grateful that men of their status often kept stacks on them when they went out. She had waited in the lobby of the hotel until a group of people left, and she had gone out with them, in case Brown or Trav had set up a lookout, but she hadn't really thought that was the case. They had underestimated her, and they had been stupid, which was why Trav was dead and Brown would be, too. one day.

Zuri had chucked her phone when she first left the hotel. There wasn't a lot that she knew about technology, but she knew that people could be tracked by phones, and so she'd thrown it down a sewer drain as soon as she was sure nobody was watching her. She had realized then that beyond the privacy a hotel room provided for a murder, it also allowed for a quick cleanup. Zuri had been able to walk through the city unnoticed, since she'd just looked like another girl out on the town, with her nice dress and heels. The only thing that had looked out of place was the pillowcase with the stacks and guns she had, but she had solved that problem quickly by buying a plain-looking backpack at one of the random gift shops that stayed open all night long for the New York City tourists that truly believed the city never slept. Once she had the backpack, she'd blended into the city seamlessly.

The money she had taken off Trav and Dame had ended up being a godsend. She had walked for a long time, had found a nice hotel, and had been able to get a hotel room that first night to rest and collect her thoughts. Using the complimentary notepad, she had made a list of all the things she would need to do the next day. If she got out early, she would be able to buy some casual clothes, a new phone, and even a wig. She hoped that she had at least until the original checkout time for the room Dame had rented for him and her to hook up, about eleven o'clock in the morning, to do her shopping. She didn't know how hard Brown would be looking for her the next morning, but she didn't want to risk it, and she would go to any lengths to avoid being anywhere near him again. At least if it was not on her own terms.

It had taken her the whole week she spent at the hotel to figure out where Nubia was buried without raising suspicions in her old neighborhood. But she finally got the info from the aunt of one of Nubia's old friends. A gust of wind broke through the intensity of her thoughts now, and she remembered where she was. She looked down at Nubia's tombstone. Zuri was trying really hard, but she didn't feel connected to that piece of rock on the ground. In the hospital room all those years ago, she'd been heartbroken when Brown told her that she had missed Nubia's funeral. The original pain she felt recalling that moment was now compounded by the knowledge that Brown had been the one to order the hit on Nubia in the first place.

Zuri couldn't help but wonder if, in fact, Brown had spent so much time in her hospital room not because he cared on some deep, repressed level, but because he was waiting for the perfect opportunity to finish the job. It was like all the places she went in her mind for safety and happiness were tainted now. Her memories of being with Brown didn't bring her anything but blinding hot rage anymore, and her memories of Nubia only reminded her of Brown. She wished there was a way to kick someone out of her head, to block him from her thoughts. But there wasn't, and so she just stood silently in front of Nubia's headstone, trying to figure out how to say what she wanted to say.

"Hey, NuNu. I know it's been too long since I've been to see you, but I wanted you to know that I miss you and I love you more and more every day." Zuri could feel her voice starting to crack. She reminded herself that it was just a rock, that the most important part of her sister was still with her, but she was so broken up over the little things, she couldn't keep herself from crying. "I wish you were here to braid my hair and have girl talk. I have so much to tell you, now that I'm grown." She paused. "I would have listened to you talk all night," she joked and chuckled a little bit as the tears spilled over the wells of her eyes.

As she looked at the dates of the headstone, she realized that she was older now than Nubia had been when she died, and there was something about that fact that broke her heart even more. She took off her duffel bag and sat next to her sister's headstone. Zuri wished she could ask if what Brown had said was true, if she had double-crossed him, but she knew she would never get an answer, and to her, it didn't matter if Nubia had or hadn't. Brown was a monster, and he didn't deserve loyalty or respect. But Zuri did think of one thing: she went back to the last day she and Nubia had been together. She thought about how Nubia had stopped her from spending Brown's cash, how she had told her to keep it instead spending it. Now, in her bag, Zuri had more money than she could ever imagine she would hold in one place, and she had gotten it without the help of a man. Or at least, she did not consider a man who had died for her come-up as worthy of receiving credit.

"Brown turned out to be the worst thing that happened to both of us. But I promise you if it's the last thing I do on this earth, he will pay. And you will be able to rest peacefully. I know you always took care of me, and now it's my turn to take care of you. And I know that more than anything, you wanted me to learn how to take care of myself. I want you to know I did, Nubia. It took me a while, and it cost me a lot, but I learned how to handle my own shit." Zuri started to choke up, making it hard for her to speak as tears rolled down her face. She couldn't believe that in this life, she had officially outlived her sister. There was something about that knowledge that made her feel unstable.

The cemetery was silent around her. It wasn't like Zuri had expected a response, but as she sat there, the silence fell heavy around her. She had never visited a grave before, and she didn't know how long she was supposed to be there, but being near Nubia made her feel less alone, so she made herself comfortable and continued to talk absentmindedly to her big sister.

"So, uh, is Mom up there with you?" Zuri asked quietly. She didn't know why she was asking questions, though really, they felt less like questions. Her mom, unfortunately, had been buried in Philadelphia, far away from her firstborn daughter, but if her mom had taken her life to be with Nubia, then that was where she would be. What had Zuri hung up was a much harder conversation with a less easy answer, considering that the dead couldn't speak.

"NuNu," Zuri began, the words barely making their way past her lips. She didn't know why she was forcing herself to say the words out loud if she was speaking to Nubia's spirit more than anything else. But a part of Zuri knew that this was an exercise in healing for herself as well. "I messed up. I messed up really bad. I let the way Brown made me feel take over my logic. I let my guard down, and I let him in, Nubia. Your memory didn't deserve that, but I just wanted to let you know that I should've put you first, and from now on I will."

A sigh of relief escaped Zuri's lips, as she had finally got to say what she had wanted to say to her sister. That was the real purpose of this moment for her, for them to forgive each other the wrongs done. Even if Nubia wasn't around anymore to confirm it for Zuri, Zuri knew her sister better than anybody and knew that this would have made her feel better too.

"I have to go away for a little while. I don't know how long I'll be gone, but I promise, I will come back to see you as soon as I can." Zuri laid the rose down on top of Nubia's headstone, then kissed it. She took one last look, then stood up and walked out of the cemetery.

Zuri had made a promise to herself that after the last bus ride to New York, she would never get on another bus in her life. But here she was, in the long line, preparing to board the Greyhound bus. She showed the driver her ticket and got on the bus and headed straight to the back. She grabbed an empty seat by the window and put her hoodie over her head again. She removed the new phone she had purchased from her pocket and powered it on. As soon as the screen lit up, Zuri went to the internet search bar and type in the words *Murder Mamas*. It felt stupid to go about looking up on Google a deadly syndicate like the women who had talked to her at Daydreams all those months ago.

But she was officially out of any options other than that one. She no longer had a job, she no longer had Geisha, and she most certainly no longer had Brown. The only thing she had going for her now were the stacks in her bag and the knowledge that she had proved the Murder Mamas right. She was special. She had single-handedly taken down one of the most powerful hustlers Brooklyn had ever seen. Brown may have been around to groom her and give her advice, but the killing she had done all by herself, and so for her, it was a victory. She had been doing her research all night, and now she clicked on another article that talked about the deadly femmes fatales, and began reading. She thought that she could recognize the women from the strip club in the general descriptions in the article. There wasn't a person with more boss energy than a woman that took care of herself. And that was the way the Murder Mamas were described.

From what she could find online, the Murder Mamas were more of a legend than a fact. None of them had ever been caught, but wherever they were spotted, death always followed them. They didn't do little hits, like the way that Scarlett had tried to stick up Bob at the hotel in Atlantic City. No, the Murder Mamas went after the big fish, like politicians and big-time hustlers. In her search, she came across stuff about that man Greg Redd who had been killed at Daydreams the day she got fired. Like Waheed had suggested, he had been assassinated, based on the theory that he had sold some of his crew up the river for less time on his sentence. She was engrossed in a story written about the group in a newspaper article but was snapped out of her zone by the driver when he spoke over the loudspeaker. They had been at a standstill while Zuri had been on her phone, and it didn't seem like they would be moving anytime soon.

"This is the nine o'clock express bus to Miami, Florida. We are running slightly behind schedule, but we will be moving shortly," he said as Zuri looked up and briefly stared out the window at New York to take it in one last time. The bus ride would be long, about thirty hours, and Zuri was trying to get as comfortable as possible. She told herself she shouldn't be surprised that they were running late. It's not like there would be anyone waiting for her in Miami when she got there, anyway. She then turned her attention back to her phone.

The ticket to Miami had been bought because, really, she didn't know where else to go. She understood that the information she was learning online about the Murder Mamas needed to be taken with a grain of salt. But Miami kept coming up as the place where it had all started. Between the scattering of news articles and one blog she had found on Miami street gangs that, for some reason, included the Murder Mamas, she was starting to piece things together. It looked like they had been led by a woman named Miamor, who specialized in training young, beautiful women to use their looks and potential for seduction as ways to lure men into traps and kill them.

For Zuri, this was not much different than what she had done with Dame. In fact, it was exactly what she had done with Dame. She felt as though she had seen both sides of what could happen with that style of attack: she'd experienced how she and Scarlett had almost been taken out by the naked Bob, and she'd read the details of the brutality that the Murder Mamas themselves inflicted. If Miami was where she needed to be to learn how to hone her newfound talent and craft, then Zuri would go there. She had nothing left anywhere else and nothing to stop her. New York and Philly had been ruined for her by betrayal and deception, and there weren't too many places on the East Coast that she could run to. Plus, Miami was warm, and she had never lived in a place with a good climate.

Either way, she would figure it out when she got there. It wasn't like she would be able to walk into the Murder Mamas' office somewhere and sign up. She would have to make them come to her. The positive reaction they had had with her back at the club in Philly let her know that if she had been invited by them once, she could be invited by them again. There were a couple of clubs in Miami that were popular that she could dance at, King of Diamonds being the most popular one. Zuri had a lot of options, and even though she was all alone, she was confident that she would be able to make money and start building the semblance of a life until she landed on her feet. As the bus stalled to accommodate stragglers, Zuri planned out the rest of her life in her head.

Zuri had once wondered how someone could be hellbent on destroying someone else's life, but now she understood that feeling. She felt that way about Brown, and she was not going to rest until he lay in the ground, along with any and everyone connected to him. During the past week, she had tried to keep her ear to the ground, tried to figure out if Brown knew what she had done, or if he thought that one of Dame's men had come to check on his boss and, upon seeing what Zuri had done, had killed Trav and taken Zuri. She was hoping that if they had underestimated her before, they would do it again, and she would be able to live under the radar until she was ready to strike. But there was no way to know. Zuri just had to have faith. If there was anything that Zuri had learned from Brown, it was to wait to strike until you were ready to take on your opponent. And even if it took Zuri years, she would wait until she was ready to not only end Brown's life but also destroy every part of it.

Another young woman ran onto the bus, interrupting Zuri's deep introspection. Like Zuri, she was very beautiful, with brown skin and blond braids held away from her face by a ponytail. She looked around the bus for an empty seat, and because Zuri knew that she had the last one, she started shifting her bags to make room for the new passenger. The girl hurried down the aisle, presumably the last person that needed to board, as the driver wasted no time in hopping back on the speaker.

"Thank you for your patience," the driver said. "We will now be starting our journey to Miami. Please get comfortable, and if you need something, please don't ask."

There were a few laughs around the bus, and the new passenger gave one of them as she landed in the seat next to Zuri.

"Hey, is it cool if I sit here?" she asked Zuri in a sweet, bubbly voice. And Zuri couldn't help looking at her like she was crazy. "Oh yeah, that's my bad. I am already sitting down . . . ," she noted awkwardly and trailed off. It was so awkward that Zuri actually found it funny, and she chuckled a little bit before turning back to her phone.

"No worries," she said. "Don't even think about it." Zuri wasn't good at speaking to strangers that weren't men, and there was a lot more research that she wanted to do before she got to Miami. But her new seatmate didn't seem able to get the hint.

"So, are you going back or going to?" she asked, shoving her overstuffed bag under the seat in front of her and pulling out a smaller purse, which was filled with gum, candy, headphones, and a random assortment of half-finished lip glosses and receipts.

Zuri took a minute to think about her answer. If she was honest, it might get her caught up later, but if she lied, the same thing could happen. She was still thinking when the stranger answered her own question for herself.

"I'm going back. I'm born and raised in Miami, baby. Three-oh-five till I die," she said jokingly as she opened a bag of Skittles. She poured a few into her hand before she offered the pack to Zuri. It had been a long time since someone had done something so inadvertently kind for Zuri, and she felt tears welling up in her eyes. She turned toward the window and pretended to cough to make sure there was no moisture on her face.

"I got a cough drop, too," the stranger said, placing the bag of candy in Zuri's lap before she fished around for a cough drop that Zuri didn't need.

If she had to guess, she would say that she and the stranger were the same age. Whereas Zuri had been forced to be hard and cold, her seatmate was warm and open, going out of her way to try to comfort a random person on the bus. Zuri had once been like that, before everything else had gotten in the way, and having that same kindness extended to her was breaking her heart in a way she couldn't explain. She finally responded.

"I'm okay. Thank you so much, though," Zuri said in reference to the cough drop. She wasn't hungry, but she took a few Skittles as a way to express her gratitude and handed the bag back to her new, weirdly happy friend. Zuri decided that she would take a cue and take a risk and chose to be honest. "I've actually never been to Miami. I'm moving there for a change of scenery," Zuri said. It was a bit of an embellishment but not completely untrue. She was very interested in seeing the beaches they had.

The stranger was ecstatic as she listened to Zuri's plan, and as the bus rolled away, leaving the skyline of New York in the background, the stranger answered all Zuri's questions, gave her all the tips she had, and started to help Zuri come up with an actionable plan. After a few hours of talking, they realized that the rest of the bus was quiet and dark, and the stranger took a little nap, but Zuri stayed awake. From her assessment of the situation, the stranger seemed safe, just a young girl happy to help another young girl, and Zuri was excited to continue their conversation when she woke back up. It was that safety that gave Zuri pause, and as she looked out the window into the star-filled sky of the East Coast night, she thought of only one other person who had held her down like that before, no questions asked.

"Nubia," Zuri whispered to herself as she placed her hand on the cool glass of the bus window and let herself cry, knowing that her sister had somehow blessed her from above and that somehow, someway, she was going to be all right. "Thank you," Zuri whispered. "Thank you."

Epilogue

The present day . . .

The beautiful blue sky seemed to merge with the deep waters of the Atlantic Ocean. The ripples from the waves were mesmerizing, and Zuri found herself once again hypnotized by their movements. The view was one of the things she loved most about her penthouse apartment. The ocean made her feel a sense of peace, a calm that had escaped her for most of her life. There was something about looking at water that aligned her spiritually, and because Zuri had never been one for church, she treasured the daily communion she was able to make with the water. The sound of her red-bottom heels walking across the white marble floor echoed throughout the silent apartment as she glided over to the bar and removed the bottle of Domaine Ramonet Montrachet Grand Cru she had on ice. She poured herself a glass, her second of the morning, and return the bottle to the ice it had originally rested in.

It was in quiet morning moments like these that she spent time reflecting on the past few years of her life, but she always ended up in the same meditation of gratitude over her living space. It had been years since she had first landed in Miami, homeless and desperate for work. She had struggled for months, dancing at clubs up and down South Beach, renting a room from a mean Cuban lady, and saving up for a place of her own. The penthouse she had now was definitely not bought with tips from any club, but she had always been grateful for her hustler attitude and grateful for all the success the streets of Miami had brought her. For Zuri, who had spent so many years bouncing around, unhappy with her living conditions or unable to control her living conditions, her home now was very important to her.

The South Beach apartment building that she had finally landed on was forty stories high, and she was in the top unit. Her furniture was of the highest caliber, and her fridge was filled with top-of-the-line food, which often she didn't even get to eat, because she was always working. In her walk-in-closet there was only designer clothing, shoes, and purses going wall to wall. Balmain, Dior, and Hermès were her favorites, but she had a special place in her heart for Gucci after that last day that she and Nubia had spent together. The original Gucci skirt Zuri's sister had bought her had long ago been lost in all her moving around and running, but with the resources Zuri had now, she had been able to find another one in the same size, and it sat on a dress form she kept in her closet, in a place of highest honor. She didn't have photos on her wall as a security precaution, but seeing the skirt every day as she got dressed was enough sentiment for her. It reminded her of all that she had lost to get where she was, and all that she owed the memory of the women in her life. Seeing that skirt motivated her to stay dedicated to her craft and about her business.

She made her way back over to her perfect oceanfront view and spotted a cruise ship off in the distance. It had been a long time since she had been able to go on vacation, and she longed for the chance to enjoy one. Sure, she traveled. Her line of work took her many places, but there was always work to be done, and then once she did what she had to do, it wasn't wise to stick around for too long. She was the best at what she did, her services were in high demand, and she was grateful that her money kept flowing, but she would be lying if she said that sometimes she wished things would slow down. The team she was on, she really enjoyed working with, but business was always booming, and as much as she would enjoy a break, she also knew that she had to be at the ready.

So she made sure to enjoy her brief moment of relaxation to the fullest extent before she started her day, knowing that her phone would be ringing at any moment. She soaked in the blue ocean and the movement of the water one last time while sipping from her wineglass. She hated to turn away. She could get lost in the beauty of that seascape all day, and the peace it provided her was intoxicating. But work was how she afforded her luxurious way of living, and she was not ready to give that up. The penthouse apartment provided her with more than just a view. It also provided her the privacy she so desperately required and needed in her line of work.

When Zuri had first moved in, she had had remodelers come in and specially design soundproof walls, easily cleanable floors, and high-tech locks on all the doors, which only she could open with a combination of pass codes and fingerprints. It had been a strange request, but men didn't often question a woman as beautiful as Zuri. The floor-to-ceiling windows went dark at the push of a button, another feature she had specially requested for her living space. Before, she had worried about the fact that basically her whole apartment was visible to the outside eye, but she had had to remind herself that at forty stories up, the outside eye would have to be on an airplane to see anything going on inside her apartment. But the window adjustments made her feel safer all the same.

Privacy would come in handy as she took care of a little personal business. She had to admit to herself that what she was doing at the moment was not work, but how could she deny herself the years of built-up anticipation, all the time she had spent waiting and planning? Zuri placed her wineglass down and crossed the room to her state-of-the-art entertainment unit. She pressed PLAY, then increased the volume on the jazz music that had begun to play from the speakers. The music filled her apartment, and she swayed a little bit, moved her hands to the beats of the music as she fluttered over to her task. She got a glimpse of herself in the large mirror that hung on the wall behind her couch, and caught the glint of her dark, malevolent eyes as they peeked out from behind strands of her long dark hair. Her body had only gotten better with age. She wore a white satin robe over her naked form, and it gripped her in all the right places.

Zuri was so beautiful that one might not even notice that she was covered in blood and sported the murderous grin of a blackhearted villain. She turned her attention to the middle of the living room, where a bloody and beaten Brown sat unconscious, gagged and bound to a chair. She had waited years to exact revenge on him, and she was just getting started. . . .